Box of Secrets

Alan Grainger (signature)

Alan Grainger

Also By Alan Grainger

The Tree That Walked
The Klondike Chest
The Rumstick Book
It's Only Me
The Learning Curves
Father Unknown
The Legacy
Eddie's Penguin
Deadly Darjeeling
Deep & Crisp & Even
Blood On The Stones

Copyright © 2015 Alan Grainger

All rights reserved.

ISBN: ISBN-1505224233

ISBN-13: 978-1505224238

Box Of Secrets

For Maureen

Alan Grainger

Justice will not be served until those who are unaffected are as outraged as those who are.

Benjamin Franklin.

Alan Grainger

DAY ONE

Thursday 17th September 2009

Alan Grainger

4, Braithwaite Avenue,

Eastbourne, Sussex.

Annie Weaver, a tall thin and normally straight backed woman of seventy seven, was sitting slumped in a white plastic garden chair behind the potting shed at the bottom of her garden. Other than the few strands of waist-long matted grey hair which were adhering to her skin, as though she'd just stepped from her shower, she was completely naked. An off duty staff nurse at Eastbourne General, Buzzy Knight, a forty one year old, with a back garden abutting Annie's, saw her the minute she drew back the curtains; and she got such a shock she almost fainted.

It was just after seven and the newly risen sun was already casting shadows; one of them had practically obscured the unclad woman, even so Buzzy was able to make her out.

'Peter,' she yelled, turning to the duvet covered figure lying in her bed trying to will himself back to sleep, 'come and look at this for God's sake, it's that weird woman in Pendine Avenue, the one whose garden backs onto mine, the miserable so and so I was telling you about the other day who complained to the council about my trees; she's sitting out in her back garden and she hasn't a stitch on.'

'What …?'

'Oh for God's sake Peter .. she's in the buff … and d'you know what,' she said, slightly adjusting her position to get a better view … 'I think she might be dead.'

'Couldn't be.' The tousled head of Doctor Peter McFee, a twenty-six year old Junior Registrar in the same hospital as Buzzy appeared above the bedclothes. 'Dead? You're joking?'

'I wish I was; come and look for yourself.'

Reluctantly throwing back the duvet, Peter levered himself up, swung round until he was sitting on the side of the bed, yawned, and began to stretch his arms over his head.

'Oh for Goodness sake, put something on and come over here. You'll find a robe on the back of the door.'

He looked across the room; a man's red and blue striped dressing gown was hanging on the hook, and he immediately began to wonder who'd last worn it. Buzzy Knight wasn't known as 'Busy Night' for nothing.

He took down the gown and put it on. It was too short and barely met round his middle but, drawing it about him as best he could; he walked over to the window.

Buzzy's finger was pointing towards the end of her garden. 'There,' she said, 'between the shed and the fence.'

He shaded his eyes. 'Crikey!'

'Yeah, "Crikey", I agree, but what should we do?'

'Have you a pair of steps I could use?' he asked, ripping off the dressing gown and picking his clothes up from the floor where, in haste, he'd dropped them the previous evening. 'I'll go and check her if I can get over. You'd better ring the police and call an ambulance; there's something fishy been going on over there.'

Creakwood Stud Farm,
Dial Post, Sussex.

The stable yard manager, Sam Midleton, was half way across the yard when his heard the telephone ringing in his office. Cursing quietly to himself, he retraced his steps to the desk he'd just left and picked up the handset.

'Creakwood Stud.'

'Sam, it's me, has Pip Emma been picked up yet?'

'No, Mr Finnerty, they rang a few minutes ago and they're on their way. When they went to hitch up their trailer this morning it had a puncture so they were delayed. The lad told me they'd be here at eleven or so.'

'I bloody well hope they are. I want that box she's been in cleaned out, disinfected and white washed; it has to be ready for a mare I booked in for Slipstream last night. She'll be arriving the day after tomorrow. How is he this morning?'

'Slipstream? He's seems better, covered with mud of course but no sign of the limp he had yesterday, and I couldn't feel anything. I'll get Tommy to give Tracy a hand sprucing him up this morning while June's mucking out. A good blood line has she, this mare that's coming in?'

'Oh yes, stayers on both sides and five or six decent wins herself. She'll make a fine partner for Slipstream and between them we could hit the jackpot if she throws a decent colt. Anyway keep on top of it Sam, and for Christ's sake ring me if you have any problems, we don't want a slip up with this baby. And make sure our boy's looking his absolute best. I'm just about to leave for the airport and I'll ring you when I get to the hotel sometime this afternoon. OK?'

'OK Mr Finnerty.' said Sam, while displaying a smirk which illustrated how un-OK things were at Creakwood, how unhappy the staff was, and how at the first decent opportunity they'd be off. Well perhaps not all of them, June for instance, she'd stay.

As he walked back into the yard Sam found himself drifting back to the moan which always seemed to dominate his thoughts ... "The unfairness of life" ... and he aimed a kick at a bucket to emphasise his how miserable his own had been since his birth. 'And there's "His Majesty", he muttered, 'swanning off to Scotland with his "bird" to drink champagne with that crowd of messers he calls "our clients" ... all bloody wasters, not an honest one among 'em. And they'll be drinkin' champagne and smokin' cigars 'til the cows come home without giving a thought for me and Tommy and Tracy and June, working our backsides off, shovelling muck and manure, and washing down that bad tempered bastard Slipstream to make him look better than he really is. He's a messer as well ... stallion, huh, I could do better myself ... none of the foals he's fathered have ever come to anything, not one. Ah well, better make sure Tommy's on the ball before I go; the transport might arrive before I get back and the last I saw of Pip Emma she's not quite ready ... 'Tommeeeee ... Tommeeee. Where the heck are you, Tommy?'

'Coming ... coming, what's the fucking panic?' Tommy replied, emerging from Pip Emma's loose box.

'I've to go to Brighton later on to do something I was supposed to do yesterday, a job for Henry I said I'd look after while he was away seeing about ...'

'Oh, yeah, about a mare he's hoping to get, he told me.'

'Mare? Filly more like, one with two legs.'

Tommy began to giggle 'Ah, yes ... see what you mean.'

'Anyway, Sod's Law, those buggers'll turn up to collect Pip Emma while I'm missing.'

'So?'

'So if that happens *you* look after them.'

'Me? Oh no ... what if they ask questions?'

'They won't, it'll only be a couple of stable lads who don't know the front end of a horse from the back. Get a signature on the form on my desk, it has Pip Emma's photo on it, and then you can hand her over ... right?'

'What if Henry rings?'

'He won't; he'll be halfway to Scotland.'

'Yeah, OK.'

'I'll be leaving at about eleven,' said Sam, 'so make sure you always somewhere handy to the yard while I'm away.'

Tommy stuck up his thumb. 'Sure.' he answered, and went back into the loose box to finish grooming the mare.

The C.I.D. Suite, Police H.Q.
Sussex House, Brighton.

Buzzy, having walked round to join Peter who'd managed to get over the fence and confirm Annie's death, had made her way to the front of the house to wait for the ambulance and police to get there. It was coming up to seven thirty by then, and Annie's next door neighbour was just leaving for work. Backing out of his drive he gave them half a smile, and looked as though he was about to lower his car window. Buzzy thought he was going to say something, ... maybe to ask them what they were doing there at that time of the morning, but he didn't, he just nodded and drove off.

'Ha!' said Peter. 'So much for Neighbourhood Watch.'

Twenty two miles away in Brighton, Detective Chief Inspector William 'Foxy' Reynard of the Sussex Police Criminal Investigation Department was just arriving at his office.

Almost as well known for his liking of freshly brewed Costa Rican coffee and Hobnob biscuits as he is for his investigative work, D.C.I. Reynard is an impressive, well built, fifty one year old police officer of the "old school". No torn jeans and leather bomber jackets for him (or any of the team who work with him). He's generally to be found in a dark grey or navy blue suit, under which he'll have a white cutaway collared shirt and Paisley patterned tie. His shoes'll be highly polished too and, all in all, from his glistening toecaps to his close cropped curly grey air he's about as far removed from the public's perception of a detective as it is possible to get; he looks more like banker or a stockbroker. He expects, and gets, the same standards of dress from his team, all of whom, unless it's on a one to one basis, he addresses by rank and surname only.

Recently he's relaxed a little with regard to the way he lets them address him, no longer insisting on being called 'Sir'. These days he's happy to settle for 'Governor', or even 'Guv', a popular mode of respectful address beloved by Londoners and lower ranking policemen. Those who work for him willingly conform to his strict regime, and spurn the silly comments others hurl at them for being so compliant. They know the ones who scoff loudest are probably the most jealous. Being one of Foxy Reynard's team *means* something ... even as far away as Scotland Yard, for Commander Bill Simpson, National Criminal Investigation Coordinator, who works there, a man with a lot of influence in policing circles, served under Reynard years ago when Reynard was a newly appointed sergeant and he was a "just qualified" Detective Constable. It was a relationship which has been regularly serviced over the years leaving neither of them ever feeling too inhibited to pick up a telephone and ask the advice of the other; as had happened a year or two ago, for example, when Chief Detective Superintendent Dudley Melchitt was murdered under some very odd circumstances involving a Penguin.

The Second in command of this highly rated outfit is Detective Sergeant Lucy Groves, another fastidious dresser; a thirty two years old good looking woman who generally clads herself in the female version of one of the suits Reynard wears. Under her jacket she'll have on a plain pastel coloured silk shirt or a lamb's wool jumper. She's quite short; five six or so in her high heeled shoes, but her hair is long and it's blonde, shoulder length in fact, and though it seems to flop about her face prompting frequent manual adjustments and much tossing back, it's actually been expensively dressed to give her the engaging, and somewhat deceptively casual image she often uses to her advantage.

The rest of team are men; three of them, and they're all Detective Constables at different levels of seniority. They, like Groves before them, had to fight to get on Reynard's team. To ensure they remain on it, and in his good books, they're all dressed as he is. Apart from their varying heights and their different coloured hair they might have all come out of the same box. They are: D.C.s Norman Best, known as 'Next' to his pals, a fast learner and a protégé of Reynard's; Desmond Furness, 'Dessie', a recent transferee from Shoreham CID; and Welshman D.C. Taffy Edwards, a one-time Tax inspector, who was temporarily attached to Foxy's team during the Nelson Deep Murder Inquiry, and has somehow managed to get himself made permanent on it.

Reynard parked his car, entered the building, and climbed the stairs to his office. There were very few about so early in the morning; in fact, apart from the cleaners and Edwards, whom he'd seen driving in as he'd locked his vehicle, the only people present were Best, and Furness. Walking between the shoulder high blue dividing screens enclosing the desks used by the three detective teams working there, he called out. 'Anyone seen Sergeant Groves?'

Best, at his desk filling in an expenses claim, answered. 'She's with the Super, Guv. He came in here looking for you a few minutes ago, and when he saw you weren't here he told the Sarge "she'd do".'

Reynard nodded, a twitch at the corner of his mouth the only sign of the annoyance he felt. He didn't like anything, or anyone, interrupting his schedules and the daily 'catch up' meeting, for him, was one of the most important elements of it. 'Ten minutes then.' he said, 'Ten minutes, and we'll make a start whether she's there or not.'

Best, Furness, and Edwards, who'd joined them by then, answered as one ... 'Yessir.'

Still shaking his head, Reynard continued on into his office, switched on the Coffee machine, and then sat tapping his desk top with his fingertip. Before he got to working out what Chief Superintendent Bradshaw wanted though, Groves appeared. 'I've been with the Super.' she said, 'he asked *me* to ask *you* who you could spare for the day. He needs a body or two to bolster up the uniformed lads he's sent down to police The Great British Food Fayre in the Royal Pavilion Gardens; it's V.I.P. day. I said you'd talk to him later.'

'Oh God ... to do what? What's he want them for?'

'He didn't say specifically, but I gathered he'd like them to mingle with the crowd; keep an eye out for trouble makers, bag-snatchers, pick-pockets, and so on.'

'Heaven help us! We're police detectives not school prefects; we catch *villains* ... not damned hooligans. And we're going to be stretched today anyway ... I hope you haven't forgotten you and I are giving that talk at the Rotary Club lunch.'

'I haven't forgotten.'

'Got your stuff?'

Groves held up a file, on the front of which he could see she'd printed: 'Technology and Instinct - Partners in Detection.'

'I'll be straightforward, don't worry, we're there to entertain, not instruct; they're all the Super's pals. OK then ...'

he said, turning to Best, 'what have you on your plate today?'

'Well Sir, as it's quiet, I was going to catch up on a few reports and do some ferreting on the internet.'

'For what?'

'Brandon Ramage's background.'

'Him ... you think he's exaggerating, telling us things have been stolen from his gallery that he never had in the first place? You're probably right, he's done it before.'

'I know ... several times ... I've seen the files.'

'Fair enough, but put him on the back burner for today and go to this food exhibition. You'd better go with him D.C. Edwards, and we'll leave D.C. ...'

Furness smiled. 'OK, I'll mind the shop'

'Right ... all done then? Now, before we go about our business, and D.C. Best fills us in on what the rest of the division is up to, let's have an update on *our* investigations ... Sergeant?'

Groves, who always did the catch-up report on their own cases, opened a file she had on her lap. 'Cupboard's a bit bare at the moment as you all know. Since winding up the Pharmochem drugs theft yesterday, and finding that the girl who went missing at the fairground in Lancing hadn't gone missing at all, we don't appear have anything of consequence other than the doubtful insurance claim D.C. Best is looking into, and the stabbing of the Polish man in the Simon Community hostel in Pickering Street. We're still waiting for Dr Vladic's confirmation of the precise cause of his death, and I've few lines to follow up with the Polish Embassy and our own Immigration people. With luck I'll have the victim's identity established some time tomorrow or the day after. Apart from that, it's quiet. If we don't get a call soon, D.C. Edwards'll start thinking life's always like this. We haven't had a decent case for days.'

'Don't speak too soon.' said Reynard, 'Now, Constable Best, what are the other teams up to?'

Best pulled out his notebook so he could refer to jottings he'd made the previous evening.

'Well, Sir, D.I. Lawrence's team have been put on the baby snatching which happened outside Marks & Sparks yesterday. They're all out looking for the child, a two year old girl. A good few uniformed officers are with them too, which is why the Super is short of men at that Food Fayre thing at The Royal Pavilion.

D.I. Crowther's lot are equally committed; they've taken over a couple of Lawrence's cases to free up his manpower; last week's ram-raid in Worthing and a possible rape on the beach on Saturday night. They also have three older cases of their own: the robbery at the Sunshine House Chinese takeaway, they've got nowhere with that one so far; the threatening letters to the Principal of St Gerard's Primary School, no progress there either; and the theft of goods from Autospares for which they've identified the men responsible and they're bringing them in for questioning today. Last night when I was talking to D.I. Crowther he hinted that he might be coming to you for a bit of help this morning; he even asked me if I'd mind being transferred to his team until he gets his head above water again.'

'If I lend you to him I'll never get you back,' Reynard answered, 'he's tried that trick before. We'll stick to Best and Edwards helping out at the Royal Pavilion and see what tomorrow brings. Alright?'

'Alright, Guv,' they all replied.

'Perhaps I shouldn't have said "the cupboard was a bit bare" when I spoke earlier.' said Groves.

'Perhaps you shouldn't.' said Reynard, grinning.

Barton Court,

The Prime Minister's private residence, near Horsham, Sussex.

Rose Jellicoe had had an early start, the bright sunshine almost blinding her when she'd opened the casement and waved 'Goodbye' to her departing husband, James, Prime Minister of Great Britain and Northern Ireland. He'd glanced up just as she'd called, his attention caught by a beam of light reflected by the glass as the window swung back. And when he saw her wave he returned it with one of his own, wishing he was just arriving not just leaving. A few days with her at Barton Court, his parent's former home near Horsham, now his, had always seemed more attractive than taking the family to Chequers; more personal, more relaxing and, provided there were no foreign visitors to be entertained, always his first choice. Pity the opportunities to spend time in what had been his boyhood home came so infrequently.

Once the three car procession had disappeared out of sight, Rose shut the window and went back to bed, hoping the faint rattle of china she could hear outside on the landing meant her breakfast was on the way. It was, and before long she was sitting up propped by three pillows, savouring her first burst of caffeine, buttering her toast, and beginning to think of what she should wear.

She was up by nine, and by ten she was showered, made up, and dressed; her long auburn hair cascading over the shoulders of her powder blue trouser suit. She'd chosen to wear it especially, having recalled an embarrassing moment the previous time she'd been in Brighton when, to her face reddening embarrassment, a gust of wind had lifted the skirt of her lightweight dress and brought a cheer from the crowd which could have been heard three miles away in Hove. No, the pale blue linen, provided it didn't crease too much, was going to be just right; it and the floppy bowed white silk shirt, perfect for the occasion.

When she was satisfied with her choice of clothing, she slipped into a pair of white loafers knowing she be glad she'd chosen them before the day was out and then, as she walked over to the mirror, she found herself wondering how many other Jellicoe women before her had checked their appearance in that same old mahogany framed cheval; dozens probably. Happy she looked alright, she smiled; not with the face splitting beam which surfaced automatically on formal occasions leaving those who saw it doubting her sincerity, but an infectious good natured grin to match her pleasurable anticipation of what promised to be an interesting day, including an opportunity to catch up with her old college friend, Julia, wife of the Lord Mayor of Brighton and Hove.

9, Pendine Avenue,

Eastbourne, Sussex.

The ambulance, with a driver and two paramedics; and a squad car, with uniformed police constables in it, arrived together and soon everyone was gathered at the bottom of the garden looking at Annie, sitting statue like in the plastic chair. By then she'd an old tartan rug Peter had found in the shed draped round her and, in consequence, the newcomers didn't get the same shock he and Buzzy had experienced when they'd seen her from the bedroom window. A quick examination by one of the paramedics confirmed Peter's view that Annie was dead, and she was covered up again while they awaited the arrival of a second squad car bearing a Sergeant. When it got there and he saw Annie, and after he'd heard Peter's and the paramedics confirmation of her death, he ordered the body was not to be touched again, and pronounced the whole area of the house and garden a potential crime scene.

The ambulance and its crew left soon afterwards and, once Peter and Buzzy had given contact details to the Sergeant together with a description of how they'd discovered the body, they left too.

Meanwhile the two P.Cs who'd come in first police car,

having checked the house was unoccupied by entering it through the unlocked back door, taped off a route through the garden all the way from where Annie was sitting in the chair to the front gate. Outside it, neighbours alerted by the unusual presence of two squad cars and an ambulance in a road where "nothing ever happened", were standing in groups trying to guess what was going on. When one of the constables told them, they shook their heads in disbelief. 'Annie Weaver dead in her garden ... and naked? Never.'

By nine o'clock the road was quiet again and most of the neighbours had gone to work or back to their homes. Only a few still chatting at their gates and the presence of a police car drawn up at Annie Weaver's house gave any indication of the drama which must have been played out there during the night.

The Royal Pavilion and Gardens,
Brighton, Sussex.

Rose's driver, a taciturn man, had brought the car round at a quarter past eleven and, opening the rear door, delivered one of his four standard greetings: 'Lovely day for it, Maam.'

'So it is.' she'd answered on cue as she'd got into the back of the vehicle grinning at their little daily pantomime of words.

'It' for her was going to mean meeting Julia and walking round a series of exhibition stalls. For him it would more than likely mean hanging around all day drinking tea with other chauffeurs, and scanning the previous day's results on the horse racing pages of The Sun and The Daily Mirror. The information gleaned from those papers dictated his life, 'and,' she said to herself with a sigh, 'I've a nasty feeling it won't be long before it's doing the same to mine.'

The drive to Brighton through the by-roads of Sussex was un-eventful and, by a clever bit of timing the driver had worked out the previous evening, the car pulled up at the steps of The Royal Pavilion exactly on noon as expected.

Lance Henderson, the Lord Mayor, splendidly clad in a

flame red fur trimmed gown, and wearing a black tri-corn hat and the city's mayoral gold chain of office, was on the steps to greet her. On his face he'd a smile so broad a cynic might have said it was sycophantic, but it was actually genuine. Behind him, scarlet robed councillors beamed a welcome too.

Polite applause broke out from the crowd as Rose stepped from the car, a white Land Rover Evoque, and took Lance's hand. Slightly behind him Julia winked, prompting Rose to give her a just-perceptible nod as she was transported back to the day they'd first met and found they had adjacent rooms in the Women's Hall of Residence, at Trinity College, Dublin.

'Beautiful day for the Fayre, Your Worship.' Rose said, returning to formality.

'We're so pleased you could come, Mrs. Jellicoe.' the Lord Mayor answered. 'The city is honoured by your presence.'

Rose couldn't help smiling at this short, but entirely predictable, conversation knowing that behind the pomposity both showed was a genuine and longstanding friendship for, not only had she and Julia known each other at college, but Lance and her husband James had known each other since they were at Harrow. For a moment she let her concentration slip as thoughts of her student days in Dublin drifted back. Little would she have thought in those carefree times that one day she'd be the wife Britain's Prime Minister, or that the studious looking girl who'd moved into the room next to hers would become the Lady Mayoress of Brighton and Hove. So engrossed in her thoughts was she, she nearly missed the Mayor's invitation. 'So is that alright, Mrs. Jellicoe?'

'What? Oh yes, meet the committee. Certainly.'

The official opening ceremony, followed by a tour of the Fayre, wasn't scheduled to start until one, which left enough time after the introductions had been made for Lance to escort Rose and Julia through the vast and somewhat cavernous Entrance Hall into the smaller more intimate Octagon Room, a tiny architectural extravagance, where coffee was awaiting them.

'It'll be the last chance for you two to have a chat before the fun begins.' Lance whispered, 'How's James?'

'Fine, but he's having a tough time with the Health cuts. He'd much rather be here with us than stuck, arguing, in the Cabinet Room all day.'

'I wouldn't have his job for all the tea in China.' Lance said, not intending the visual pun he was creating when he picked up the thermos jug and said, 'Coffee?'

'Please ... so what am I going to see, I don't want any surprises ... anything special I should, or shouldn't do, or say?'

Lance shook his head. 'Sorry, I ought to have given you a list of exhibitors; I'll slip out and get one.'

Julia stretched across the table and picked up the milk jug. 'With or without?' she asked.

'With ... er ... just a drop, thank you. I like the dress.'

'I bumped into Ursula last week.' Julia replied, either not having heard Rose's comment, or not wanting to admit she'd bought her outfit in Marks and Spencer's.

'Ursula? Really ... where?'

'Local hotel, here in Brighton, The Feathers; she wasn't very pleased.'

'I'm not surprised. Who was she with?'

'Who d'you think?'

'Not Henry Finnerty. Oh God, that sister of mine's a pain. James has asked me to distance myself from her ... but how can I

... I don't know what to do?'

'She should have more sense than to get involved with that idiot Henry anyway; it'll come to no good, and you could be caught in the backwash. No wonder James is upset; his political opponents'll have a field day if the tabloids get sniff of any scandal they can attach to you. Have you tried talking to her? I presume you have.'

'Julia, I might as well talk to the wall. Ursula no longer cares what people think about her. Lucky she never had children; they'd be the first to suffer.'

'True ... though children might've ...'

'What, with Alex Constantanidi as their father? Do me a favour! Maybe if she'd stuck with Gareth it would have been different ... or even Milton, I liked him. As it is, any possibility of her having a conscience about her 'carryings on' rubbing off on me ... and therefore onto James ... well ... she doesn't. She couldn't care less. We had flaming row the last time we met; she even slapped me ... slapped my face ... my own sister!'

'She didn't.'

'She did; we haven't seen each other since. I rang her a week ago to try and make peace but she got shirty and put the phone down. I don't know, Julia, I'm at my wit's end. How can I pretend I have nothing to do with her when everyone knows who she is?'

9, Pendine Avenue,

Eastbourne, Sussex.

Not long after ten o'clock a Police van drove up Pendine Avenue and stopped at Annie Weaver's house. It was driven by a member of the SOCO (Scene of Crime Officers) squad, from Brighton, led by Sergeant Geordie Hawkins, a friend of Reynard's, which had been called in by Chief Superintendent Horrocks, the Officer-in-charge at Eastbourne Police station. He'd decided, after hearing from the Sergeant on the scene in Pendine Avenue, that while death due to natural causes related to the lady's age was most likely, it was also possible, that a crime, even one as serious as murder, had been committed there.

Once the van had been backed into the driveway, the SOCO boys unloaded their stuff, carried it round into the back garden, and erected a blue incident tent over Annie's body and the ground immediately surrounding it. It had hardly been put up when Dr Emil Vladic, the County Police Surgeon, who also worked from Brighton, turned up. His preliminary examination of Annie uncovered no obvious reason for her death: no wounds, no bruises, no signs to indicate she'd been attacked. He had a careful look around the area nearby, and a more cursory one over the rest of the back garden where, once again, he saw nothing suspicious.

He left a few minutes later, telling Sergeant Hawkins he'd like to arrange for the body to be picked up and delivered to the Path Lab in the Royal Sussex Hospital in Brighton as soon as it could be moved.

Hawkins nodded. 'That's alright by me; I don't think we'll need her once we've finished photographing her, and everything close to her. But it's not up to me; whoever turns up from CID will make that decision. It could be Foxy Reynard, Archie Lawrence, or Jack Crowther. We'll have to wait and see.'

'Fine,' said Vladic, I've promised to take my wife to some food thing for a couple of hours at lunchtime, but I'll be back in the lab before three to make a start on the autopsy. Perhaps you'd mention this to whoever arrives to take over the investigation.'

'Not a problem.' said Hawkins, squatting down to stare at the ground in the hope he'd spot something which would give him a clue as to what had transpired there during the previous night.

☼☼☼

About fifteen minutes later, and just as he was about to give up, he saw something that looked out of place shoved into the foliage of a Hydrangea bush next to where Annie was sitting - a ball of screwed up masking tape. As he reached to take it out he heard voices and swivelled round; Reynard and Groves had just come round the corner of the shed and were approaching the tent. 'Ah, Foxy,' he said, 'I was praying it would be you.'

'Really, I don't know that I want to be the answer to anyone's prayers, especially yours.' Reynard replied, entering the tent. 'What're you doing down there on your knees anyway? Oh yes, you said didn't you, praying.'

'Very funny, d'you know what I mean? You and I have always worked well together ... whereas with either of the other two ... well ... Archie fusses, and Jack's far too slow.'

'Vladic been yet?'

'And gone; he wants the body ASAP. I told him you'd release it when you're ready. He didn't find a thing ... went over her thoroughly but didn't see any marks so he couldn't say how she died. I saw nothing either, have a look yourself, you might do better.'

Reynard turned to Groves and waved his hand towards Annie's body. 'Your job I think, Sergeant.'

'Yes Guv.' Groves replied, going over and slowly peeling back the rug Peter had used to cover the woman's nakedness. 'How bizarre, poor soul,' she said, 'she must be eighty if she's a day, and to end up like this. What was she doing out here with no clothes on?'

'What indeed?' said Reynard, checking the time on his watch. 'Maybe she was just forgetful and went out into the garden looking for them. Old people do odd things all the time.'

'You in a hurry, Foxy, I see you looking at the time?' said Hawkins, standing up and wiping his hands on the rug.

Reynard gave him a disapproving look. 'Don't do that!'

'What? Oh yeah ... are you two off or not then?'

'We are, we're giving a talk to the Rotary Club in the Feathers Hotel at half past one. Can't miss it. Boss's orders.'

'Bradshaw?'

'Who else? Yes. But we'll be back here sometime after two. I just wanted to have quick look around before we did the talk ... get some idea of what happened.'

'I don't think much did happen; I've found nothing to suggest anything but natural causes. Anyway, I'll be examining the area inside the tent later, photographing as I go. Why don't you have a quick shufti outside before you leave?'

'Anyone been in the house?'

'Just the lads who checked to see if there was anyone else there, which there wasn't; only piles and piles of rubbish. They're outside waiting for orders from whoever's in charge; you I suppose.'

'Give him a coconut, Sergeant!' said Reynard, laughing.

'Yeah ... and when they found the house unoccupied they locked up and took the key. They'll give it you if you ask them.'

'Groves can do that after she's checked the victim and Vladic can have the body whenever he wants. After that we'll push off and get this lecture out of the way, hopefully being back here around two or two thirty. Before that another of my team'll be here.'

'Fair enough. Watch where you put your feet, I'll be looking for foreign footprints when I'm finished in here.'

'What d'you mean, foreign?'

'Ones that aren't the old woman's of course, the ground's nice and soggy, so I might get lucky.'

The Royal Pavilion and Gardens,
Brighton, Sussex.

When the Mayor came back into the room he had three programmes the size of weekend newspaper supplements in his hand. 'Sorry I took so long ladies, there's just enough time for you to have a quick glance at these and then I think we should be on our way; the natives are getting restless.'

'It's not one o'clock surely.'

'Yes it is; it's gone one.'

As if he'd heard the Mayor's words the Town Crier arrived to collect them and lead them back through the Entrance Hall into The Long Gallery where the rest of the entourage was waiting for them: Councillors, Committee Members, and 'hangers on' who, having finished their coffee were edging towards the door so as to be close to the mayoral party as it toured the stalls and display stands. At a nod from Lance the door opened and they all trooped out into the garden, the Town Crier in the lead, ringing his hand bell and calling for the waiting crowd to 'Make Way for His Worship the Lord Mayor and his honoured guests.'

As they emerged into the sunshine Lance turned to Rose.

'Here we go! Got your seat belt on?'

'Of course!' she replied.

☼☼☼

The Great British Food Fayre had been Lance's idea from the start, and he was banking on it to bolster both his personal and political image. But by the time he'd discussed it with his fellow councillors and milked his contacts for all the help he could get, the idea of making it a shop window for the best of British food had been embraced by the whole industry with such enthusiasm it began to gather a momentum of its own. The Sussex Tourist Board also saw possibilities in the idea and was soon deeply involved in building the project. In the months since he'd first thought of it, the concept had become a major event; a shop window for British food, and a tourist attraction which would bring people from all over Britain and the continent hopefully, to spend money in Brighton. Its success would guarantee him a second term.

☼☼☼

The scene in the gardens was impressive; rows of tents lining a path which encircled an array of stalls pitched around a huge red white and blue striped marquee. Garlanded maypoles festooned with silk ribbons stood on every corner; Union Jack flags fluttered in the light sea breeze, and there was bunting everywhere.

'I'm not looking forward to this.' Rose muttered from behind her hand as she spied a six foot high pyramid of pork pies inside the first tent they entered.

'It'll be alright.' Julia answered.

Rose shook her head, 'I'm not *usually* nervous, Julia, but for some reason I'm worried to death. I just hope I don't get asked to eat things I don't like.'

A man dressed as a butcher in a blue and white striped apron and wearing a straw boater appeared from nowhere. He was holding a circular tray covered with a starched white napkin on which bite sized pieces of pork pie had been interspersed with sprigs of parsley in a series of concentric rings. Right in the middle of the wheels of pie and parsley was a tiny blue porcelain pig. Oddly, it appeared to be grinning! 'Can I tempt you Mrs. Jellicoe?' The man said, shoving the tray closer to her.

Rose took a piece and nibbled a bit off the edge. 'Lovely.' she said, politely, and then, with a slow nod of approval as the excellent flavour and texture came through, added. 'Yes, really good.'

The man's eyes lit up.

In the meantime Julia had also eaten a sample and was mumbling compliments too.

'For the Prime Minister, with my compliments,' the man said, handing Rose a little box which his assistant had brought out when she'd seen the approval on Rose's face. 'And here's one here for His Worship.' he added, giving another to Julia.

Rose grabbed Julia's wrist. 'How many stalls are there?'

'I think Lance said there were a hundred and thirty, but you don't have to sample every one. This lot trailing along behind us in their fancy dress'll demolish whatever we don't take, just taste the things you like the look of, don't try them all.'

'Thank God for that.' said Rose, pausing a moment and bringing the whole procession behind them to a halt.

Lance grabbed her arm. 'Are you alright?'

'Yes, fine, I was just wondering how you'd gone about choosing the exhibitors when there are so many food producers.'

'I didn't select them ... what it boiled down to was that each segment of the industry invited a few of their more committed members to take a stand. The National Federation of Master Bakers took twenty six for instance, and The Cheese Makers Association took twenty, as did The Worshipful Company of Master Butchers and The Society of British Fruit Growers. The Brewers Guild brought a dozen or so. In addition we asked a selection of small up-and-coming 'prepared meal' companies, craft beer brewers, jam manufacturers, flour millers, fish and shellfish farmers, honey producers and all sorts of others. But we'd better get on; we've a lot to see in the next hour or so.'

'And to consume, I expect! Where do we go now?'

'We'll keep to the path, stopping whenever you want. All the exhibitors we pass will be fighting for your attention, trying every trick in the trade get you to take a sample, pressing as close as they dare in the hope of being photographed with you or seen next to you on the television. And then, apart from the food on the stalls, there'll be people drifting around dressed as waiters and God knows what ... I spotted a fellow dressed as a cucumber just now, and they'll all be trying to entice you to sample their stuff.'

'Like Simple Simon did?'

'Simple ...? Oh the Pie-man, yes. So shall we go?'

'Lead on McDuff.' said Rose, and they and the rest of the followers set off, only to stop again almost immediately at a towering display of wedding cakes.

☼☼☼

By two o'clock they'd been right round the path and were

heading for the stalls scattered around the marquee; they'd tasted smoked salmon, liquorice allsorts, quince jam, goat's cheese, wild boar sausages baked in honey, fish fingers wrapped in seaweed, spring onions, Bakewell tart, curried lamb, cocktail canapés, and scones. In between, they'd drunk buttermilk, Jersey milk, real ale, sparkling wine, and raspberry cordial.

They'd inspected almost every stall, admired almost every display and, by the time they'd got near the end of the tour, walked round almost every tent except the marquee; *it* had purposely been left until last so the stage inside it could be used for the presentation of the 'Best in Category' and 'Best in Show' prizes, and the announcement of the winner of a children's art competition which had been run in conjunction with the Fayre.

'Is there much more?' Rose asked, as they finally seemed to be approaching the big tent.

Lance, noting the fatigue showing on her face, said 'No, we're nearly done; another few minutes, that's all.'

Julia, who'd also noticed Rose wilting, linked her arm. 'Why don't we to sit down for a few minutes before we do the prizes; you're looking tired.'

'I will I think, I *am* feeling a bit light headed.'

'Chair!' barked Lance, who'd heard Rose's answer. And one of the councillors following them darted off to find one. Before he got back though, Rose had begun to sway and then, before Julia could get her arm round her properly, she slipped to the ground apparently choking, and gasping for breath.

For a split second nobody moved, and then it was all action. Julia dropped to her knees and turned Rose, wild eyed by then, onto her side, put a finger into her mouth and fished out the oyster she'd seen popped in only moments before. At first, when Rose smiled weakly, she assumed she'd solved the problem, but when Rose continued to struggle for air she panicked.

'There's something else stuck in her throat or her windpipe, Lance. Oh God what'll I do?'

Her husband, still all but paralysed by the shock of seeing Rose collapse, didn't react at first.

'Oh for *God's* sake, do something.' Julia cried, 'Get a doctor … she can't breathe.'

Lance turned to the crowd 'Any of you a doctor? We need a doctor urgently. Is anyone here a doctor please?'

A man, who hadn't seen Rose collapse but who'd spotted there was something amiss in the middle of the group of people in scarlet robes ahead of him, heard Lance's call for help and pushed forward. When he got to the front of the crowd and saw Julia kneeling at Rose's side, he dropped to the ground beside her and offered his help.

9, Pendine Avenue,

Eastbourne, Sussex.

Detective Constable Desmond Furness had been quietly "ferreting" away at his computer when D.C.I. Reynard telephoned him and told him to leave everything and go to 9, Pendine Avenue in Eastbourne, where a woman had been found dead in her garden, and to start looking around it for hints of what might have gone on there the night before. He was not to go into the incident tent unless Sergeant Hawkins of SOCO, provided he was there, said he could. Nor was he to enter the house.

Within half an hour of getting the call he was pulling in behind the squad car and, after a brief discussion with the two men sitting in it, and determining Sergeant Hawkins had already left, he was combing the garden for clues. Half hour later again his search had only produced another rolled up ball of masking tape and a feeling that the garden hose, still connected to a tap in the side of the shed and lying unwound on the lawn, was somehow wrong. Why was she watering the garden when it had rained so hard the previous day the ground was still soaked? And why had she cast the hose to one side so haphazardly; everything else in the garden was neat and tidy; there wasn't as much as a blade of grass out of place? Surely it should have been disconnected and coiled round the empty reel fixed to the back of the shed.

With nothing else obvious on the ground, and the house and tent forbidden territory, he decided to go round to the next door neighbour at Number 7 to find out what, if anything, they knew. His knock was eventually answered by a small timid woman who took flight the minute she saw him, backing into the hall again and slamming the door behind her. When he tried a second time she came back to the door but refused to open it.

'I'm a policeman,' he said, 'Detective Constable Furness; I'm in plain clothes because that's how we work. We're trying to find out what happened next door during the night.'

'You'd better ask the person who lives there then. It's got nothing to do with us.'

'She's been hurt I'm afraid; attacked possibly, and it's in everybody's interest we find out what was going on. Here ... I have my identity card, you can see it if you open the door.'

'If I open the door I might be next. Are you with those policemen in the car parked outside?'

'In a manner of speaking I am. Would it help if I got one of them to come over here and identify me?'

'I'm not dressed.'

'Oh.' he said, just stopping himself from adding "you're not the only one on this road"! 'I'll be back in fifteen minutes then, and I'll have one of the uniformed men with me. Alright?'

'It is if he's a proper policeman with a helmet on you can. You can't trust anyone these days.'

Furness was inclined to laugh but changed his mind when he realised his grandmother was just the same. 'I'll be back in fifteen minutes then.' he said, making his way round to try the neighbours on the other side of Annie's house at number 11.

The House of Commons,

London.

James blanched when the news of his wife's mysterious collapse was whispered in his ear. He'd been about to leave the Commons chamber to vote, in the company of the Member for Ipswich North, whose bill he was supporting, and he all but passed out he got such a shock.

When he recovered he dropped everything, including his mobile telephone, and raced off to Brighton to be at Rose's side. In consequence of leaving his 'phone behind he didn't get the information in Lance's second call until his secretary finally got it to him in the police car taking him to Brighton, at which point he was south of Croydon and heading for the M23.

☼☼☼

He'd left Barton Court at seven thirty that morning, having been up at six, gone down to the kitchen and made himself a pot of tea and then, sitting at the kitchen table, spent an hour skimming through the dispatch boxes a courier had brought down from Downing Street during the night. The cook had come in at six thirty, made his breakfast, and served it to him in the little dining room as he'd written a few scribbled notes to be given to his speechwriter when he got to Number 10 later on.

His journey to London through the early morning traffic had been speedy, thanks to the police car preceding his Jaguar, and he'd been in a good mood when he'd entered his office at nine having finished the dispatch boxes as they drove over Westminster Bridge.

☼☼☼

'The list please.' he'd said, as he'd walked through to his office where he'd taken off his jacket and handed it to Mrs Armitage, his secretary, who'd seen the car draw up through the window. 'And when does the damned heating come on?' he'd called out, rubbing his hands and looking at the radiator suspiciously.

'Any minute, Prime Minister; it was put back from seven in the interest of economy, just as you asked last week.'

'Did I ... well ... alright ... that was last week and it was warmer. Someone should use their loaf when we've an unseasonal chilly start like today. Now where's the list?'

'I have it here.' Mrs Armitage had answered, passing him a hand written list of his tasks for the day. Without it in his pocket he floundered; with it he worked like a Swiss watch. A man of lists, he frequently had to defend himself from the jibes of his opponents *and* his own colleagues. 'That your crib sheet Jim?' they'd say with a loud guffaw every time they saw him with a bit of paper in his hand.

'Yes,' he'd reply 'and your name's on it.'

Silly banter which disguised the fact he was actually a no-

nonsense man of steel.

The hour he spent with Mrs Armitage, a woman who was half as old again as he was, a treasure without whom he'd be lost, had been followed by another with Peter Arbuthnot, the Foreign Secretary, who'd brought him up to date on the collapse of the Middle East peace talks in Geneva the previous evening.

A meeting in the Cabinet Office, which he and the Foreign Secretary joined after their own discussion, had gone on until he'd had to leave for a private lunch appointment in the Naval and Military club in St James's Square, better known to its members as the 'In and Out'. Here he'd joined the Chairman of the Confederation of British Industries, George Natrass, a personal friend for years and, more recently, having married his sister, Amy, his brother-in-law. Their friendship was long one and went back to the early eighties when they both rowed in the Cambridge boat which twice lost to Oxford by a canvas.

'Sorry George,' James had said, looking up at the clock in the bar as he'd entered, 'I hope you didn't mind my suggesting an early lunch but I'm a bit pushed, and if you don't mind we'll go straight in. And please, please, please, shove me out as soon as we're finished. I have to be in 'the house' for …'

'Yeah, yeah, yeah … Question Time, I know.' Natrass had said, holding out his hand. It's just that I must talk to you about Rose's sister; I'm worried. By the way I've ordered you an orange juice … Is that OK?' he'd added pointing to the Britvic standing beside his Gordon's.

'It's fine. Just make sure you chuck me out by one fifteen. Now what's this about Ursula, I'm not her keeper you know.'

'It's tricky.'

'What is … Ursula? Huh, I damned well know that already, she's been the bane of my life ever since I got married. Rose is always digging her out of some mess or other. If Ursula wasn't Rose's sister, I'd throttle her. What's she been doing now?'

'Well it seems she's getting a bit too involved with that bloody man Finnerty and you know where that'll lead.'

'You mean Henry Finnerty who lives near you?'

'Yes, he has a little stud farm about four miles from us, just off the A23, outside the village of Dial Post, it's called Creakwood. Nice house, terrible land, and a bunch of shady horses of questionable pedigree ... know what I mean? It used to be a good business, one with a decent reputation, but since Finnerty's father died, and he took over, it's gone to pot. There're all sorts of rumours going round concerning dodgy schemes he's got going, "guaranteed to win" betting systems, all that sort of thing, the backlash of which, if true, might somehow damage you.'

'I see what you mean ... "P.M.'s sister-in-law involved in horse racing scam" ... Yes, I could do without that. Tell you what, I'll mention it to Rose tonight, we're on our own as it happens, and I'll find out what she knows. Thanks for the tip, any sort of scandal like that would be blown up by the papers if they found a link to me, however far-fetched.'

☼☼☼

Most of the time they were at the table they talked of Ursula, of her irresponsibility, and of the fact she'd already lived with and left two men, been married all too briefly to a third, and at the same time continued seeing Finnerty in a relationship which alternated between intense and indifferent.

Any sort of connection to him, via Ursula and Rose, however tenuous, had the potential of being disastrous: the infamy attached to Finnerty's horse breeding business was legendry, the reputation he had as a gambler was even more so, and his extravagant life style ... well it was like manna from heaven to the tabloids and the tittle tattlers of society.

As far as James was concerned, Henry Finnerty was bad news. Not that the man was openly dishonest, more that he was one who could work the system while giving a two fingered salute to the rules of acceptable behaviour. That he was "a character", no one could deny, but he was one to be observed from a safe distance. Only those looking for trouble got into bed with him, actually or figuratively. What the papers would make of Ursula openly attaching herself to him while she was still married to Alex Constantanidi, and what headline they might employ to indicate her relationship to Rose and James, was a worrying prospect.

As he returned to 'the house' after the hurried and disturbing lunch, James was trying to think of a tactic he might employ to put a distance between Rose and her sister; he wasn't expecting to hear she'd been taken ill and was on her way to hospital or that, within minutes, he'd be on his way there too.

Departure Hall,

London Airport, Gatwick.

Ursula Constantanidi, a tall, fashionably dressed and stunningly good looking recently married woman of thirty six, was sitting in a café on the mezzanine looking down on the Check-in Desks in Terminal One.

She was pensively sucking the spoon she'd been using to scoop froth from the top of her Cappuccino, and she was waiting for Henry Finnerty. He'd gone to park his car, having told her he'd be back in ample time for them to catch their flight but it was twenty minutes since she'd been dropped off and she was getting concerned about being too late to check in. She took out her 'phone and rang him on his mobile, but there was no answer.

They were on their way to Ayr, via Glasgow, with the intention of attending the Ayr Gold Cup Meeting where, at the nearby Old Racecourse Hotel, Henry would be hosting a cocktail party for a dozen or so of his northern clients, an annual affair.

The reception was likely to be hard going though, due to Henry's name currently being associated with a horse racing scam that had nearly come off. Nobody knew for sure whether he'd *actually* been involved, though there was a strong suspicion he had, for it was a plot to fleece bookmakers not unlike one which had taken place some years earlier with which he'd definitely been associated. On that occasion, like the more recent one, a number of very fast horses had been held back to give the impression they were very slow. They were then entered in races at a number of small meetings up and down the country which were taking place on the same day, and at the same time.

When the original scam was set up there were no mobile phones, and bookies depended on landlines to communicate. By ensuring every instrument at the race courses involved was in use for the ten minutes prior to "the off", the bookies were unable to lay off a number of last minute long odds combination bets and they lost a fortune. Actual illegality was hard to prove and nobody was charged, though it was said Finnerty was behind it all.

The very recent, equally innovative, attempt to fleece bookmakers had failed, however, when an over eager punter, who'd got wind of the operation seemingly by chance, placed a large bet too soon, thereby alerting the bookmakers and scuppering the operation. Henry was said to be hopping mad as a result of the losses sustained; woe betide the punter who'd jumped the gun should Henry catch him.

Ursula picked up her cup and put it down again as she tried to make up her mind as to what she wanted to do. Finally, she took her mobile from her handbag and rang him a second time. Again there was no response, which only further upset her and she stamped her foot. Ten minutes later, during which time she'd got progressively even more worked up, she tried a third time but still he didn't answer. 'My God, who does he think he is, thirty five minutes to park a damned car; we're going to miss the plane.'

She stood up and looked down on the Departure Concourse, hundreds of people … but no sign of him.

She shook her head and sat down again. 'I don't know

why I'm doing this,' she mumbled, 'it's not as if I want to go to the stupid races, or to bloody Scotland. And it's not that I particularly want to be with him for the weekend either. I don't know what I was thinking about when I said I'd go. Maybe it was meant to be … him not turning up, that is. It's not as if I really like him all that much either. In fact, if the truth were told, I'm a bit scared of him … and I certainly don't trust him. They say he looks like his father and acts like his grandfather, "Stirrups" Finnerty. He was a *monumental* tearaway … monumental. His father went by "Stirrups" too … I wonder why Henry didn't? She took in a deep breath and let it out in one long despairing sigh. 'Oh come, you great oaf, our check-in queue's down to two.'

She looked at her watch, took her 'phone out of her pocket for the fourth time and sent him a text.

Five minutes later he still hadn't replied.

The Royal Pavilion and Gardens,

Brighton, Sussex.

The man who'd pushed through the crowd, and joined Julia on her knees beside Rose, used his finger to check there were no more obstructions in her throat. Even as he did so, he began to suspect there was something much more serious going on than a bit of shell fish stuck in her windpipe.

'Well?' The anxiety on Lance's face was mirrored on Julia's as he asked the question.

'She needs to be taken to hospital immediately,' the man said, 'her breathing's dangerously shallow and her pulse is erratic; this woman's very seriously ill and needs urgent hospital attention, and I mean *urgent*.'

'D'you know who she is?'

'No I don't; not that it makes any difference. I can't feel anything else in her throat which would to cause such a sudden collapse. Who is she?'

'She's the Prime Minister's wife, Rose Jellicoe.'

'Oh … I see … that's awkward.'

'Yes, and she was alright one minute and the next she was

on the ground struggling to breathe. You *are* a doctor I presume, not a pressman?'

The man smiled, 'I'm a police surgeon, a forensic physician.'

'Here in Brighton?'

'Yes, I work from Police Headquarters in Sussex House but I also have a facility at The Royal Sussex.'

'So you *are* a policeman?'

'Of sorts, yes, though I'm here in a private capacity today; my wife wanted to see the Fayre. What happened to Mrs Jellicoe?'

'She said she felt light headed, and we'd just sent for a chair so she could sit down, when she collapsed.'

'So she'd not complained of feeling ill before?'

'No ... not as far as I know. What's your name doctor?'

'Vladic, Emil Vladic. Has an ambulance been called ... and ... er ... can you get the crowd back a bit, she needs all the air she can get?'

Lance nodded.

'And while we're waiting we might try one thing which works sometimes. Can you help me get her to her feet?' Vladic said, standing up from the ground.

With the assistance of two councillors, Lance brought Rose upright again and Vladic, by then behind her, locked both his arms round her waist and gave her a sudden tight squeeze. If there'd been anything stuck in her throat it would surely have shot out. But nothing came up other than a small trickle of vomit, and she was still in breathing difficulties.

Vladic shook his head. 'It was worth a try.' he said.

Lance smiled his thanks, and then turned to the councillors behind him. 'Move them back would you, I'm going to ring the police myself to ask them clear the way for the ambulance which, if I'm not mistaken, is arriving already. Miraculous ... only a minute or two since it was called and it's practically here.'

'It's a private ambulance Your Worship;' the Town Crier told him, 'we've had one here since the exhibition opened.'

Minutes later a procession of vehicles led by a squad car, and including the ambulance with its patient in the care of Doctor Vladic and the paramedic, was weaving through the still crowded gardens to head for The Royal Sussex Hospital. Julia was in the back with Rose too. And Lance, who'd insisted on going with them, and had enough clout to ensure he was allowed to do so, was in the front with the driver, his head metaphorically in his hands. What had started as great day had become a calamitous one.

In the back, Julia, recollecting the slow shake of his head Vladic had given the paramedic when he'd arrived, had been watching his face for a hopeful sign that Rose was responding to the emergency treatment she was getting; but none came. She was failing fast and, if the present look of gloom on the face of the paramedic was anything to go by, they'd all but lost the battle. All the way, as they roared through the streets of Brighton, the paramedic and the doctor continued trying to get oxygen into Rose's lungs, but they had no detectable success, and there was a palpable air of despondency in the ambulance when it pulled up at the A&E entrance to the hospital.

The Feathers Hotel,

Sea Front, Brighton, Sussex.

D.C.I. Reynard and Sergeant Groves didn't quite walk out of The Feathers Hotel hand in hand but they *were* feeling good about themselves. Their lecture, which had turned out to be halfway between a talk and an entertainment, had gone down very well and member after member of the Brighton Rotary Club came up to them afterwards offering congratulations.

Reynard had taken Chief Superintendent Bradshaw's advice and, assisted by Sergeant Groves, delivered a highly informative and entertaining address which had been much appreciated. They were only on their feet for twenty minutes, though to them it had seemed much longer and, during that time, they'd outlined the workings of Sussex's C.I.D., illustrating their talk with examples of unusual and amusing cases. So genuinely spontaneous was the response of the audience to what they were hearing that Bradshaw was already thinking of offering the possibility of repeating the talk to other Rotary clubs. Sussex C.I.D. didn't often get a chance to blow its own trumpet and Reynard and Groves had done the department proud.

As they left the dining room, Reynard felt an arm descend on his shoulder. He didn't need to turn his head to know who it was, for he'd spotted Bradshaw's guest when making his speech. 'Good afternoon, Sir,' he said.

'Well done, Foxy, and you too Sergeant, I'm glad I came; glad C.S. Bradshaw invited me as his guest.'

As a trainee detective constable, years before, the speaker, Bill Simpson, had been introduced to the art of detection by Reynard, at that time a lowly sergeant. Currently National Criminal Investigation Coordinator, and working at Scotland Yard with the rank of Commander, Simpson joined the police force straight from law school, and was fast tracked up through the ranks as his abilities were recognised. Despite the high circles in which he currently moves, he's never forgotten those who helped him get there. Prominent among the shadowy figures from those early days when he was a young copper learning his craft, is his first, and maybe his most, influential mentor ... Foxy Reynard.

'Cup of coffee before you go back to London?' Bradshaw asked Commander Simpson, hoping he'd say 'No'.

'Why not? I'm not in a rush. Let's all have one.'

'Fine.' Bradshaw replied, trying to sound enthusiastic, despite wanting to get back to his office to clear his desk.

'I won't Sir, if you don't mind.' said Reynard, 'The sergeant and I are on a case and we need to get back to it.'

'Oh ... right ... what sort of case? asked Commander Simpson. 'I haven't been at the sharp end for so long I've nearly forgotten I used to be a detective. Let's abandon the coffee ... I'll go with you.'

C.S. Bradshaw breathed a sigh of relief, and was about to offer his hand to Commander Simpson in farewell, when he felt the silent throb of his mobile telephone in his breast pocket.

The roundabout on the A23,
London Airport, Gatwick.

Henry's lovely car was wrecked, his favourite toy, and it was ready for the scrap yard; he was boiling with rage. He'd been on his way to park it, having dropped Ursula off at the entrance on the Departure Level, and had only a few hundred yards to navigate before he'd be on the slope leading to the multi-storey car park. He never saw the van until it hit him; it seemed to have come out of nowhere. He'd barely entered the cars circling on the roundabout when the unmarked white Ford Transit came charging up a service road and rammed straight into the passenger side of his shiny black Porsche 911, jamming all the doors, distorting the chassis, and crumpling the bodywork from back to front.

The van was full of money and had been stolen only minutes earlier when it had arrived with a consignment of Norwegian bank notes destined for Oslo. The thieves had attacked it as it backed into the discharging bay, emerging from their hiding place in a large empty packing case. They'd dragged the driver and his helper from the van, secured them with cable ties, and nailed them, together with two warehousemen, into the packing case they themselves had just vacated. They'd then driven off at breakneck speed, up the service road and straight into Henry's vehicle. Two of them were knocked unconscious and the police had them in handcuffs before they knew what had happened, a third got away, leaving Henry, semi-conscious having hit his head on the car window, slumped over the steering wheel behind jammed doors.

He hadn't been seriously injured by the impact, but he *had* been temporarily stunned and, as he slowly recovered his senses and began to look round, the full realisation of what had happened began to sink in. A knock on his window soon brought everything back into focus, and he turned to see a man tapping the glass with his key ring.

'You alright mate?' the man asked.

For a moment Henry said nothing, and then he nodded.

'I can't open the door, is it stuck?' the man asked.

Henry checked the handle and nodded again.

'You can't open it?'

Henry shook his head, somehow speech wouldn't come.

'Cover your face then, I'm going to break the window.'

Henry nodded once more, and was about to do as requested, when he saw others running towards the car. Heading them were two young policemen.

'Is he alright?' he heard one of them say to the man who'd tapped on the window.

'I think so, but all the doors are jammed and he can't get out. I was about to try smashing the glass.'

The policemen reached under his tunic and pulled out his truncheon. 'Here ... let me.'

By this time Henry had completely recovered his senses. 'Go on, whenever you like.' he said, leaning forward and pulling his jacket over his head to protect himself from flying shards.

The younger of the two policemen drew back his arm and hit the window as hard as he could with his truncheon; it bounced off. 'Jesus.' he said, changing it to the other hand and shaking the first one to get rid of the pain.

Another man appeared with a car jack, thumped it against the window without saying anything, and showered Henry with pieces of glass.

'Are you hurt?' the policeman asked, 'Will you be able to get out if we give you a hand?'

'I think so; it's just the door's stuck.' Henry told him, as he wriggled out of the seat and gradually manoeuvred himself out of the car through the window. 'Thanks for your help.' he said, when he was out. 'That bloody lunatic in the van never looked. I was on the roundabout and, although I saw him come racing up the service road, I thought he'd stop, not crash into me. You can see, from where the vehicles are, it wasn't my fault. He should be locked up.'

'And I dare say he will be Sir, and his mates ... for stealing a van and a load of foreign money ... if nothing else.'

'Foreign money? How come?'

'Oh yes; these laddies are for the high jump, the van's full of Norwegian bank notes. We were waiting for 'em down the road - a tip off. In fact we were about to block 'em off and catch 'em red handed when we saw them come roaring up the service road and run straight into you.'

'So you were waiting for them?'

'We were, and we were hoping to catch 'em without too much fuss; they're not known to be a particularly violent lot.'

'Until I showed up.' said Henry, wryly.

'Ah, yes indeed. Anyway, we've got two of 'em and we'll soon have the third.'

'Now about …'

'Your car?'

'My ex-car!'

'There's a tow vehicle on its way now to sort this mess out. I'll ask the guys to haul your Porsche onto the verge ready for picking up if you like. And while we're waiting we'd like to go over to our vehicle where we'll take your statement. After that you can make whatever arrangements you want to get your car home.'

'To a scrap yard you mean,' said Henry, thoughtfully tapping his fingertips on his lips. 'But first I have to do something. I'm supposed to be getting a flight to Glasgow and a lady who's going with me will be waiting for me in the Departure Hall, wondering what's happened. I'd better ring or text her, and tell her what's what. Perhaps you'd help me get into the car boot; my 'phone's in it, in one of my cases.'

'You're not going to get in there, Sir; not without some sort of lever or jemmy. It's jammed shut like all the other doors.'

'Oh hell … well I'd better nip over on foot and find her, or she'll think I've deserted her. Once I have her sorted and I've changed my flight to a later one, I'll come back.'

The policeman nodded. 'Fair enough, Sir, get in the car and we'll run you round.'

'No, it'll be quicker on foot; I can cut through the cars dropping off passengers.' Henry replied, setting off at a slow jog trot and quickening as he got nearer the building. Hardly had he got beyond the ring tone range of his mobile, buried somewhere in the boot of his car, than it started tinkling, demandingly.

The Royal Sussex County Hospital,
Brighton, Sussex.

As the ambulance drew up a swarm of helpers arrived to get Rose out of it and into the A&E Department where, in a small side ward packed with resuscitative equipment, Professor William Smithson, consultant cardio-vascular surgeon, and head of the hospital's Cardiology Department, was waiting to attend her.

Vladic, who knew the professor well, gave him a quick résumé of what had happened and told him what he'd found and suspected but, even as he did it, he knew it was too late for, by his reckoning, Rose had probably died a few minutes earlier, just as the ambulance was crossing Freshfield Road.

Because he knew he'd never be forgiven if he didn't do his damnedest to snatch her back to life, the Professor and his team tried every "trick" they knew. Their efforts were to no avail though and, with considerable regret and a lot of foreboding, the sheet was finally pulled over Rose's dead body fifteen minutes after her arrival. Everyone in the room was deflated; what had seemed a possibility, despite the odds, had failed to materialise, and they were left trying to untangle the thoughts racing through their minds in silence. True Rose's death was going to be no more devastating to her family than it would be to any other. But she was the P.M.'s wife, which meant the whole nation was going to be in some way affected by her passing.

The professor had quickly realised there was also another delicate concern with which he must deal. News of Rose's death had to be kept from the public, and especially from the press, until the P.M. had been informed. Knowing he was on his way, and might appear at any minute, the professor left the room to meet him, telling those who remained to stay where they were until he came back. Under no circumstances were they to speak to anyone or to use their telephones.

As he went out into the corridor he saw James Jellicoe and the Hospital Manager hurrying towards him. They were at the head of a group of people, including the Lord Mayor and Lady Mayoress, whom he knew slightly.

They stopped. As did he. It was his worst moment ever. He was about to destroy the look of hopeful anticipation on the Prime Minister's face

The Feathers Hotel,

Sea Front, Brighton.

There was a puzzled look on the face of Chief Superintendent Bradshaw as he closed the lid of his mobile telephone and replaced it in his breast pocket, and it prompted D.C.I. Reynard to ask if 'everything was alright'.

'That was your man Best, bright young fellah, there's been some excitement at The Great British Food Fayre, the P.M.'s wife who's there to …'

'Oh yes, it was in the paper.' said Groves unable to stop herself bursting into the conversation. 'She's going to be there to present the prizes today …'

'She's been taken ill,' said the superintendent, 'and she's just been carted off to hospital in an ambulance.'

'So why did Best ring you and not me?' asked Reynard, slightly annoyed the "proper" channel of communication had not been used, and probably more upset on that account than the fact the city's most important visitor had been hospitalised.

'He tried, but your 'phone was switched off.'

Reynard blushed, actually went red in the face. He'd turned his 'phone off while he was giving the talk, as had Groves, and he'd forgotten to turn it on again. Groves told Best afterwards it was the funniest thing she'd seen in years; the Governor wrong footed in front of his bosses. Reynard was furious though and, snatching his 'phone from his pocket, turned it on, only to see there *was* text and it *was* from Best. It said 'For your information, the P.M's wife, Rose Jellicoe, here today, has been taken ill and is now on way to The Royal Sussex County Hospital, upset by something she ate. The Fayre is to carry on as planned.'

Bradshaw held out his hand 'Here, let me see.' As he took the mobile he saw that, out of the corner of his eye, Commander Simpson was trying to stifle a smile. 'What is it? he asked.

'I'm trying not to laugh.' Simpson replied, 'But isn't it ironic that the great VIP guest, at The Great British Food Fayre, winds up in hospital suffering from food poisoning.'

'Oh ... I know ... the papers'll have a field day.'

'You're dead right there. OK let's go to this house in Eastbourne and do some detecting, Foxy. I'm looking forward to it taking me back, if you'll pardon the pun. And ...' he said, turning to Bradshaw, 'I can see you'd rather be in your office ... so go. No need to worry about me; I'm going down Memory Lane looking for clues with my friends here, I'll be alright.'

'And you'll be returning to London later this afternoon?'

'As a matter of fact I won't. No, I'm half local you know, married a girl from Brighton when I was serving here twenty years ago ... Foxy was at the wedding. Mildred and I are staying overnight with her parents, who live on the seafront at Hove. We'll go back up to London in the morning.'

As they left the hotel they split. Bradshaw walked back to his office on his own, while the other three got into Reynard's car and headed for Eastbourne.

Departure Hall,
London Airport, Gatwick.

Absentmindedly stirring the last of the practically cold coffee, Ursula let her mind drift back to when she'd met up with Henry again after years of not seeing him. He was beginning to make a name for himself as a breeder at that stage for, despite his wayward approach to most things in life, he *did* know about horses. He also knew about women, in spades, she reckoned, and could, and did, have his choice of dozens.

In many ways it was no surprise they hit it off; they were so self-centredly similar; each using the other like a tightrope walker uses his equilibrium pole, balancing their lives with each other's sensuality. It was a curious relationship, exciting even, but it was never going anywhere … 'like right now, for example,' she muttered, 'he's blown it properly this time. He's either met some floozy he knows, or one of his drinking pals … and I know what he'll do. He'll come dashing up here at the last minute and expect me to *run* to the bloody plane with him. *"Run"* … in these heels! Well I'm not doing it.'

She slapped the table so hard her cup and saucer almost bounced off it. 'What beats me,' she continued, 'is why the hell he went careering off down to Brighton before coming here. "I have to see a man about something; it's important. I missed him by whisker yesterday. It's on the way, don't worry." he'd said, "You can wait in the car, I won't be long."

Who does he think he is? I should have said there and then I wasn't going to Ayr, that I'd changed my mind. I wish I had now.'

✺✺✺

A short tubby woman, in a ridiculously bright blue track suit with a picture of Minnie Mouse emblazoned on it, who was carrying a plastic supermarket bag and pushing a trolley loaded with pink and grey striped suitcases, stopped beside the table and put her hand on the back of one of the chairs. 'Is this free, dear?'

'Er ... yes.'

'Do you mind if...?'

'No, take it.'

The woman nodded and sat down; placing the supermarket bag on the ground beside her. 'My hubby's parking the car.' she said, 'We're going to Tenerife; it's our fortieth. You ever been to Tenerife?'

Ursula shook her head but said nothing. The woman, not to be put off, even by the lack of a spoken reply, said, 'He's gone halfway to France to do it. I told him he was daft. All that way to leave the car in a field instead of the car park ... and how much does he save? Three pounds, that's all ... three pounds. Barmy I call it.'

Ursula gave her a hint of a smile; just enough to avoid being unmannerly but insufficient to encourage conversation. The woman took the hint, dived into the supermarket bag and pulled out a shrink wrapped sandwich. 'Missed my breakfast.' she said, removing the film and taking a bite.

Ursula ignored her and kept her eyes fixed on the concourse below. 'He could be in trouble,' she said to herself, 'but then he'd have telephoned, and he hasn't. No, I know what he'll do; he'll come barging in here at the last minute. Amazing the way he *barges* everywhere, never walks like anyone else. He bursts into a room even if it's full of people and they're all screaming their heads off. They soon shut up when he arrives. He's like that in everything really ... *and* he gets away with it. Not with me though, oh no, he's not going to go steamrolling through my life and expect me to take it lying down. He *is* a character mind you, and women love him. And it's not just for his money, though he has plenty of that ... at least he acts as if he does. I like him when he pays attention to me but I hate him when he doesn't, when he ignores me. And I'm damned if I'm going to let him think he owns me ... which he's inclined to do. I don't want to be owned by him or anyone else.'

She took out her 'phone again and tapped out another text while continuing with her thoughts ...

'Pity about yesterday; I gave him the wrong idea. Didn't intend to, just got carried away when he appeared out of the blue and kissed me. Well I hadn't been out had I? Not since I walked away from Alex four weeks ago. I fancied a bit of fresh air and ... well ... seeing a bit of life again. What better place to do that is there than in the American bar at the Savoy, or Kaspar's? Huh ... marriage. And to Alex! I should have had my head examined. A month, that's all it took for me to realise I'd picked the wrong man ... not his fault I suppose but he should have told me, not let me assume everything would be ... well ... normal.

It was strange seeing Henry again though ... chance really. I'd hardly touched my first gin for days when he breezed in with that bitch Pippa Tomlinson on his arm. I don't know what made me call out to him; *she* was furious, I really enjoyed that.

Anyway Henry guessed I was ... well, lonely, and somehow before the evening was much older Pippa was out and I was in.

He was treading very carefully of course, knew I was ... well ... not quite myself. And then I went and ruined everything. Typical of me, flirting with him just to spite Pippa, and of course I wound up in his bed instead of hers. It shouldn't have been the end of the world even then; wouldn't have been, except he took it as a major signal and asked me to go to Ayr with him.

"Come on," he said, "it'll be fun."

And I said "yes" ... I can't think why ... I wish I hadn't now. I never gave it any proper thought at the time. I mean I'd no clothes, no make-up, nothing.

"Oh don't worry about that," he said, "we can pick up a few things on the way."

Pick up a few things on the way! Me! No thank you! I shouldn't have had so much to drink of course, my own fault. I mean what was I thinking about? Ah well, I suppose I knew the risk I was taking, yet I ignored it. It won't happen again.'

A new queue was building at the desk which had checked in the Glasgow passengers. The overhead sign read "Belgrade".

She got up from her seat to get a better view of the people milling about on the concourse, wondering if she wanted to see Henry amongst them or not, unsure of whether she should wait a bit longer or go.

'Ah to hell with him, if he doesn't come soon I'm off.' she said to herself after receiving no answer to yet another text message, her third. 'I hope he loses his skin at Ayr ... the bastard.'

☼☼☼

A short fat man dressed in a bright blue Lycra track suit appeared out of the milling crowd and came to stand at the side of the woman eating the sandwich who, by then, had almost finished it. He didn't say anything, just stood there.

'Well,' she said, 'Have you got them?'

He tapped his back pocket, and continued to say nothing.

'Good, let's go then.' she said, shoving the last quarter of her sandwich in her mouth, holding it there with her teeth as she got up from her chair and waddled off, followed by him, still silent, and pushing the trolley.

As they disappeared into the mass of people Ursula, getting progressively edgy, began tapping the table with her fingernails. And then, suddenly, she stopped. 'That's it,' she said, in a voice so loud several heads turned ... 'he's not making a fool out of me.' And without further hesitation stood up and made her way down to the concourse and out of the Departure Hall down a long corridor with a travellator, hoping she wouldn't bump into him coming towards her.

When she got out into the open she saw a single decker bus marked "Victoria Coach Station". It was just pulling up at a stop just a few yards in front of her. As soon as the exiting passengers were clear of it, she got on, taking a window seat at the back.

Moments later the driver released the brake and edged away from the kerb. As they picked up speed she turned round and took one last look towards the Departure Level entrance ... and there he was, Henry, red faced and running towards it as if his life depended on it

'Ah, you poor thing,' she whispered with exaggerated sympathy, 'you've done it again ... you've missed the bus!'

The Royal Sussex County Hospital,

Brighton, Sussex.

When he saw the professor come out into the corridor and stop, facing them, the Hospital Manager grabbed James Jellicoe's arm and halted him too. 'It's Professor Smithson,' he whispered, and James immediately knew; the expression on the man's face told him what he dreaded … Rose was dead. He'd had some warning as to what he might find on his arrival at the hospital fortunately, because Lance had got a message to Mrs Armitage at Number 10, saying Rose was in a far more serious condition than had first been thought. She'd then managed to contact him in the police car as it approached the end of the M23. Even so, to find the wife who'd seemed so alive when he'd waved her goodbye at seven that morning was dead before three thirty in the afternoon was very hard to take in.

'May I introduce Professor Smithson?' said the manager. 'He's Head of Cardiology, the most experienced heart man in the county. He's been with Mrs Jellicoe since she was brought in.'

'Perhaps …' the professor began. But, before he got as far as inviting James into one of the waiting rooms so he could have more privacy in his moment of sorrow, James asked if he could have some timewith his wife, on his own.

The roundabout on the A23
near London airport, Gatwick.

By the time he got back to his car Henry was fuming. He'd looked everywhere, but couldn't find her. 'She's gone off in a sulk, the so and so.' he muttered. 'Bloody woman.'

A low loader had arrived and, having towed the Porsche up onto the grass verge, was slowly winching on the stolen van. A policeman he'd seen earlier was watching; he had Henry's luggage at his side.

'Is this what you wanted? he asked, when he saw Henry approaching. 'Your bags don't seem to have been damaged.'

'Thank God for that.' Henry replied, picking up his brief case, taking out his mobile, and flipping it open. 'Oh ... shit!'

'Something the matter, Sir?'

'No, I couldn't find my friend waiting for me inside, and I'll bet these text messages are from her.' Three were. One wasn't.

The three from her were at around ten minute intervals, and went progressively from 'anxious' to 'angry'. The last finishing with a very terse and biting threat: 'If you can't be bothered to reply, I can't be bothered to wait.'

'Eff you too.' he said, angrily, scrolling down to the final text message. It was the shortest one of all. 'Job done. Went OK.' was all it said. There was no signature but the words seemed to please him, for he calmed down and began smiling.

'Must be good news, Sir.' the policemen said.

'Er ... yeah, not bad.' Henry answered.

The policeman nodded. 'Want any help getting your car sorted. I dare say this man'll take yours as well if you ask him. Mind you he's only going to Crawley.'

Henry thought for a minute 'No, I'd better get my own garage to see to it. I'll call them.'

'Far is it?'

'Near Horsham - Town and Country Cars - they're the people I bought it from. But I'm going to Glasgow - have to.'

'Ah, so you managed to get your flight changed?'

'Four o'clock.' Henry said, glancing up at the clock which showed it was coming just after three. 'I'm going to get someone to drive up from my place and keep an eye on the car and so on until the tow truck from Town and Country gets here.'

'Very wise, Sir,' the policeman said, strolling off to join his colleague who was signalling they should be on their way.

It had started to rain by then and Henry's raincoat and umbrella were lying on the back seat of the Porsche. He went over and tried to yank the door open but it wouldn't budge. 'Bugger, bugger, bugger.' he shouted, kicking the back wheel a couple of times for good measure. Then, taking out his 'phone from his pocket, he dialled his yard manager. It seemed an age before Sam Midleton finally answered. 'What kept you, for Christ's sake?' Henry asked, not bothering to hide his annoyance.

'Sorry, Boss, I couldn't pick the phone up, my hands

were all mucky ... something the matter?'

Finnerty told him.

'Oh my Goodness, are you alright, you're not injured?'

'No of course I'm not. But I want you to drop everything and get here as quick as you can. You'll have to look after the car until Town & Country pick it up. I can't do it myself; I've got a plane to catch.'

'OK, I'm on my way.' said Sam, not attempting to prevent the smirk which was fast developing on his face from becoming an outright laugh.

The Royal Sussex County Hospital, Brighton.

Thanks to the professor's fast thinking when he'd asked the staff to stay where they were, and the fact that they, respecting the delicacy of the situation, still hadn't used their phones or revealed to anyone that their attempts to resuscitate their patient had failed, James was going to have plenty of time to think of his next move once he'd spent a few precious last moments alone with Rose.

When he came out after his short vigil, he asked the Hospital Manager if there was a room available.

'Of course, we've already anticipated you'd want to talk to Professor Smithson, and he's waiting for you to call him on the house phone; his number is 3124. Dial him when you're ready and he'll join you in this small waiting room.' the hospital manager said, pointing to an unmarked door. 'The Lord Mayor and his wife are in another one nearby; they can be with you as well, whenever you want. You have their number I presume?'

'Yes I have, very thoughtful of you, thank you.' said James, going into the room the man had indicated, taking out his telephone, and ringing Lance to say he'd need a few minutes with the professor after which he and Julia could join him. By the time the professor got to him James had already telephoned the Queen to inform her of Rose's passing, handed over his political responsibilities to his deputy, and rung the head at Cranleigh School, where his two boys boarded. He asked the headmaster not to reveal what had happened until he got there to tell them himself, having decided to collect the children and take them to Barton Court, where they could stay until he sensed some sort of recovery from the shock of their mother's death. He gave no thought to her funeral until the professor raised it.

'The ... er ... funeral, Prime Minister,' he began.

'Oh God ... yes the funeral ... now let me think.'

'I don't know how to say this, Sir, but Doctor Vladic, the man who first tended your wife, and I, have been discussing some ... well ... inconsistences concerning Mrs Jellicoe's death which, perhaps, ought to be ironed out before you think of burial.'

'It'll be at St Oswald's our Parish Church.'

'That's fine, Sir. It's just that I thought I ought to mention these slight difficulties after Doctor Vladic pointed them out to me, and I'm glad he did. Your wife died of heart failure, Prime Minister, but he, and now I, cannot see why a woman of her age and undoubted fitness succumbed so quickly. The oyster which had been choking her initially had been expelled and one would have expected her to recover speedily, not to have a regressive heart attack.'

'So what are you saying?'

'I'm not saying anything, I'm asking. Did your wife have a heart condition? And if she did what treatment was she having?'

'She had an irregularity which she knew nothing about until it was discovered during her annual insurance check-up four years ago. She takes pills for it. I have a similar problem; we take the same tablets. Why? Has this got something to do with it?'

Smithson slowly shook his head. 'That's the trouble, Sir, we don't know. We'd need to look more closely before we rule out your wife's existing condition as being one of the reasons for her ... well ... let's face it ... unlikely *and* untimely heart failure.'

'You mean the oyster mightn't have caused her death?'

'It might not ... and then again it might.'

'Ah come on Professor if you're having reservations about issuing a death certificate tell me what they are, and what I should do. I can't be seen to dither on this, and I'm not going to. If you can't issue a death certificate what happens?'

'Well a post mortem examination is generally required.'

'And in my wife's case?'

The Professor raised his bushy eyebrows and threw open his hands as much as to say 'In her case too.'

James thought for a moment before answering. 'What do I have to sign then? Give me the form and I'll do it. Maybe there *is* something. I never saw a fitter and happier woman in my life than Rose ... there has to be a better explanation for her death than having a damned shellfish stuck in her gullet. Have you any particular suspicions Professor, you or Vladic?'

'I haven't, but Doctor Vladic has, and he's probably the one who'll be doing the examination. Can you give him your wife's doctor's name, the one who put her on the medication she was taking? He can then give Vladic the reasoning behind his diagnosis and suggest what to look for ... and ...'

'You mean other than her heart?'

'Yes ... if necessary ... for example it might be

worthwhile examining her stomach contents.'

'She could have been poisoned? God Almighty ... is that what you're saying? Where is this going? My poor Rose.'

They talked for few minutes more after which James signed a form Vladic brought in.

As he left, the professor made one final observation. 'The very thought of a post mortem examination being made on a loved one is a difficult thing for anyone, Prime Minister, but remember this ... the result could throw light on something which will ultimately save someone else's life. It's a thought which often gives comfort; hopefully it will give you some too.'

When Lance and Julia appeared a few minute later, James seemed to be strangely composed even though he must have been in turmoil underneath. He told them of his conversation with the doctors, and of his intention to collect the boys and break the bad news to them himself before they heard it from anyone else.

'It's a sad day, Jimbo ... sad.' said Lance, slipping back, without thinking, to the nickname James had when they were both at school.

9, Pendine Avenue,

Eastbourne, Sussex.

They were looking at the ground inside the incident tent when Commander Simpson's 'phone rang. They'd arrived a few minutes earlier and gone straight through to the back garden after failing to find Furness who, they'd have discovered had Reynard texted him, was next door at Number 7 drinking tea with Alison Dandy, Annie Weaver's elderly neighbour.

'What?' said the commander, 'Dead?'

He took the 'phone from his ear and looked at it as though he was doubting the information he'd been given. But the response he got seemed confirmatory, for he began to look very serious. 'And when did this happen?'

The answer which came back seemed complicated and Reynard and Groves, quickly losing track of the conversation, resumed their ground search. 'OK.' said Simpson, 'So what d'you want me to do, Sir?

'Sir' ... Reynard and Groves both looked up with renewed interest. Who was this big nob talking to the Commander ... and who'd died? It had to be someone important.

'No, I'm in Eastbourne at the moment. I'm with D.C.I

Reynard of the local C.I.D. but I can go back to Brighton if you'd rather have me on hand.'

There was another pause during which the commander continued to nod and say, 'Yes', until he got to what was clearly the end of the call when he said. 'Alright, I'll carry on as planned.'

'Someone you know died?' asked Reynard, as casually as he could manage.

Commander Simpson, not normally a man to display his emotions, nodded. 'Yes, it is, Foxy. It's someone we all know; it's the Prime Minister's wife.'

'What?' exclaimed Groves, unable to suppress her shock, 'That's awful, Sir, what happened?'

'We won't know for some time,' he replied, 'there'll have to be a lot of tests. The problem is it's almost certainly something she ate at The Fayre.'

Groves's eyebrows shot up in surprise. 'Food poisoning?'

Reynard, whose thoughts were racing through *his* head, could see a bigger picture emerging. 'There's going to be a huge Public Safety issue with this, Sir ... and a risk of panic. Everyone who ate at the exhibition yesterday will be worrying. Some'll talk themselves into feeling ill even if they're not. It'll be a hard task keeping this from turning into mass hysteria. Thank God *we* won't be involved.'

'Huh ... don't speak too soon.'

'You mean she was poisoned deliberately? Never!'

'She may have been. I mean it has to be a possibility until we know more. Is that fellah Rogers still the Police Surgeon here; I've lot of time for him?'

'Fred Rogers? No, he retired a long time ago; we've had

two since him. The present guy's called Vladic, he's Pole, nice chap, knows his stuff.'

'You'd better start praying he finds a quick explanation for Mrs Jellicoe's death then, or we'll all be dragged in.'

'Oh great.' said Reynard, who immediately felt guilty for having said so.

Victoria Coach Station,
London.

Descending the steps from the bus which had brought her from the airport, and then looking around to make sure there was nobody about who knew her, Ursula ran as best she could in her high heeled shoes, to a taxi which had just dropped off a fare. 'Savoy Hotel' she said, getting in.

The driver nodded, glanced up into his mirror to make sure she was seated, and pulled out into the traffic: 'Savoy Hotel … hmm … that'll be worth a decent tip.'

As they threaded their way through the traffic Ursula found herself wondering what Henry had done when he got into the Departure Hall and found her gone. 'I'd better write him off for a while,' she thought, 'assuming he hasn't written *me* off!'

He had though, high above the clouds and heading north for Scotland on his own, Henry Finnerty was muttering into a plastic 'glass' of whiskey and vowing never again speak to her.

'Never, never, never.' he kept repeating. And doing so, so vehemently, the man sitting next to him flinched.

'What a day', he said to himself, 'his fabulous 911, his "Porsche to beat all Porsches", was wrecked; he'd missed his flight; and his date for the weekend with a girl who should have been sympathising with him over the demise of his car had evaporated, abandoned him, buggered off and gone.

'And look at my bloody suit,' he muttered, 'ruined. I got soaked to the skin in that downpour and I still haven't got a coat or an umbrella because they're locked in the back of the flamin' car. Ah, to hell with it …' He signalled a stewardess coming down the aisle. 'Another Scotch, darling … no make it two, these bloody bottles are getting smaller.'

The Savoy Hotel,
London

Ursula had hardly got seated in the strategically advantageous position in the American Bar she often took, and ordered her first Bombay and Ginger, when she heard a man at a table behind her, telling the woman he was with, that the Prime Minister's wife had died.

At first she thought she'd misheard what he'd said it was so preposterous. How could the Prime Minister's wife be dead? Rose was the Prime Minister's wife and she wasn't dead. Obviously they were referring to the Prime Minister of another country ... and yet? She turned round to see who was talking and found herself facing the most English looking couple imaginable and somehow, instinctively, she knew it was Rose they were talking about.

'Excuse me,' she said, I couldn't help overhearing you just now, is it Rose Jellicoe who's died?

The man seemed to see something which told him she was connected to Rose. Maybe it was a tiny mannerism of which she was unaware, or the way she held her head. Whatever it was he spoke gently, sensing his words would bring a reaction.

'I'm afraid it is, yes.' he said, 'She died a short while ago in a hospital in Brighton; she'd been attending big some food exhibition I think. It's on every radio and television station according to the Hall Porter.'

Ursula shook her head to rid herself of his words. Then leapt from her seat, grabbed her handbag, and made for the Ladies Room as fast as she could, where she burst into tears.

'Are you alright?' It was the attendant, a big black girl, pretty, and kind looking. 'Something I can do?'

Ursula shook her head; nothing made sense. How could Rose be dead … how could she be? She reached into her handbag and took out her phone, but before she'd switched it on she was overwhelmed by another bout of tears. The attendant took her arm and ushered her to a chair. 'Can I call someone?' she said.

Ursula shook her head again, and dabbed her tears. 'No thanks I must go; it's my sister, I've just heard she's died.'

'Oh dear. I'll get you some water … alright?''

Ursula nodded and, somewhat more composed after a sip or two, thanked the girl for her kindness and gave her a five pound note.

'I couldn't.'

'Go on take it.' Ursula said, 'Have you got a sister?'

'I've got three.'

'Don't ever fall out with them. I said some awful things to mine the last time I saw her and now she's dead and I can't say sorry. I'll never be able to say sorry.'

And with that, tears still streaming down her face, she slowly walked out through the Foyer and out into The Strand.

At first she'd intended to grab a cab from the rank at the hotel and go straight to the room she'd taken in the hotel in Bloomsbury where she'd hidden herself in the past, but when she felt the need of air and space and time to think, she walked on past the cabs into The Strand, and turned for Trafalgar Square.

After a few yards she saw an alley down to her left she'd never noticed before. She went into it as if she'd been drawn into it, and down the few stone steps leading to Carting Lane.

Ahead she could see the green shrubs and trees of Embankment Gardens. Just the place.

She walked on, calmer with every step and, when she got to the gardens, she took a seat facing across the river to the National Theatre and the Festival Hall, and then, only then, was she able to find enough courage to ring James.

Alan Grainger

DAY TWO

Friday 18th September 2009

Alan Grainger

The Pathology Department,
Royal Sussex County Hospital.

Two trollies were parked in the centre of the floor; each had a woman's body on it. One was completely covered with a sheet and was just about to be removed into temporary chilled storage. It was that of Annie Weaver. Doctor Vladic had completed his preliminary un-intrusive examination of her long before going to the Food Fayre and he'd found nothing to suggest a violent attack; no wounds, no bruises, nothing, and he'd left his assistant getting ready for them to make a start on the examination of the organs when he returned.

During the short cursory examination he had the opportunity to give them before leaving to collect his wife, he'd discovered two minor things he'd missed in the poorer light in the garden: a pair of very faint red marks on Annie's cheeks, just in front of her ears, and two almost invisible ones on the backs of her wrists. Along the edge of the mark on one of her cheeks he found an inch long extremely thin white line of a rubbery substance. Guessing what it was, immediately he sent a sample to the analytical laboratory for positive confirmation.

Once Annie's body had been temporarily wheeled away, various capped and gowned observers with specialist knowledge, drawn from the hospital staff, moved into the space on which she'd been parked and began to watch two similarly clad men standing on either side of Rose's body.

One of them, who'd recently arrived at the hospital, was short and rotund and, from the little of his face which was visible, appeared to be about sixty years of age. He was Professor Sir John Goodfellow, a senior pathologist from the Home Office who'd been rushed down from Crawley, leaving a job there unfinished. The figure standing beside him was Doctor Vladic, who'd been in no way offended when Sir John was brought in, and more than flattered when he'd been asked to assist.

Things had developed rapidly the previous afternoon. Hardly had the news of Rose's death been released than rumours started flying round: she'd choked to death on an oyster, she'd got food poisoning from one of the samples she'd eaten, she'd had a heart attack, she'd been assassinated in some way yet to be discovered in response to her husband's unrelenting stand on the ruling regimes in Syria, Iraq, Iran, and Israel. The rumour mongering had to be stopped, and James agreed.

He'd already come to the conclusion that Rose had actually died from the effect, or the secondary effect, of something she had eaten at the Fayre. Dr Vladic concurred, and Professor Smithson, though a heart specialist and not well qualified to make a dependable judgement of that sort, also agreed.

The question was 'how many other people had eaten the same things and how many of them had weak hearts and might collapse and die as Rose had done'? The risk of a full scale disaster could not be ruled out and, it was agreed, the only way to avoid other tragedies occurring was to find out exactly how Rose had actually died.

James, while not having thoughts as far-fetched as some around him, needed no persuasion to agree to an autopsy and would have been happy enough to let Doctor Vladic do it, indeed he'd said as much the previous day. But, within an hour of Rose's death being released via a statement to the press, other and wilder reasons for it started to appear on Facebook and Twitter. To keep any sort of control on this dangerous development the best in the land had to be brought in to find a definitive answer. Sir John Goodfellow was the obvious choice, a senior pathologist in the Home office, a man with years of forensic experience, a wide knowledge of the protocols which were going to be have to be observed and currently doing a job in Crawley not forty minutes from Brighton.

The autopsy took most of the night and Sir John and Vladic, exhausted at the end of it, were found beds in the hospital so they could get a few hours' sleep while some leafy matter they'd found in Rose's stomach was rushed up to a special laboratory in the Botanical Gardens at Kew for identification. They were awakened at six when the answer came back ... Rose Jellicoe had eaten hemlock.

One might have thought such news would have been a surprise to the two men who'd done the autopsy, but it wasn't; Vladic had suspected something of the sort from the start and had told, first Professor Smithson, and then Sir John, both of whom, after carefully questioning him, were inclined to agree with him.

As it happened, Vladic when a student, and having decided on a career of forensic science, had chosen 'Natural Poisons' as a topic for his final year project. In consequence he'd become something of an expert on them and, though it had been some years since he'd given the subject a thought, it had occurred to him that the symptoms Rose was displaying as her life drained away might be put down to the onset of a creeping paralysis which was closing down her breathing muscles; a distressing situation liable to happen when alkaloid poisons like hemlock or curare are ingested; one which can be particularly dangerous if there's a weakness in the heart function.

'What now? Let the P.M know?' said Vladic.

'It's a bit early. Any chance you can rustle up some coffee while we go over the information again? We have to get it right.'

'Er ... yes ... and then ...'

'You have a number, you said?'

'I do.'

'Right. We'll go over it once more and then, if you call him, I'll speak to him.' said Sir John.

'Yes, but first I'll get the coffee.'

The C.I.D. Suite, Police H.Q.
Sussex House, Brighton

Autumn was showing its hand; carpeting the ground with red and gold leaves as D.C.I. Reynard drove away from his house at seven. He'd left his wife, Cathy, carrying a second cup of tea back to bed, where she was planning to finish her book before getting up "properly" and dressing. She'd some shopping to do after that, and she ought to bake a cake, but most of the day would be spent in the garden. With no children to care for she and Foxy led a quiet life at home, which nicely counterbalanced the pressure his work brought.

'Awful that business about the Prime Minister's wife isn't it Guv?' said Sergeant Groves, who met him on the stairs as he arrived at Sussex House twenty minutes later. 'Her death's the headline in every newspaper and on every newscast, and poor old Brighton is going to suffer by association. It just shows you how vulnerable we all are. Luckily I don't like oysters; I don't know how anyone eats them. I certainly can't imagine myself swallowing a whole one.'

'Ah, you don't know what you're missing, Lucy.' Reynard said, addressing her in a way he wouldn't have if they'd been in the company of others. 'But it *is* sad about her dying so needlessly, and you're quite right about the town's reputation. The guys who make up those tasteless jokes which always appear when something like this happens will be working full time, never giving a thought to the hurt they create.'

'They've kids of school age haven't they, the Jellicoes, two boys? They'll take it hard.'

'They will, and James Jellicoe's in for a rough time too.'

'I wonder if our two heroes, Best and Edwards, saw what happened, I suppose not; one of them would surely have rung you.'

'You can ask them yourself, they're just coming in.'

Groves had been taking out the porcelain mugs while she was speaking and Reynard, a Cona Coffee jug in his hand, was waiting to pour when D.C.s Best and Edwards knocked on the glass panel in Reynard's door. There was no sign of Furness but, just as everyone else was picking up a mug and taking their seat he rang, saying he was outside number 11, Pendine Avenue, having received a message from the occupier, Mr Aubrey Winters, the man who'd *nearly* spoken to Buzzy Knight and Peter McFee the day before, but had driven off without doing so.

Mr Winters, apparently, was now ready to talk.

The Pathology Department,
Royal Sussex County Hospital.

Sir John and Doctor Vladic, in the latter's office, off the Path Lab, had finished the coffee and toast Vladic had persuaded a nurse to make and were studying a print out of the email Kew had sent confirming the information they'd given verbally half an hour earlier. It looked even more explosive when written down.

'We've got to keep this tight, Emil,' Sir John said, 'P.M. only. It's red hot and only he can decide what's to be done.'

'Looks like murder doesn't it?'

Sir John sighed wearily and nodded his head. 'I'm afraid so, I can't think how the damned stuff could have got into what she ate unless it was put there deliberately.'

'I agree.' Vladic answered, 'It's common enough round here, grows everywhere, so I suppose it's theoretically possible it got into the food she ate by accident … but I doubt it.'

'What's it look like, hemlock? I don't think I've ever seen it growing in the wild.'

'You must have, Sir John, you just didn't recognise it. It's a member of the parsley family: two or three feet tall, small parasols of tiny white flowers, and often confused with what's known as Queen Anne's Lace, Cow Parsley, or Wild Carrot. You can see it growing in roadside verges and ditches all over Britain provided they haven't been trimmed or cut.'

'I was wondering if she was given it deliberately as part of a malicious campaign aimed at the P.M.; something to hurt *him* by taking *her* life.'

'Or a warning to the government in connection with a policy decision at home or abroad.'

'Or even a disgruntled ex-employee, exacting revenge on one of the food manufacturers who'd fired him, a spiteful and petty act which backfired.'

'Backfired?' said Vladic. 'It backfired alright ... it killed the Prime Minister's wife!'

'Ah no, that's not what I meant, I was thinking of ... but wait a minute, we'd better get this information to the P.M. pretty damned quick, You have that number don't you?'

'I do ... one he gave me last night before he left. It's actually his home number I think, his own home, the house near Horsham in which he was brought up. He was going to collect his sons from boarding school before taking them there. I heard him talking to the headmaster. Do you want me to try him?'

'Yes.' Sir John answered, watching as Vladic, looking very apprehensive, telephoned the number he'd jotted down.

James answered; he'd not been to bed, as they had surmised, though he'd tried to nap in an old velvet chair in what had once been his father's study and was now his Barton Court office.

'Sorry to call you so early, Prime Minister, it's Doctor Vladic. I have Sir John with me and he'd like to talk to you.'

Sir John reached across the table, took the 'phone, and for the next five minutes, read from the email and the notes he'd made when 'Kew' first called him, departing from both occasionally to expand on passages needing additional explanation.

Vladic sat back, listening, trying to judge from the expression on Sir John's face and the occasional monosyllabic responses the P.M. was making, how he was taking it. When Sir John was finished, the questions came thick and fast, culminating in one final and searching, one. 'Was my wife murdered then; your honest opinion, Sir John?'

'Sadly, Prime Minister, I believe she was. I'm so sorry.'

After he put the telephone down James sat in silence, trying to grasp the meaning of what he'd been told, attempting to work out the whys and wherefores, and contemplating the action he needed to take. But it was no good; his thoughts were racing through his head so fast he couldn't marshal them, and he got up from the chair and began pacing about the room. The motion seemed to calm him down and, after a few minutes, he returned to his desk and wrote down all the queries which had flashed through his mind. When he was satisfied he'd gone as far as he could he went through to the kitchen and made himself a mug of tea, took it back into the office, squared the list in front of him, and began telephoning. It was still only half past six in the morning.

By seven Sir John was on his way to Crawley to finish the job he'd left in a hurry the previous day, and Doctor Vladic, having pulled Annie Weaver back out of the temporary storage chamber, was getting ready to complete her full examination.

Four hundred miles away, Henry Finnerty was lying on

his back, snoring, in the Old Racecourse Hotel in Ayr. He was giving no thought whatsoever to what was going on at Creakwood, where the day was getting off to a normal start: Tracy, mounted on Slipstream, was on her way out to the exercise paddock watched by Tommy and Sam. And June, the girl who was so mad about horses she worked for nothing, had begun mucking out the stallion's loose box and telling herself she was enjoying it.

Ursula Constantanidi, lying on her bed in the room she'd rented in Bloomsbury was staring at the ceiling. She was wishing she could turn the clock back and wondering what she was going to say to James when she got to Barton Court later in the day.

The Path Lab staff, the specialists being sent down from London, and most of Sussex Constabulary other than D.C.I. Reynard and Sergeant Groves, who were already at their desks, were on their way to, or from, work.

None of them, other than Sir John and Doctor Vladic, had any idea what was ahead.

The C.I.D. Suite, Police H.Q.
Sussex House, Brighton.

'Did you get anywhere?' Reynard asked Furness, after he'd telephoned him, telling him not to leave Pendine Avenue without checking with the office first.

'Why,' Guv, something up?' he asked.

'No, but I've a feeling there might be. So how did the interview go, did you get anything?'

'With Mr Winters? Well ... I did and I didn't, Furness answered. 'He knows nothing of what went on next door the night before last, either in Annie Weaver's house or in her garden. On the other hand his wife might. She's a very timid lady and when I went round to talk to her yesterday she wouldn't speak to me. Then she changed her mind and said she would if I brought a "real" policeman in a helmet with me. I thought she was genuinely nervous so I agreed and, at her request for "a few minutes to get herself dressed properly", said I'd be back in twenty minutes. I was going to return with one of our lads from the car at the gate, hoping she'd settle for him being in uniform and not insist on him wearing a helmet. Unfortunately it was more like half an hour before I got there though, as I was delayed talking to the neighbour opposite.

When I eventually arrived, Mrs Winters had gone to work, leaving a note stuck on her front door saying she'd not be home 'til late, and that she, or her husband, would ring me if I left a number. I shoved one of my cards through the letter box and he called me late last night, suggesting we meet early this morning before he went into town to open his chemist's shop. I'm with him now so I'll not be in until around ten if that's alright with you?'

'Of course it is. Get as much out of them as you can.'

'What was that all about?' asked Groves, curious to know what Furness had discovered.

'*That,*' said Reynard, 'was the only member of this squad who's actually working at the moment. It was Furness, and he's about to interview one of Annie Weaver's neighbours who wasn't at home when he called yesterday. He spent the whole day in and around Annie Weaver's place as far as I know, so we'd better wait to hear from him. He'll be joining you at the Royal Pavilion Gardens once his meeting with the man next door, is over.'

Groves smiled. 'He'll not get much; in fact I don't reckon there's much to get. It was just a poor old soul suffering from dementia who wandered out into the garden during the night, with no clothes on, and died of exposure. It's sad but it's not complicated. Geordie found nothing of consequence, neither did Doctor Vladic, Geordie told me. We might as well hand it back to 'uniform' to tidy up, because no crime's been committed.'

Neither Best nor Edwards, who'd first been listening to Reynard talking to Furness and then to the exchange between him and Groves, knew anything about the Annie Weaver or her bizarre death; they'd been in The Pavilion Gardens all day eating free samples. After Groves had said her piece, however, they asked to be told about the death of the naked woman.

Reynard was on the point of elaborating, when Groves intervened. 'Are we having any coffee or not, Governor?'

'Of course we are.' said Reynard, handing her the jug. 'You can pour it while I check the biscuits.'

'Checking the biscuits' was enough to trigger a dutiful laugh from the others, but not from him; he took the morning routine seriously, seeing it as team building exercise. As he spoke he pulled out the top drawer of his desk and ran his fingertips across the packets, counting them out loud as he went. Every day began like this; a bit of fun to get things off to a good start.

When he'd finished checking them, he picked a pack out, opened it, and took out a biscuit. 'Right,' he said, taking a bite, 'back to Annie Weaver then. A neighbour spotted her in her garden at dawn yesterday, she was wearing no clothes and, because the circumstances were so unusual, we were asked to check to make sure there'd been no funny business. Doctor Vladic and SOCO were on site when we arrived and we were there about an hour, during which time none of us saw anything to make us think a crime had been committed. Sergeant Groves and I had to return to Brighton to speak at a Rotary Club lunch but D.C. Furness was there all day, poking around outside and talking to whichever of the neighbours was at home. The doctor's examining the body this morning; he might even have done so already; we'll get Furness's report in a couple of hours and the doctor's later today ... and that's it. Once we've heard from them we're out of it and 'uniform' can do the tidying up. Now ... how did you two get on? Did you see Mrs Jellicoe actually collapse?'

'No, Guv, we didn't,' said Best, 'neither of us. I was at the back of the crowd following the Lord Mayor and the council. Mrs Jellicoe was ahead with the Lord Mayor's wife but, with so many people, all I could see was the top of their heads. When the shout for a doctor went up I was concentrating on something else, well ... someone else really: Barney Truscott he was ...'

'Barney Truscott?' Reynard put down his mug. 'Barney Truscott? Is he out already?'

'He must be unless he's got a double. No, I was more than close enough to recognise him.'

Reynard saw the blank look on Edwards's face. 'Truscott's a man every copper in this division comes up against sooner or later: a pathetic little pickpocket who gets caught in the act, a house-breaker who leaves so many clues he might as well have signed the visitor's book, and a wife beater who once wound up in hospital with a broken jaw when his "better half" rode his punch and whacked him with an empty beer bottle. He fancies himself, mind you, a little tubby guy, he swaggers about the town trying to look 'the boyo' ... which doesn't impress anyone. Even the kids round where he lives think he's a joke.'

'Sounds like quite a character.' said Edwards.

'Oh he's that alright, but he's often on the wrong side of the law too. If he *is* out, and it *was* him, he could have ...'

Best raised a finger to stop Reynard, speculating. 'It was definitely him, Guv, believe me. He was my first "collar", I'm not likely to forget him.'

'What was he doing?' asked Groves.

'Talking to a tall man with his back to me. He gave him something which he put in his pocket without even looking at it.'

'A letter?'

'Couldn't tell.'

'Here we go.' said Reynard. 'Let's not get side tracked. We know where to find *Mister* Truscott if we need him so ... anything else to tell us ... anyone ... come on, speak up?'

Nobody said a word so Reynard continued, 'OK. let's have the updates on what our esteemed colleagues are up to.'

'They found the child, Guv,' said Best, 'she'd wandered away from her mother and somehow got into the warehouse at the back of the shop at Marks and Spencer's; one of the staff must have left a door open.'

'Did nobody hear her shouting for help or crying, the poor little mite?' asked Groves.'

'That was the trouble, she didn't shout, or cry; she was so frightened of what her mother would do to her if she caught her, she hid. She was found around lunch time yesterday, unharmed, in a cardboard box containing men's pyjamas.'

'Pyjamas ... God Almighty ... but it's good news for us; it'll take the pressure off the uniformed branch and we'll get you two back.' he said, nodding in turn at Best and Edwards. 'What about the other cases?'

'Not much to report, Guv, everyone was out looking for the child. The only other thing that happened was that the girl who was alleging rape has withdrawn her complaint.'

'Is that it then?'

'Yes, Sir.'

'OK Sergeant what about our stuff?'

'The same ... not that we have much on, the cupboard's a bit bare at the moment.'

Hardly were the words out of her mouth than she wished she'd never opened it, for she could straightway see a glower developing on Reynard's face. For a moment she thought he was going to explode but then, to her utter surprise, he started laughing. 'Alright we'll leave it at that.'

They were all on their feet and beginning to leave when Reynard's in-house telephone rang. He was in the middle of asking Best how his trawl for information on Mr. Ramage was going, and signalled to Groves to take the call. She picked the phone up and almost immediately put it back down again. 'The boss is looking for you urgently; he has Commander Simpson with him.'

'Really, that's odd? I thought he'd be on his way to London by now. I had a drink with him last night, Cathy and I went round to see him and his wife, they were at her parents, and he said nothing to me about staying on.'

'Must be important the way he spoke, you'd better go and see what he wants.'

Reynard threw his coat across his desk and retraced his steps to the main landing, off which Chief Superintendent Bradshaw's office was situated. When he got there and reached for the door handle he could see through the glass panel that D.I. Archie Lawrence and D.I. Jack Crowther, the leaders of the other two teams of detective who worked out of Sussex House, were there ahead of him. Presumably they'd got into work before him and received their summons first. They were sitting at a round side table the Super kept for small meetings, and they were talking to Commander Simpson, Chief Superintendent Bradshaw, and Chief Superintendent Pollard, his counterpart from the uniformed branch.

'Take a seat, Chief Inspector,' said Bradshaw, 'something's come up and, now we're all here, I'll ask Commander Simpson to elaborate.'

'Good morning everyone,' the Commander said, 'you may have thought you'd seen the back of me when I left yesterday and, apart from knowing my wife and I were going to meet my friend D.C.I. Reynard and his wife for old time's sake last evening, so did I. We, that is to say my wife and I, were staying the night in Hove with her parents and, at about six fifteen this morning, I got a very disturbing telephone call from the Chief Constable of the Metropolitan Police. He informed me that Mrs Jellicoe's death was not by choking, as we all thought yesterday, but by poisoning, which makes it a very different matter. Coincidentally, and at around the same time, Chief Superintendent Bradshaw received a similar telephone call from Commander Mustard your own Chief Constable. We've been asked to 'stand by' for further orders concerning the investigation into Mrs Jellicoe's death and, in the meantime, to see that all steps are taken to ensure nobody else gets poisoned the way she did.'

'But we won't know that until Doctor Vladic's report comes in.' said Reynard.

'Precisely,' Commander Simpson answered, 'Which is why I rang him about ten minutes ago. He and Sir John Goodfellow, a senior Home Office Pathologist, who came down to perform the post mortem at the request of the P.M., checked the stomach contents and discovered Mrs Jellicoe had eaten hemlock. He's gone back, but Doctor Vladic and his assistant are preparing to …'

'Hemlock!' exclaimed Reynard, 'that's Agatha Christie stuff.'

'Well it looks as though it's this killer's stuff too,' the Commander replied. 'and right now, as I was about to say, Vladic and his assistant are trying to work out which of the foods contained it. Once we know that we can check to see if there's any left and confiscate it. We must ensure we eliminate any danger of anyone else suffering the same fate as Mrs Jellicoe. Once we're sure we have that secured a full investigation will commence.'

'Carried out by some high flier college boy from the Met, I suppose,' said Lawrence. 'we'd not be considered good enough … They think we're a bunch of seaside cops who couldn't even catch a kid nicking an ice-cream.'

'On the contrary, Inspector, this'll be my call and I'll be

putting the best detective I know on the job ... D.C.I. Reynard.'

'Me!'

'Now don't start blushing, Foxy, my head's on a plate, and you may be sure I wouldn't appoint anyone I didn't think could do the job. As the man on the spot, as it were, it'll make many things much easier to organise and it'll give us a better chance of completing the investigation successfully and quickly. Any questions?'

Not a word was said, even the Super seemed surprised.

'Well? asked the Commander, '*Anyone* got anything they want to say?'

They all shook their heads except Chief Superintendent Bradshaw. 'You've done us proud by asking D.C.I. Reynard to head up this enquiry, Sir,' he said, 'and we'll not let you, or him, down. You may rely on that, and on all the support we can give him. He's only to say the word ... and we'll be there to help him in any way he needs.'

'Fair enough, so it's down to you Chief Inspector,' said Simpson, turning to Reynard. 'You're the boss. Now go away, think about what I've said, and come up with a plan of action. And get on with it *now*, get rid of all your other responsibilities, your colleagues here will help with that, I'm sure, and start thinking on how you're going to tackle this tricky and very sensitive situation. I'll talk to you in one hour ... Go.'

The Cabinet Office,

10, Downing Street, London.

'I shall be standing in for the Prime Minister today for obvious reasons,' said the Stephen Padgett, the Deputy Prime Minister, 'and, before we get into our business, I'm going to read you a message I got from him a short while ago … It is addressed to 'My dear Cabinet friends' …

"Thank you all for the messages of sympathy you have sent me and for the support you have offered.

I shall be at home with the children for the next few days, at least, but in touch and available all the time through the Cabinet Office Secretariat and through Stephen. Do not hesitate to contact me if you feel the need.

As to what happened to Rose, we're not sure at the moment other than that she appears to have swallowed some food tainted with a toxic material which triggered respiratory failure.

Whether the offending stuff was there by accident or design we do not know at this time, though an investigation to determine exactly what happened was set up immediately.

Steps are also being undertaken to ensure there is no repetition of what I hope will prove to have been a dreadful accident. You'll be briefed through the Cabinet Office regularly by the investigation team, which'll mainly be drawn from Sussex C.I.D. and senior Home Office and Security Service personal.

At this stage there is no reason to assume the incident which has had such a devastating effect on my family was other than a very serious misfortune.

If this perception changes you will of course be told.

Yours,

James.'

The C.I.D. Suite, Police H.Q.
Sussex House, Brighton.

Commander Simpson and Chief Superintendent Bradshaw were at the table facing him when Reynard returned to the room. Simpson had his armed folded across his chest, his eyes were glazed, and he looked as though he was only two blinks away from being asleep. Bradshaw, on the other hand, was wide awake. He'd been writing copious notes on a block of yellow paper, and was wondering if he should write more when he looked up and saw Reynard.

'Ah.' he said.

Simpson opened his eyes at Bradshaw's exclamation, only to find Reynard standing in front of them 'What have you got then?' he asked, pointing to a chair. 'Got it all worked out?'

Reynard smiled and sat down. He knew they'd have their own ideas as to how the situation ought to be tackled and by asking him, they were simply giving him the impression his views would be taken on board. Not that they would be ... or at least that's what he thought. In actual fact his cynicism was misplaced; both men had a considerable amount of respect for his judgement and ability, and *really* wanted his opinion.

'I haven't got it worked out yet, Sir,' he said, 'not in

detail anyway, and you wouldn't believe me if I said I had. I might have something to show you this afternoon. I'd like to raise one particular aspect which is troubling me though. This whole business is a major issue, it's not just the death of a woman who might otherwise have lived another thirty years, it's the death of the wife of a nation's leader. That merits special treatment and we must not only give it, but be *seen* to be giving it. Yet, paradoxically, we mustn't appear to be treating it in any way different to the way we'd treat the killing of any other citizen, not give the impression we consider one life more valuable than another. It'll be a fine a balance.

Public utterances coming from us will have to be honest and accurate, and tell of the immense effort we're putting in to close the case as quickly as possible, and yet they must also reassure the public that the effort we will be employing is no different to that we'd put in for anyone else. I can see this case throwing up a lot of pot holes in this respect, and I'll need constant guidance to keep me from inadvertently putting my foot in one of them by making an embarrassing blunder which will do nothing for the case and might put you both in 'hot water'. Other than that, I can only say I'm flattered you think me capable of conducting what will one day be a famous investigation. I'd love to take it on.'

Bradshaw, a look of astonishment creeping across his face, said, 'Gracious, where did all that come from?'

Simpson, however, with a tiny wink in Reynard's direction, which Bradshaw didn't see, said, 'Fair enough.'

For a moment or two there was silence as the three men mulled over Reynard's words, and then the Commander began to voice his thoughts. 'You're dead right of course, this death will be like no other as far as we're concerned and yet … at the end of the day … it *is* the same as *all* the others … someone has unlawfully killed someone else and we must find the perpetrator or perpetrators and see them in court. That's always been our mission and always will be ... no matter whom the victim is. The hunt for Mrs Jellicoe's killer must be no more, and no less, relentless than it would have been if that poor woman suffering from dementia you showed me yesterday had been the one who's lost her life. We *will* be putting in the extra effort of course, because we'll be *told* to do so; but we must be circumspect in the way we do it. We can't afford to hand ammunition to the P.M.s' opponents ... we'd be damned stupid if we did. What do you say Chief Superintendent?'

Bradshaw nodded, wiggled the muscles on his face, which might have meant anything, but remained silent.

Reynard saw his chance to raise another matter and took it. 'With respect, Sir, I have another point troubling me; I doubt an officer of the rank I hold being put in charge will impress the public. This operation ought to be headed by a more senior person. I don't mind doing the work, but we'll need a higher ranking man or woman to be in charge, even if it's only nominally "for show", as it were.'

'Good point, what level of seniority would do the trick d'you think. How high up the rankings would we need to go to cement the credibility you feel is necessary?'

That put him on the spot. 'Oooh ... I don't know about that Sir,' he said, with uncharacteristic hesitancy, 'it's not up to me to say.'

'But it is ... I'm asking your opinion.'

'Well, in that case,' he continued, rapidly running through in his mind all the people he'd be happy like to see appointed, someone he could work under ... as well as one or two with whom he couldn't. Ach ... I suppose someone with the rank of Superintendent ought to ...'

Bradshaw began to grin as Reynard struggled, and ought

to have gone to his rescue; but he didn't, he left it to the Commander. 'We were discussing that just before you came back in,' he said, and we've got the very man in mind.'

'May I ask who it is, Sir? Only I ...'

'Of course you may ask ... it's you.'

'Me?'

'Yes, *Superintendent* Reynard, you.'

'What?'

'*Acting,* of course, at this stage.'

Reynard, a man never completely stumped for words before, was speechless. Genuinely, it was about the last thing on earth he expected the Commander to say.

If he hadn't been so surprised at the decision to lift him a rank, he probably wouldn't have missed the question the Commander asked or needed the prompt Chief Superintendent Bradshaw gave him when he said, 'So ... er?'

'Sorry, you've thrown me, and I don't know what to say.' Reynard eventually said, 'What was it you wanted to know?

Simpson answered him. 'I wanted to know if you'd had time to give any thought as to what your first moves in the investigation will be ... we mustn't lose any more time in securing the scene in the Pavilion Gardens.

I know the movement of food was stopped, and all the sampling cancelled yesterday afternoon on the orders of the Lord Mayor. A fortunate decision he took even before he left to follow the ambulance taking Mrs Jellicoe to hospital, a precaution he deemed necessary to prevent the spread of what he thought might be food poisoning from something which had "gone off", rather than choking on something she'd failed to swallow properly. I doubt the *deliberate* poisoning of food crossed his mind.'

Reynard gave a confirming lift of his chin. 'True, Sir, which is why I sent Sergeant Groves and two of my three D.C.s to do much the same as you are now telling me the Lord Mayor ordered last night. The third man will follow then shortly.

Let me check to see how they've been getting on and what the current situation is, bearing in mind it's still only eight o'clock in the morning and the Fayre won't open until ten.'

The commander leaned forward and crossed his arms on the table top. 'Yes, go on, call her. Get an update and let us know what, if anything, has transpired overnight.'

'I will, Sir, and … er .. thank you.'

The Royal Pavilion Gardens
Brighton, Sussex.

Groves was at the main gate talking to one the security men who'd been on duty in the gardens all night when her 'phone blasted out "We are the Champions", a ring tone of which Reynard disapproved. He was a plain bell man.

'Are you there yet?' he asked.

'Yeah, we've been here a while, Guv.' she answered, flipping a switch on her mobile so the others could hear. 'We made it quite quickly because there was no traffic and everything was still locked up when we arrived. During the last few minutes though, the exhibitors have started to dribble in and set up.'

'What have you got sorted so far?'

'I've put Edwards on the main gate; he'll be there in the hut with the regular man until you decide how we're going to tackle the situation, or the "uniformed" men turn up to take over. Edwards'll tell everyone who comes in there's a security clamp on until further notice, and that all opened foodstuffs have to be bagged and delivered to the marquee which, luckily, won't be needed until this afternoon's closing ceremony.

When Furness gets here, I'm putting him with one of the

gardeners; they'll stay in the marquee until further notice keeping an eye on the bags. You did tell him to come here didn't you?'

'I left a message; he'll be there.'

'Good. And Best will be with another gardener on a mini tractor/van thing, emptying the refuse bins by removing the liners and taking them to the marquee. And that's it really; I'll be roaming around keeping an eye on everything until you get here.'

'I'll be a while, but you seem to have everything covered.' Reynard said, 'Just make sure there's no other way anything which was open yesterday gets anywhere near the public today.'

'Of course. Anything else?'

'Will you have everything done before the Fayre opens?'

'We will ... What d'you want me to do next?'

'Do next? Get back here as soon as the uniformed lot arrive and take over. Any of them there yet? '

'Are you joking Guv? Uniformed officers around at this time of day ... with the streets not aired ... do me a favour!'

'Call me again in an hour if you're still there. I'll have a plan of action sketched out by then,' said Reynard, 'and make damned sure you have all the bags safely to one side and secure.'

'In the marquee?'

'Yes, once you're satisfied they're isolated in the marquee, and the uniformed crowd have taken over from you, come back here; we've plenty to discuss, OK?'

'Not a problem, Guv.' she replied, flipping down the lid of her mobile again and putting back in her pocket.

Alan Grainger

The C.I.D. Suite, Police H.Q.
Sussex House, Brighton

After speaking to Groves, Reynard left the Commander and the Super chatting and returned to his own office to think; his new rank more a source of amusement than a matter of pride. He didn't want to be anything other then what he was, what he'd always been - a detective. Even the paperwork he was obliged to complete at the end of each investigation bored him to distraction. And he didn't need the extra money that would go with his promotion; he and Cathy lived modestly and with few indulgences. His father had left him enough to get rid of his mortgage, her mother enough to fund a small portfolio of unit trusts and government bonds. They had no children, hated foreign holidays and, in truth, didn't even spend the salary he earned as a D.C.I. The extra money which would be coming in would make no difference at all to their life, but the challenge of the Jellicoe investigation would, it'd be a reward he'd really enjoy. Pitting his wits against those of a criminal and winning, was goal enough for Foxy Reynard, being a Superintendent no more than a means of getting there. If the cross he needed to bear was that of unwanted promotion, he'd bear it. He could put it down again when the game was over.

As his thoughts circulated, he started to pluck them from

the air and fit them together as he would if he was building a jigsaw puzzle. Detection was like that, he reckoned ... or maybe it wasn't. Maybe it was more like tackling several bits of the puzzle at once, with the half completed segments stubbornly refusing to come together until those last few unidentifiable pieces suddenly saw their home and magically pulled the whole thing together. That's what he liked; finding those last few frustratingly meaningless fragments and using them to complete the picture.

'Hey!'

He opened his eyes ... and blinked. It was Archie Lawrence, the self-appointed clown of the department.

'I hear you'll have to get a new one, Foxy.' he said, tapping on the name plate fixed beneath the glass panel on the office door which read 'D.C.I. William Reynard'.

'Go away.'

'Charming!'

As Lawrence ambled off, Reynard's telephone started to ring; it was Vladic. 'So you've got the Jellicoe case ... no better man, you'll be even more famous at the end of this one.'

'Infamous more like. Anything I can do for you?'

'Other way round. I've some more information on Annie Weaver but I don't think you're going to like it.'

'Nor do I from the sound of your voice, what is it?'

'She'd been gagged and tied up before she died.'

'Oh no ... I didn't need that. Tell me more.'

Vladic launched into a long description of his finding the faint red marks on her face and wrists, and of the bit of rubbery substance on her cheek. 'It was an adhesive, the sort used on masking or parcel tape. I missed it, and the marks, when I examined her in the garden because her hair was plastered all over her.'

'Which's why I didn't see anything either, I suppose. So you think she was …'

'Tied up, yes; and gagged. I don't think she was taped to the chair or I'd have seen some of the adhesive on it, its arms weren't hidden by her hair. No, it seems more likely to me she was tied up to stop her defending herself or screaming rather than to keep her sitting in the chair.'

'So … no dementia?'

'Can't be sure about that until I talk to her G.P. One of your boys was there all day wasn't he? He might have found out who her doctor was … can you ask him?'

'He's on his way to the Pavilion Gardens at the moment I think, but, yes; I'll call him and get him to ring you back. Even if he doesn't know the doctor, he interviewed a neighbour so there'll be a contact of some sort for you.'

'Thanks *Superintendent*, I look forward to your call.'

'Don't you start! I'll ring you as soon as I can.'

The Royal Pavilion Gardens,
Brighton, Sussex.

'I thought you said you'd ring in an hour, Guv, have you finished your meeting?' It was Sergeant Groves; she'd just seen the last of the rubbish bags going into the trailer and was congratulating herself on doing a job which should never have been a C.I.D responsibility in the first place; detectives detected, they didn't shift rubbish.

'No,' he said, 'I just wanted to tell you a couple of things. First … it just might be that Annie Weaver didn't die of exposure while hunting for her clothes in the garden after all. I've been speaking to Vladic and he reckons there's more to it. She'd been tied up for a start.'

'How did he know that?'

'Deduction from clues we missed: pale red marks on her wrists and cheeks and some rubber adhesive of the type used on masking tape and parcel tape stuck to her skin.'

'Furness found some masking tape chucked in a bush, didn't he? It was all balled up as if it had been torn off something. Geordie found some too.'

'They came from her wrists and face probably. Is D.C.

Furness anywhere near you? I want him to ring Vladic and tell him how to contact one of the neighbours he was talking to yesterday; make sure he has their numbers handy.'

'Crikey ... so this could be another murder.'

'It certainly could. Now the cupboard's not looking so bare, is it?'

'I'll go and find D.C. Furness.'

'You do that.' said Reynard, chuckling as he put the telephone down.

✵✵✵

The early morning passed quickly for Groves and her team working in the gardens and, long before the public came in, they had everything needing a closer examination stacked in the marquee. The uniformed detachment arrived half an hour before opening time, and took over policing duties for the rest of the day, the last one of the Great British Food Fayre. It had highlighted the British food industry alright ... but not in the way intended.

The Lord Mayor, the head of the Council, and the Chairman of the Organising Committee, arrived together just before the gates opened. All seemed satisfied at the progress which was being made, and at the size of the crowd pressing to get in. As they began a short tour of the tents, hoping to encourage the exhibitors and to lift their spirits, they passed Sergeant Groves who, with Best, Furness and Edwards was making for the exit.

'Aren't you ...?'

'C.I.D. Sir. We met you yesterday.' said Groves. 'All the

opened food has now been removed and put to one side ready to be taken away for examination and we're about to leave too.'

'Oh, so who's …?'

'There'll be plenty of officers here Sir, uniformed men and women, not plain clothes coppers like us.' replied Groves, smiling as she and the other three headed for the gate.

Creakwood Stud Farm,

Dial Post, Sussex.

Henry walked back into the yard with a face as black as thunder. Nobody had turned up at the party when there should have been a dozen. The only one who'd bothered to telephone told him he couldn't afford to risk being seen to be connected to him until things cooled down. 'You were singing a different song last time we spoke, you miserable creep.' Henry said to himself, as he put the 'phone down, 'You were twisting my arm to let you "in" and I, damned fool that I am, did.'

He didn't risk going to any of the hotel's public rooms to be humiliated or ignored by people who knew him. Instead, he spent the night alone drinking whisky in his room, checked out of the hotel first thing in the morning, took a taxi to Glasgow airport, and was back in Gatwick not much more than twenty hours after he'd left it. A minicab soon had him home and, after a quick wash and a change of clothes, he strolled out into the yard to see if the mare had arrived.

'You're back early.' It was Sam Midleton, he was hosing down Slipstream having lunged him in the paddock, the first step in preparing him for his beauty treatment, and he was pushed for time because the mare was due at midday.

'The people I was going to meet scratched at the last minute, the card looked dull, it was pissing with rain, and I was worried about my bloody car. Have you heard from the garage?'

'Not a dicky bird.'

'Everything ready for the mare?'

'Everything ship shape as you ordered.'

'Anyone ring ... Mrs Constantanidi, for example?'

'Wasn't she with you?'

'No she bloody-well was not.'

'I suppose you heard about the Prime Minister's wife?'

'Yes, ate something at an exhibition I believe.'

'You were in Brighton yesterday weren't you ... before you went to the airport ... did you see anything?'

'I didn't go.'

'Oh ... only I thought you said you'd be pushed for time to do Brighton and get to Gatwick in time for the flight.'

'I did, but then I cancelled Brighton and did the job another way.'

'Erm ... I meant to ask you ... is it alright if I take a bit of time off, I've something to do ... family business?'

Henry stopped and swung round, glowering. 'Like you did yesterday you mean?' he said.

'Yesterday? I was here yesterday, you rang me don't you remember, and told me to go to Gatwick and see to the car. And I did, I got there the same time as the breakdown truck and followed it back to Crawley. I do need some time off though. A day at least; I'll make it up some other time.'

'I'll think about it.' Henry said, as he reached the back

door and took out his keys.

'Miserable sod.' Sam mumbled under his breath. 'What the hell's got into him?'

Hardly had Henry disappeared into the house than Tommy and June came back into the yard leading two Creakwood mares, pregnant by Slipstream and shortly due to foal. 'Boss is back early.' said Tommy, leading Black Coffee into her loose box. 'Saw him getting out of a minicab.'

Sam nodded 'Yeah, whole thing got fucked up and he's in a shocking temper so keep clear of him.'

'It's him who needs to keep clear.' answered Tommy. 'I'll take that bastard down a peg or two one day, watch me.'

Sam didn't answer; he'd never understood the animosity between Tommy and the boss and didn't want to get involved. Instead he turned to June and warned her against speaking to Henry the way he was. 'Watch what you say when he's in this sort of mood; he can fly off the handle for no reason at all.'

June smiled sweetly, but she didn't mean it; she'd built up the most ridiculous belief that Henry fancied her and that, in some amazing way which would surprise everybody, he was going do something about it. She wasn't quite sure what she meant by "do something" and she didn't care, though the way she flaunted herself in front of him, there was every possibility she'd find out. Sam had warned her over and over again, as had Tracy.

'He'll take advantage of you one day, June.' he'd told her, 'He'll use you, and throw you away; he's done it before.' But she didn't believe him; Henry loved her. Even Tommy tried to knock sense into her, told her of other girls who'd worked there and fallen for Henry's charms and then been ditched when he'd had enough of them. But June wouldn't have it ... he *did* love her ... she could see it in his eyes. But then, she'd never seen the eyes of a lecher before.

144, Peabody High Row,
East Jutland Street, Brighton

Barney Truscott stole downstairs and out through the front door without his wife seeing him. She was cooking thick yellow curry sauce she'd bought in a packet (only needs water) at the corner shop. When it was ready it'd go over the chips little Rocky had picked up from the fish and chip shop in the next street. The Truscotts were 'eating in', at least she and Rocky were. They ate in every day in truth, and almost always on their own. Barney took his meals out of a glass, an idiosyncrasy which had run in the Truscott family for generations. Three days back Barney had "got off work early"; at least that's what he told his wife. What he really meant was that he'd spent his dole money and the barman would no longer serve him. But then, out of the blue, things changed miraculously; he'd never been so flush. So well off was he, he could hardly believe it himself. Even as he walked down the street on his way to the Red Lion he still couldn't credit it, though the cash was in his pocket. He tapped it to make sure he'd not been dreaming and then, unable to resist it, he took the money out and counted it again. So much for so little ... and four Hundred and fifty five quid of it still left ... even after all those pints ... unbelievable! He shoved the money back in his pocket, quickened his step, and began to whistle. Life was good ... fucking good.

The C.I.D. Suite, Police H.Q.
Sussex House, Brighton.

Yesterday morning', as Sergeant Groves so eloquently put it,' said Reynard, 'the cupboard "was a bit bare". You may wish it still was, but if you do you're in the wrong place. My teams thrive on being busy, and busy we will be over the next few weeks, even if no more crimes are committed which, knowing Brighton as I do, is very unlikely. So ... what have we got? I'll tell you, we've got two probable murders, one high profile and one relatively low profile. Two chances to make a name for ourselves or torpedo our careers, and I'll be overseeing both of them.

Now you were all picked by me because I saw potential in you, and this is the time for me to see that potential realised. A few words on how we're going to tackle the investigations first though ... and you may take it what I am about to say has been approved right up to the top, and I mean the top. The Prime Minister himself has been made aware of the way we will be approaching the killing of his wife and of the old lady form Eastbourne. He's expecting quick results in both cases, and I emphasis *both* cases. Mrs Jellicoe's death is sure to prove politically sensitive, Annie Weaver's will not ... or at least we have no reason to believe it will. We'll progress both cases with equal vigour, give them equal weight. When issuing statements to the public or the press this must be emphasised.

As to details ... the five of us will be the main investigators, though we will have technical back up available from various Home Office and Security Service personnel. A public relations officer from Commander Simpson's staff will be seconded to us for the duration of both cases, so you and I will be spared the risk of accidentally making an unguarded comment and seeing it twisted into something totally different. Got all that?'

'Yes Sir.' they replied, as one.

Starting from now we split into two teams. D.C. Furness and D.C Edwards will be with me investigating Rose Jellicoe's death. Sergeant Groves and D.C. Best will take on Annie Weaver's. All our present cases will be handed over to D.I. Lawrence or D.I. Crowther ... alright? We'll meet in this office daily at the usual time *and* at six thirty p.m. though we'll be on duty all day, every day, until both crimes are resolved.

OK. Go and get a bite to eat and report back here in an hour so we can get started. *I'm* waiting for a call summoning me to C.S. Bradshaw's office where I'm expecting to meet the Medical, Communications, and Security personnel I've told you about. If I'm not back in an hour you can start parcelling up your notes on the cases you're handing over. Right off you go.'

As they left, Groves hung back and, when they were alone, she began to smile. 'Congratulations, Foxy. Well done'

Embarrassed at his unsought promotion, all Reynard could manage was, 'Huh.'

☼☼☼

Detective Superintendent Ian Good from Scotland Yard, and Henry Allerton from MI5 both said much the same to Reynard, after Chief Superintendent Bradshaw had introduced them. They'd stay in the background, they said, only becoming active in the Jellicoe investigation if it showed signs of being in any way connected to James in his capacity as Prime Minister. They discounted Annie Weaver's death as not having any political relevance, but said they'd keep an eye on developments. Inspector Jane Everett though, on secondment from Commander Simpson's staff, was likely to be of direct help to Reynard no matter which way the investigations went. An experienced press liaison officer, she undertook to stand between the reporters and the investigating officers, to give the briefings, to make the statements, and to leave Reynard with the process of detection only.

☼☼☼

By the time Reynard had clarified his position with the "outside help" the Commander had arranged, the rest of the team were back from the canteen and ready to get on with the two jobs.

'We'll start with Annie Weaver,' he said, turning to Furness. 'How did you get on, you spent most of the day in Pendine Avenue. Give us a brief outline of what you found.'

'OK, Guv, and it will be brief because I haven't much to say. I think you know I found some balled-up masking tape close to Annie's body. It had been shoved into a hydrangea and looked as though it had been done recently and deliberately; in other words it hadn't just blown in. I understand from Sergeant Groves that Doctor Vladic found traces of marks which might indicate Annie had been tied up and gagged.'

'And Geordie Hawkins found more tape.' said Groves.

'Well,' Furness continued, 'I don't think I mentioned this yesterday but there was another thing which bothered me - the garden hose. It was ...'

'The garden hose, what about it?' asked Reynard.

'She'd been using it to do some watering but it's been raining on and off for the last three days and the ground's soaking.'

'Hawkins mentioned that.' said Reynard. 'So what are you suggesting?'

'Suggesting? ... Nothing. It just looked wrong somehow. Anyway, apart from the hose and the tape there wasn't anything in the garden of interest. I was told not to go into the house, which is likely to be a lousy job if what the guys in the squad car told me is true. They went in briefly to make sure there was nobody else there and found the place full of junk. I looked through a few of the windows and from what I could see they're right. Annie Weaver was a serious hoarder; there was stuff there she must have been saving for donkey's years: newspapers, clothes, bits of furniture, boxes and boxes all piled on top of each other, it'll take ages to search through.'

'A pleasure in store for you and D.C. Best I think, Sergeant. Better make the house a priority.'

Groves smiled. 'Oh yeah, lucky me! So what did you do if you didn't go into the house?'

'I got on with 'the door to door'. First I tried ...'

'The Winters?'

'That's right ... Mr and Mrs. He'd left for work, I think you know about that, Guv, and she wouldn't let me in.'

'Yes, yes, go on; I told the others you'd had a problem seeing her at first, but then she relented didn't she?'

'She did but, in the meantime, I'd got delayed and she'd gone by the time I arrived at her house. I didn't see her in the end until this morning. In fact I saw both of them today because Mr Winters had waited for me to arrive so I could talk to him.'

'What delayed you getting there?' asked Groves.

'I was with another neighbour, the one on the other side; Alison Dandy. She was very helpful and we might get more out of her. The Winters, though, have only lived there a few months and hardly knew Miss Weaver.'

'Miss?' asked Best.

'Well that's what Alison Dandy, another Miss, told me. And it was confirmed by the only other people I found in the road who seemed to know Miss Weaver well enough to be of help to us in determining her background.'

Reynard, stroking his chin and nodding as he followed Furness's account, said, 'It's normal; neighbours fall into one of three or four categories: those who've just moved into the district and don't know the victim at all, those who know the victim by sight only, and those who know the victim well having lived near them, or next to them, for years. This latter lot will have become familiar with their neighbours and their ways. The Winters are clearly in the first category, but they *do* live next door so it's possible they saw or heard something.'

'They didn't, Guv; it was the first thing I asked them. Miss Dandy's a different matter, she's worth another call. And the Colberts in Number 1, the house on the corner, might be helpful; they've known Miss Weaver for a long time and they're definitely worth a second visit. As to the rest, forget them.'

'Forget them? Not likely, I want every single house in that road called on … it's a cul-de-sac isn't it?'

'Yes, of about fourteen houses, maybe sixteen.' Furness

replied. 'D'you want me to continue?'

Reynard shook his head. 'Only if you've anything more of substance. If you haven't, Sergeant Groves and D.C. Best can carry on from where you left off. And,' he said to Groves, 'make it the house first, and the rest of the people in the road after. Try and have something for us when we meet up tomorrow. OK?'

'Fine by me, Guv.' said Groves.

'Me too.' added Best.

Furness closed his notebook and returned it to his pocket 'And I'm with you and D.C. Edwards now, Guv, correct?'

'Oh blimey, what time is it?' asked Reynard, totally ignoring the question.

Edwards answered him. 'It's getting on for four, Guv.'

'Ah.' said Reynard, who was already thinking ahead to an appointment he had to meet the Prime Minister at his home at Barton Court. The Commander had suggested it, believing that by introducing the man he'd put in charge, and letting *him* present his plan of action, the P.M would gain comfort and confidence on a personal and a political level. On the way to the P.M.'s house, and at Reynard's suggestion, they were intending to call on Doctor Vladic to see if he had any further news as to how the hemlock had got into Mrs Jellicoe's system.

'It's almost four, Guv.' Groves said, tapping the table when she saw Reynard's attention wavering.

'What ... oh yes, four ...right ... so we'll leave Annie Weaver for the moment and move onto Rose Jellicoe. I'm meeting the P.M. at six so I need something to tell him. What have we?'

'Crikey, Guv,' said Edwards, 'not much. We've been concentrating on making sure the poisoning doesn't turn out to be a public health issue and surely, until we hear from Doctor

Vladic, we won't know whether it's murder or accidental death.'

'True,' said Reynard, 'but I don't see any harm in … what is it Furness calls it … "ferreting around". We might spend the time, while we're waiting for Doctor Vladic's report to come through, doing a bit of … "ferreting around".'

'Yeah, you never know what might turn up.' said Furness, 'I'll get onto it straight away, and if D.C. Edwards helps me, we could cover a lot of ground. What d'you say Taffy?'

Edwards agreed and soon afterwards the meeting broke up, with Groves and Best making for Pendine Avenue, and Furness and Edwards opening their laptops.

Alone in his office, and thinking about the meeting he was to attend, Reynard suddenly awoke to the fact the Cona coffee machine was quietly bubbling away in the corner.

'Hmm.' he thought, 'that's a good idea, a nice cup of coffee'll go down well. He got up from his chair and bent to pick up the jug … and then he stopped, his hand poised mid-air. 'Hang on; I don't want to get caught short on the way, that'd be too embarrassing.'

Creakwood House Stud Farm,

Dial Post, Sussex.

Henry Finnerty sat at the kitchen table, alone. The woman who came in and "did" for him had gone, her tasks for the day completed. Not that they were onerous for Henry spent as many nights in other people's beds as he did in his own. Even when he was at home he never cooked anything, unless heating up in the microwave could be called cooking so, apart from tending to his personal hygiene, his domestic responsibilities were few. People said he led a lonely existence but he didn't see it that way As far as he was concerned, it was far less stressful living on his own and doing whatever he wanted, than being tied to a wife and family who expected him to live life the way they wished. No, with no responsibilities to anyone other than himself he did as he chose, and it was in such a self-righteous frame of mind he was working his way down a bottle of whisky, thinking about Ursula and Rose, and cursing them both. Ursula had gone too far this time though ... God Almighty ... standing him up at the last minute and humiliating him like that, and for what ... because some bloody bank note robber had wrecked his car? Why should he feel guilty about that? And as to Rose, well she'd paid the price, stupid woman, and all he had to do to keep out of trouble was keep his head down. Nobody would know the strength of her connection to him, not a chance.

The Pathology Department,
Royal Sussex County Hospital.

Doctor Vladic beamed at them when they came in. 'I was about to ring you.' he said.

'Have you got something?' Commander Simpson asked, practically running towards him, he was so keen to hear his findings. 'Something that'll shed light on Mrs Jellicoe's …'

'A spicy little food parcel with hemlock hidden inside it.'

'Not an accident then?'

'Oh it could still be an accident, but the chances of it being put there on purpose are much more likely. It was almost certainly in a samosa she ate towards the end of the tour round the exhibits. The incomplete disintegration of the filo pasty in which it was wrapped indicates as much.'

'Good work.' said Simpson, 'Please pass my thanks to your colleagues; this is an important breakthrough. Right, Chief Inspector?'

'It certainly is.' Reynard replied, before hesitantly asking to be reminded of the appearance and taste of a samosa.

Simpson smiled. 'I can tell you that; I love 'em. They're

little pastry things full of spiced vegetables and herbs and so on: carrots, peas, onions, chillies, coriander et cetera, et cetra, a perfect disguise for something with an unpleasant or bitter taste.'

'Whether it was there on purpose or by mischance.'

'Exactly. So we must find out who made them and make sure there are no more still out there where the public can get hold of them. The exhibition's not closing until six. That's another hour. Are you absolutely one hundred per cent sure the hemlock got into Mrs Jellicoe's stomach this way, Doctor, absolutely sure?'

Vladic began to shake his head from side to side. 'No, Sir, I'm not; there's no way we can be absolutely one hundred per cent sure at this stage of our examination but, from what I've seen in the last half hour, I'm personally convinced the poison which killed Mrs Jellicoe was delivered into her body in a samosa.'

'Good enough for me.' said Simpson, 'Who do you have at the exhibition at the moment Chief Inspector … sorry, Superintendent? Whoever they are, get them chasing round to find and confiscate *any* samosas of *any* sort they come across.'

Reynard's face wrinkled up in disappointment. 'Ach, I've no one there at the moment, Sir, but D.S. Pollard, has uniformed men swarming all over the gardens. I'll ring him and ask him to set up a search. My two officers, Best and Edwards, are back in the office looking up things on their computers.'

'Things, what things?'

'Information on Rose Jellicoe, background stuff. They're trying to find something pointing to a reason for her death.'

'Fair enough, so ring Pollard now; I want people hunting down those samosas without delay. You can tell him I asked you. What about the stuff in the marquee, who's dealing with that?'

'I am, Commander.' said Vladic, 'I've already spoken to the most senior man in Health and Safety and they're going to remove all the bags from the marquee tonight and take them to their depot where they have an analytical facility capable of identifying the presence of hemlock. If they find anything of interest I'll go down and join them.'

'Sounds as if that side of things is tied up then.'

'It is and, luckily, each bag was tagged as it was collected; if they come across anything of interest they'll know which exhibitor was nearest to it.'

'Excellent, and ...?'

'And tomorrow morning they'll start sorting it and putting to one side any food scraps they find so they can be visually analysed first. They've also left a skip beside the gate lodge and all rubbish which turns up today will have to be dumped into it so it can be examined later, if necessary.'

Simpson turned to Reynard. 'So far so good, are you happy with all that, Superintendent?'

Reynard, unused to being addressed by his new rank, grinned. 'I'm more than happy, Sir, I'm relieved; this is an area where we could slip up ... but not now. Doctor Vladic and I always work well together and I've no problem with him dealing with all things associated with the technical side of the poisoning. We all know what he uncovers will determine whether we're looking for a murderer or not. Once we're aware of that we'll act accordingly.'

'Fine.' said Simpson 'And now we must be on our way. We cannot keep the Prime Minister waiting.

Barton Court,

the Prime Minister's private residence, near Horsham, Sussex.

The P.M. was in the sitting room talking to his sister-in-law when Simpson and Reynard were ushered in. They'd spent the whole time they were travelling up to Barton Court discussing what they might tell him when they arrived, and it was only as they were drawing up at the gates that they finally agreed to say the least they could get away with in case they wound up being tripped by their own words later on in the case.

As it happened, James was still in shock and, though he was keen to know how they were planning to handle the investigation, the meeting was quite brief. Simpson made the introductions 'I'm Commander Bill Simpson, and … erm … I'm from Scotland Yard where I'm the coordinator of all the C.I.D. activities in the U.K.. And this is Detective Superintendent William Reynard, he's with the Sussex Constabulary and stationed in Brighton. He'll be taking responsibility of managing the investigation into the circumstances of your wife's death. Please accept our sympathy for your terrible loss; the whole nation will share your distress when the news gets out.'

'How do you do, gentlemen?' James said, 'Thank you for coming to see me and for your kind words. May I introduce my wife's sister, Ursula Constantanidi, she's come down from London, to help comfort my two boys. They're very distraught as you can imagine.'

'Pleasure to meet you. I'll leave you to have your discussion with the Prime Minister.' Ursula said, smiling just a little too sweetly.

'Take a seat.' said James, sitting himself as soon as Ursula had left. 'Anything come to light yet? I was in Brighton yesterday afternoon as you probably know … met the Professor and Doctor Vladic, a capable fellow. And of course I met Chief Superintendent Bradshaw who seemed to have already lined you up for the investigation, Superintendent. By the way are you *'Foxy'* Reynard, you must be?'

Reynard smiled and nodded.

'I always read the local paper you know, and your name often pops up in it. So what have you found out so far?'

'Very little Sir.' Simpson answered. 'We called into the Pathology Laboratory on our way here and spoke to Vladic. They've discovered the hemlock … you know about *it* don't you?'

'Yes, he and Sir John rang me early this morning.'

'Good. Well they've found it in a samosa Mrs Jellicoe had eaten not long before she collapsed. We've got men scouring the gardens as I speak, looking for any more that may still be around.'

'There couldn't have been many exhibitors giving away free samples of samosas.'

'Exactly, Sir, so we have high expectations of finding any that are left over and confiscating them.'

'Which might solve the problem of further victims, but it doesn't tell us why my wife was chosen as a target. I mean is it me who's being got at d'you think?'

Reynard, who'd been waiting to get back into the conversation, saw his chance. 'The view I take, Sir, is one orientated towards finding out how the poison got where it did in the first place. With that known, we might get a lead to whoever it was put it there, and find out why. That is to say we'll have pretty good idea whether you *or* your wife was the primary target We will, of course have to follow several different and parallel lines of thought in order to establish the 'how', the 'who' and the 'why'.'

James nodded; clearly these were similar to thoughts to the ones he was having. 'Any help you want from me?'

'There is, Sir, we need to know as much as possible about your wife, her life in and out of the public eye, her background, her early years, and so many other things directly associated with her. I realise you're not easily able to find the time, but we do need to have a chat with you and as many of her friends and relatives who you think might help fill in the gaps in what we already know.'

'Of course. Well I'll make myself available whenever you want, but you also ought also to talk to Rose's only sibling, her sister, Mrs Constantanidi, whom you've just met. And you may find it worthwhile interviewing Julia Henderson, the wife of …'

'Our Lord Mayor! Of course they were together when the poison struck.'

'Ah, Superintendent, it's not just that, they've been close friends for years; they were even at college together. In fact, come to think about it, Julia knew my wife longer than I did. Talk to her she'll know all Rose's little secrets.'

'Did she have any?'

'Secrets? No, no… manner of speech.'

'Hmm. And as to the investigation, Sir, I'll be involved in every aspect of the case. Chief Superintendent Bradshaw has relieved me of all other duties so I can concentrate on solving the mystery of Mrs Jellicoe's death, and that of one other person.'

'The lady who was found, unclothed, in her garden yesterday morning? I'm pleased about that. I want it to be seen that Rose's death, tragic as it may be for me and my family, is being treated the same way as that of any other citizen.'

'I think you'll find it'll not be quite like *any* other citizen, Sir, but rest assured it will look that way. We are of one mind in that regard. How may I contact you?'

'Through my secretary for non-urgent matters and directly to me through my private mobile for urgent ones.' said James, handing Reynard a business card. 'And now I must ask you to excuse me, I have a lot of calls to make.'

'We'll do our level best to find the answers, Sir,' said Simpson, 'and thank you for seeing us.'

As they left, Reynard glanced back. The Prime Minister was standing just inside the front door. He'd shrunk ... and looked a picture of total misery.

The R&R Fine Arts Gallery,

West Pallant, Chichester, Sussex.

It was getting on for seven in the evening and Ben Stone, the owner of the bookshop next to The R&R Gallery, was standing on the pavement outside his premises admiring his attempt at an eye catching window display: a spiral of books, entitled VORTEX, rising from a random scattering of the same author's other works. It was stunning and, he reckoned, more than worthy of the new publication which was being launched the next day.

Being early evening, as opposed to early afternoon, there was only a handful of people passing along the curiously named 300 year old street but, gratifyingly, most of them stopped to inspect his window.

All in all, 'a good day's work', he thought, and resisting the temptation to make further adjustments, went back into the shop and began to lock up.

Once he'd checked and double checked all the windows and doors, and ensured only the display lights in the front of the shop had not been extinguished, he had a last look round and went out to his car through the rear entrance.

It was the only vehicle left in the big square yard serving

the ancient buildings as a loading area and car park. Groping for his keys, the sound of music coming from the flat over the adjacent R&R Gallery made him glance up. Morgan Ramage, the gallery's owner, was standing on his balcony. He'd one hand on the wooden rail and in the other a glass of red wine. When he saw Ben, he raised it.

'Good luck for the book launch tomorrow.' he shouted, letting go of the rail and going back into his sitting room to telephone his brother.

A letter from the company's insurers, which had come in that morning, had mentioned "excessive valuations in your recent claim", and it had him worried. As far as he was concerned they'd made no claim. His brother, Brandon had nearly brought the business down once before by fiddling the insurance …surely he wasn't at it again?

He let the phone ring for ages but nobody answered. In the end he left a message. It was short and unequivocal. 'What the hell have you been playing at, Brandon? I want you over here tonight or we're finished.'

DAY THREE

Saturday 19th September 2009

Alan Grainger

14, Malvern Gardens,
Brighton, Sussex.

Foxy Reynard turned restlessly, opened his eyes, and looked at the digital clock on his bedside table. "Four thirty a.m."

The last time he'd done it, it had been three fifty five.

It was pitch dark in the room apart from a thin shaft of light from the street lamp which, having stolen through a gap in the curtains was dividing the ceiling in half. It wasn't like that in his mind though; in it the two killings were stubbornly resisting division and coming together in a bewildering congestion of questions. He sighed, quietly, and immediately felt Cathy move. 'D'you want some tea? She asked, knowing from past experience that a cup of tea was all he needed to send him off; odd really, when caffeine bearing substances are generally thought to promote wakefulness.

'I'll get it,' he replied, 'd'you want any?'

'No' she murmured, sleepily, turning her back to him and pulling the bedclothes over her head.

Downstairs, ten minutes later, beside the kitchen stove with his three month old black and white mongrel puppy lying across his feet, and a mug of hot tea in his hand, Foxy began to drift, not into sleep, but into clarity, knowing that what eluded him when he was in bed, often became obvious to him when he was in the old basket chair. It was in such moments, when everything magically became clear, he couldn't help wondering if the steadying hand of his late father, D. C. I. Charlie Reynard, who was also known as Foxy, the original owner of the chair and the nickname, was somehow still guiding him.

'Right,' he said to himself, 'first things first ... finding the source of the samosas ... that's our top priority. Until we know where *they* came from we've little chance of finding out how the poison got into them, and none at all of discovering how they then got into Mrs Jellicoe's stomach. The samosas, provided we can get our hands on a few, will lead us to the truth; they'll show us whether or not Mrs Jellicoe was murdered.

The whole nature of the enquiry, and the way we pursue it, is going to hinge on those damned samosas. It'll have to be heads down tomorrow, tracking them. Everything else must wait: interviews with the P.M. with Mrs Jellicoe's relations, and with her friends, must all be put off unless they have a direct bearing on what she ate and when she ate it. This means the Lord Mayor and his wife have to be at the top of the list of the people I've got to interview. I'll talk to them while Furness and Edwards are at the exhibition cross-examining the stall holders.

With the other death there's a similar situation; we don't know the circumstance which brought it about, so working *that* out has to be the main thing in this case too. A thorough search of the house, coupled with talking to *all* the neighbours will be the best way to start.'

As he mulled over his thoughts with his eyes shut, his empty mug on the top of the stove, and his dog by then comfortably curled up on his lap, he finally drifted off to sleep.

Cathy came down at six thirty, found him "out for the count" with his mouth open and, knowing the importance of the day, set about making his breakfast. In consequence he woke, not to the swish of the curtains being pulled back as he usually did, but to the smell and sound of frying bacon. By seven he'd finished his food, and was showered, dressed, and looking for his keys. By seven twenty, a little later than usual, he got to the office where, to his horror, and everyone else's amusement, he found he was the last one in. With difficulty, Groves restrained herself from saying 'Good afternoon,' and settled for smiling and asking if they could have coffee before they started.

Reynard nodded and then, changing his mind, held up his hand. 'No coffee for me, I'll have mine later; right now I have to contact D.S. Pollard in The Pavilion Gardens; I need to know what progress he's made in his search for samosas.

'Ah, I was about to tell you, Guv,' said Groves, 'he rang a minute or two ago. It seems it was chaotic there last night; just as the Fayre was on the last lap hundreds of people turned up.'

'And I can guess why … they went to see where Mrs Jellicoe had been poisoned. I can never understand how some people just can't …'

'No Guv, they went to get bargains.'

'Bargains … what sort of bargains?'

'Cut price ones. D.S. Pollard told me the public was let in free for the last two hours to buy the stock on the display stands at knock down prices; half Brighton turned up. Some of them even brought empty prams they were hoping to fill '

'And D.S. Pollard let this happen?'

'He didn't have much choice, apparently it's the way most exhibitions based on perishables end. The Chelsea Flower Show's much the same. What made this one worse was that details were put out by Brighton's local radio stations.

Reynard nearly exploded, 'And, as a result, a potential

Crime Scene got trampled to bits … great.'

'Ahhhh … it mightn't be all that bad Guv, don't forget we already have all the opened stuff at the Health and Safety depot.'

'Yes … true. Anything else?'

'Just one thing which, in a way, might be the most important one of all; none of the exhibitors admitted to having samosas on their stand at any time during the Fayre.'

'Hang on.' said Best, 'if no one had any samosas on their stand, where did the one Mrs Jellicoe ate come from?'

'Where indeed?' said Reynard, with a "just noticeable" grin beginning to light up his face.

R & R Fine Arts Gallery, West Pallant,
Chichester, Sussex.

Morgan Ramage's body might have remained undiscovered in his back yard for another hour if a courier, with a parcel marked "Very Urgent - Deliver At Any Time", unable to get an answer after ringing the bell on the front door of the gallery, hadn't walked down the arched passage running between it and the next premises looking for a rear entrance.

It was coming up to eight o'clock in the morning and, as he advanced through the dark alleyway to make his first delivery of the day, he spotted a door tucked into a recess at the far end of it and almost out of sight.

When he got nearer, he saw the feet, two of them; toes to the sky, and motionless ... even when he coughed to announce his presence. More and more apprehensive, he inched his way along the wall of the passage and around the end of the building until he could see the whole body lying in the yard. Morgan Ramage, to whom he often made early deliveries, was lying flat on his back in a pool of partially congealed blood.

It appeared to have come from his head though there were no obvious wounds. Instinctively he looked up.

Above him, and with a broken hand rail swinging dangerously in the breeze, was the balcony serving the flat over the R & R Fine Arts gallery. It wasn't hard to conclude that Ramage had fallen from it; probably after having one or two too many, for he still had the stem of a wine glass in his hand.

The courier dropped his knees and checked for a sign of life. There was none. He got to his feet and took out his mobile

9, Pendine Avenue,

Eastbourne, Sussex.

Groves and Best couldn't help feeling they were in the halfpenny place when they were given the Weaver death to investigate; the excitement was going to be with the Jellicoe killing; *it* had an international dimension. Being sent to find out why an old woman had died in her garden would hardly see print. The squad car with the two coppers in it was still outside the house when they arrived and collected the key.

'Anyone else been here?' asked Groves.

'Two sparrows, and the Archbishop of Canterbury.'

'Of course ... I should have known. No one else?'

'A newspaper delivery boy. But he only called into four and ten on the other side; obviously on this side they can't read.'

Groves nodded, but didn't react to the pathetic attempt at humour. 'Come on "Next",' she said, 'let's get on.'

'You'll need a gas mask,' shouted the driver, as they walked up the path to the front door 'and gloves ... it's disgusting.'

'One hour max then.' said Groves, handing Best the key.

Sussex Police Headquarters,
Sussex House, Brighton.

Reynard had watched Groves and Best departing with a slight feeling of guilt; he knew they were fretting over being put on the less important case, but there wasn't much he could do about it. 'At least they'll get a chance to shine on their own.' he'd said to D.S. Bradshaw, who'd asked if he thought they were ready to fly solo.

'If they can't do it now, they'll never do it,' Reynard had answered him, 'And anyway, I've devolved a few hefty responsibilities onto Groves in the past and she was well able for them. What worries me is that she'll probably make a spectacular success of this investigation, get promoted, and I'll be left starting all over again with D.C. Best.'

'Such are the trials we have to endure, Foxy, look at you, you're a Super now, same as me. How d'you think that makes me feel, with you breathing down my neck?'

'Not as uncomfortable as me, that's for sure!'

'Ha … so how're you going to start?'

'We *have* started, Groves and Best must be inside Annie Weaver's house by now; they'll be there all day unless they decide to do a few more house interviews to get away from the smell that's stinking the place out.'

'What smell?'

'The smell of mustiness at best, the smell of filth at worst. We've already been told the place is a tip inside. The other two, Furness and Edwards, are on their way to The Pavilion Gardens to interview the exhibitors again, while I'm ...'

'Trying to track down the last few samosas ... right?'

'No, no, none of the exhibitors were offering samosas, as it's turned out, so now we're looking for a maverick trader, a free rider who muscled in to promote his goods at the expense of the authorised exhibitors.'

'Cheeky. So whoever gave Mrs Jellicoe the one she was poisoned with was taking advantage of the crowd drawn in by the organisers ... well I'm damned.'

'This is guesswork at the moment, of course, but by tonight, if my two men get something out of the questioning they're doing, and I get something from a meeting I'm going to have shortly with the Lord Mayor and his wife, followed by another with the P.M. later in the morning, we might be better position to know exactly what went on the day before yesterday. Once we're sure of that we can determine whether the inclusion of the hemlock was due to sloppy kitchen management or a specific attempt to kill Mrs Jellicoe.'

'You've got your work cut out.'

'And a good team to help me do it.' said Reynard, getting up and making for the door, 'I'm off to see the Lord Mayor and his wife in a few minutes and, as I said, I'm hoping to find they've remembered something of significance.'

Bradshaw gave him a rueful look; 'Sounds like *you're* going to have an interesting day then.'

'Oh yes … and it'll be non-stop.' Reynard replied, turning away to hide a smile he couldn't hold back when he realised Bradshaw was jealous. The sharp end excitement which everyone else in the department was feeling hadn't got through to the boss. They were all out hunting for villains while he was stuck in the office waiting for phone calls.

'And that,' said Reynard to himself, 'is not the sort life I want … far from it.'

9, Pendine Avenue,

Eastbourne, Sussex.

As soon as they entered the house they got the smell. It was like the one often found in Old People's homes and came as a result of personal neglect and poor air circulation.

'Leave the door open,' said Groves, pulling a handkerchief from her pocket and putting it over her nose. 'and let's open all the windows.'

Best, following her into the hall, immediately reacted to his first intake of tainted air. 'Good grief!' he said, 'What a stink.'

'Got to get the air circulating before we do anything else.' said Groves. 'If you open the downstairs windows and the back door, I'll go up and do the bedrooms.'

Best stuck up a thumb and reached for the nearest door which he expected to be either the sitting or dining room; it was neither. The sight which confronted him was more that of an indoors dump comprised of boxes and bags stuffed to overflowing with old clothes, well used domestic ware, kitchen gadgets, blankets and books.

There was no way he'd ever have got through to the windows without climbing over everything, and he was forced to shut the door and check the one on the other side of the hall. It was locked so, before trying the one at the end of the passage which he assumed led to the kitchen, he shouted up the stairs, narrowed to a fifteen inch passage between stacks of newspapers standing on either side of each tread. 'How're you doing up there, Lucy?' he bellowed. 'I've given up on one of the front rooms; it's full of junk just as we were told; and I can't get into the other, it's locked. I'm going to try the kitchen. '

'I'll be down in a minute.' Groves answered, 'It stinks to high heaven up here as well, I can't imagine how the old girl managed to live in a place as cluttered as this. The bedrooms are bad, but the bathroom's the worst by far; it's full of tableware: glasses, cutlery and so on and there are about six tea services between the wash hand basin and the window sill. Even the bath's full, it's packed to the brim with Christmas decorations, including a wreath for the door and four plastic Christmas trees. It's a total nightmare up here, but I've managed to get a bathroom window open, so I'm leaving the rest and coming down.'

Best, waiting for her at the bottom of the stairs, cast his eyes around and gradually began to realise the hall was not as congested as some of the other parts of the house he'd seen; in fact it looked relatively normal apart from the newspapers lining the stairs, and even they were only partially visible as there was a turn on the bottom step which practically obscured the rest of them. The actual passage from the front door to what he presumed was the kitchen had only a hallstand and a small telephone table in it and would have looked uncluttered to any callers seeing into it through the entrance.

As soon as Groves appeared round the bend in the stairs, Best headed down the passage and opened the door at the other end. It *was* the kitchen, and it was spotless; absolutely nothing like the parts of the house they'd just inspected. A large room with three doors in it, it ran across the full width of the house. The first door was the one they'd just come through, the second was the back door and it gave access to the garden through a full width conservatory containing comfortable basket chairs and potted plants. The third opened into a pleasantly furnished bedroom off which was a tiny en-suite bathroom. In the corner of the bedroom was another door; it turned out to be the one Best had found locked when he'd checked it from the hall.

Rendered speechless as each surprise was uncovered they began to laugh the minute they looked at each other. Who could ever have imagined two such contradictory worlds existing side by side like that?

Within twenty minutes the air was sweet, the strong draught sweeping through as soon as they opened the doors quickly dispersing the staleness.

'It'll niff again in the morning, I expect.' said Best, as they finally got down to looking for clues.

Seaforth House
Adelaide Terrace, Brighton.

Lance and Julia Henderson, the Lord Mayor and Lady Mayoress, met him at their door when Reynard arrived at their elegant white Georgian terrace house. Each had a cup of coffee in their hand. 'It's Nespresso, would you like one?' Julia asked, leading the two men into the drawing room

'Not for me thanks, I've to be at the Prime Minister's house mid-morning so, if it's all the same to you, I'll pass. What I need, as I mentioned when I rang, is a first-hand account of what happened, and the opportunity to ask you a few questions which might help us find out who did this dreadful thing to Mrs Jellicoe.'

'As to "an account of what happened", Superintendent, I've written down everything I can remember for you,' said Julia, handing him a sheet of paper, 'but as to who put the hemlock in the thing she ate, or who gave it to her … well I know no more than you do.'

'Hmm. I see … and have you, Mrs Henderson, or you Lord Mayor, any idea who might have had a grudge against Mrs Jellicoe, someone who'd threatened her perhaps; I gather you knew her well.'

'Very well, and for years,' Julia answered, 'in fact she and I were at university together, adjacent rooms in the women's hall of residence; but that was back in ... oh I don't know when ... the early nineteen eighties I guess.'

'And you've kept in touch.'

'We have ... though infrequently. You know how it is, Superintendent, you see someone week in week out for ages and then for some reason or other you don't see them for months. We do telephone each other regularly though, don't we Lance?'

The Lord Mayor, sitting with his eyes closed, nodded.

'Did she ever mention anyone she wasn't getting on with,' asked Reynard, 'someone with whom she'd fallen out?'

'Her sister, Ursula. But I can't imagine *her* being involved in any sort of *real* violence, can you Lance?'

Henderson shook his head but still kept his eyes shut.

Not that Reynard noticed, he'd smelled a rabbit. 'What do you mean ... *real* violence?'

'Oh God, why can't I keep my mouth shut.' said Julia. 'It's just that on the day of the Fayre, and prior to our going out into the garden, Rose said Ursula had hit her in the face during an argument they'd had recently.'

'Regarding what?'

'Regarding an unsuitable liaison which Ursula had rekindled with a man who has a shocking reputation; the sort of relationship which could easily become embarrassing for James if the papers got hold of it.'

'James ... the Prime Minister you mean?'

'Yes, it could be very awkward for him.'

Lance took an immediate interest when James's name

was mentioned and opened his eyes. 'Rose's death'll have nothing to do with Ursula carrying on ... not a chance.' he said.

'I know it won't,' Julia answered, 'it was just Superintendent Reynard wanted to know why Ursula and Rose had fallen out.'

'Who was the person involved?' asked Reynard.

Julia sighed; she wished she'd never said anything about the two sisters arguing. 'His name's Finnerty.'

'Not Henry Finnerty the race horse man?'

'Yes ... him.'

'Then I'm not surprised Mr and Mrs Jellicoe were apprehensive;' said Reynard, 'Finnerty's bad news. He lives on our patch and I was marginally involved in a Fraud Squad enquiry into a betting scam he'd set up a few years back. It never got anywhere in the end, unfortunately, because he hadn't actually broken the law. I wouldn't trust him an inch though. And it's no wonder to me Mrs Jellicoe was upset if her sister was getting close to him, and worried the press might find out and use the information to discredit the P.M.'

'Is that it then, Superintendent?' Lance asked. 'Only I have meetings in town, I still have a practice you know'

'Indeed I do Lord Mayor, one of your partners called my wife and I in regarding our wills the other day. Yes, this has been a very useful meeting and I've learned some extremely helpful back ground stuff, but I doubt any of it had much directly to do with Mrs Jellicoe's death. There'd need to be another explanation altogether if Finnerty's moved from fleecing a few bookies to murdering his girlfriend's sister.'

'Exactly Superintendent, so are we finished?'

'Just a moment or two more, if I may. So, any other ideas as to why Mrs Jellicoe was targeted? If indeed she was targeted at all? I've already worked out that it could have been a random prank, one not directed at anyone in particular that went wrong. It could also be some sort of warning to the Prime Minister concerning his attitude to a power group here in the UK, or in some country abroad. It could even be an assault on the food industry as a whole, or on one firm in particular; there are endless possible scenarios?

'True; we've been wondering about all that too, Superintendent, but we can't think of anything in her life which would have precipitated her death.'

'Mmm, pity; I was hoping you would. So for the moment we'll stick with the facts we have then … see where they lead. I'm going to Barton Court now to see The Prime Minister, but I'll have a chat with Mrs Constantinidi as well if she's there; none of this arose when I spoke to her briefly last night … which is not surprising, I suppose. Oh yes there's one more thing … can you write down on a piece pf paper all the things you and Mrs Jellicoe ate yesterday, I'll call back later and pick it up.'

It had been a productive meeting he reckoned, as descended the steps and made for his car, one which slightly lifted the lid on the high and mighty, showing that they too sometimes had human failings.

Sussex Police Headquarters,

Sussex House, Brighton.

Luckily D.I. Lawrence was still working in the building when D.S. Bradshaw came out of his office looking for him. All the other detectives on his team other than Acting Detective Constable Leonard Riggs, a new man who'd 'graduated' into his outfit from the 'Uniform' branch the previous week, were out on cases; as were the those of D.I. Crowther and D.S. Reynard.

'You're just the man, Archie,' said Bradshaw 'got a little job for you. It's in Chichester and they've asked us for help.'

'Oh come on, since you landed Jack Crowther and me with all those cases of Foxy's, we're up to our necks. I'd be out on one of them myself now if I didn't have to complete some paperwork for the D.P.P.'s office before midday.'

'What about the new lad?'

'Who ... Riggs ... what about him?'

'It's just a routine check to see if there's anything suspicious in relation to what'll probably turn to be an accidental death. A chap fell off his balcony during the night and landed in his back yard.'

'And you want …'

'Someone to have a look, yes. The man who found him and raised the alarm told us that from the state of the body the fall probably took place around three.'

'Forensic scientist is he?'

'Nah … an ex-fireman who's seen plenty of dead bodies. He also reported blood was coming from the back of the victim's head when he found him. I've alerted Doctor Vladic; he'll get down there as quick as he can, and Geordie Hawkins and his SOCO boys are on their way. Surely Riggs can make a start until you get there yourself? Go on … throw him in at the deep end.'

'Well he's keen to get into his new work, and he's not short of confidence. Alright, he'll be on the road in five minutes.'

☼☼☼

As a result of the conversation between Bradshaw and Lawrence, twenty two year old Acting Detective Constable Riggs was soon on his way to Chichester where, proud of having been chosen, and full of his own importance, he came round the corner of the building into the yard where he found Doctor Vladic and Sergeant Hawkins deep in conversation. A few feet from them two SOCO men were preparing to erect an incident tent over the body of a man who was lying flat on his back on the concrete. Nobody seemed to have noticed Riggs was there, though at six foot nine he was fairly hard to miss. He gave a polite cough.

'Yes?' said Hawkins, turning to discover he was facing a tall slim school-leaver in what was clearly a new navy blue suit. 'What're you doing here, son, didn't you see the tapes. You'll have to go back.'

'D.I. Lawrence sent me, Sir;' Riggs answered, with a

beaming smile. 'I'm Acting D.C. Riggs.'

Hawkins, a man renowned for badly timed and often insensitive leg pulling, couldn't resist the opportunity to get a laugh at the young man's expense. 'Blimey,' he said, 'a brand new Sherlock; we'll have to watch our step.'

Vladic, who'd suffered from Hawkins verbal jabs in the past, smiled at Riggs and winked. 'Take no notice of him, Constable, he rarely bites. Who's with you?'

'No one, Sir, but D.I. Lawrence told me he'd be here mid-morning. What time did all this happen?'

'Hello! It asks questions as well.' said Hawkins, in a second attempt to get a laugh.

Vladic ignored him and answered Riggs's query 'Sometime after midnight I'd say; I'll have a better idea when I get him to the lab.'

Riggs nodded and, walking past Hawkins without looking at him, peered into the partially erected tent the SOCO men were by then anchoring to the ground. Hawkins didn't like it, and was about to say so, when Riggs swung back round again. 'Fine.' He said, 'I'll leave you gentlemen to it while I go up into the flat and see what's been going on up there. Any idea how I get in?'

Vladic was inclined to laugh; it was obvious Riggs hadn't sensed how patronising his words had come out. Hawkins had though, and he was incensed. 'How d'you bloody think?' he said, 'through that flamin' door … and don't touch anything. I'll be up in a minute.'

'Okey doke.' Riggs replied, cheerfully, as he made for the door pointed out. 'And don't worry, I won't touch a thing.'

Vladic was spluttering by then and soon Hawkins was unable to resist doing the same. 'Ah, I suppose he's alright,' he said, 'he reminds me of me the first time I was let off the leash.'

Barton Court,

the P.M.'s private residence near Hastings.

Before he and the commander were half way back to Brighton the previous night, Reynard had been chiding himself for not having made a proper appointment for an interview with the Prime Minister and, when he'd told Simpson how annoyed he was with himself, he'd received no sympathy.

'So ring him,' Simpson had said.

He'd made the call a few minutes later, and it had produced the invitation he was currently taking up so, after the hour he'd spent with the Lord Mayor and his wife at their home in Adelaide Crescent, Reynard was on his way to see the P. M. in Barton Court.

☼☼☼

The front door was open when he got there; the security man in the mobile sentry kiosk outside the gate lodge having telephoned ahead to advise of his arrival. Standing in the doorway was another security man, and he conducted Reynard to the P.M. who was sitting at his desk.

'Good Morning Superintendent,' he said, rising to offer his hand and pointing to a chair. 'You ask, and I'll try to answer.'

'Thank you, Sir,' Reynard began. 'I've already had a preliminary meeting with the Lord Mayor of Brighton and his wife this morning, and I'll be having a fuller one later on. They gave me a lot of important background information which'll help me build a picture of your wife and I hope you'll be able to give me more. They're presently preparing a list of all the samples Mrs Jellicoe ate and I'll pick it up when I return to Brighton this afternoon. With luck, they'll have remembered something which will lead me to the person I'm after.'

'The man who killed my wife?'

'Or woman ... precisely. So, if I may, I'll take notes as we talk. The information we collect from you, from the Lord Mayor and his wife, and from any other party, including your sister-in-law, who has any knowledge relevant to our enquiry will be gone over again and again until we have the person responsible for giving Mrs Jellicoe the poison.

After that it'll be a matter of finding him or her; a long hard slog during which we'll work through the facts, comparing the different accounts as we go, and all the time looking for a common thread that'll lead us to the perpetrator. Be assured Sir, no stone will be left unturned; a crime is a crime irrespective of whether it be committed by accident or design.'

'Alright, Superintendent, what d'you want to know?'

'In a nutshell ... everything. But before we start down this path I wish to ask you a very important question. Have you any idea, any theory however far-fetched, as to why your wife should have been killed or who might have done it?'

'None.'

'No one who bore her a grudge, even a trivial one.'

'I can't think of one.'

'Fair enough Sir, so let's start with your knowledge of your wife's personal details: her date and place of birth, her date of marriage ... all that sort of thing. Summarise the story of her life as you know it ... and take your time.'

The interview with the P.M. lasted an hour, and when it was finished Reynard asked if he could talk to Mrs Constantinidi.

'Sure, Superintendent, I'll take you out to her, she's in the garden watching the boys playing tennis.'

The garden at Barton Court, the pride and joy of the P.M.'s late mother is divided into three sections: nearer the house are long flower beds backed by shrubs, beyond them is the tennis court and, at the end and running up to two five acre paddocks is the kitchen garden. James took little interest in the garden other than to enjoy it, not that he had much time to spare for it anyway but Rose, like James's mother, was a keen gardener and the scene Reynard found himself facing was magnificent and colourful.

Ursula was sitting on a comfortable looking lounger and had what he thought was a gin and tonic in her hand ... she hardly looked as though she was mourning! James introduced him to her and left.

'James has forgotten we met yesterday.' Ursula said, giving him a big smile. 'You're Foxy Reynard, aren't you?'

So surprised was he, at her response, he didn't answer.

'I'm trying to make the best of a horrible situation.' she said, raising her glass. 'I still can't believe what's happened.'

'May I?' he asked, pointing to a wrought iron chair facing her, and sitting on it when she nodded. 'I'm trying to get some background regarding ...'

'Yes, James told me; he said you needed to acquaint yourself with everything about Rose; I'll tell you all I know.'

Encouraged by her eagerness to help, Reynard took out his notebook, but before he got a chance to question her she was talking about their childhood and their age difference.

'No,' he said, 'whatever triggered your sister's death is much more likely to be associated with something more recent and, in any event, the Prime Minister gave me a summary of Mrs Jellicoe's early life. What I'm interested in is what she's been doing, or who she's been seeing over that last couple of years say. If I get nowhere with that, then …'

'Rose wasn't "seeing" anyone, Superintendent, that's scandalous things to say.'

'My apologies; I'll rephrase my words. What I need to know is who, apart from her immediate family and her usual circle of friends, has she met or had dealings with recently?'

'You do use odd words. "dealings". What d'you mean?'

Reynard smiled and shook his head; this was bad start … the talk wasn't going as he'd either intended or expected. Ursula was a beautiful and attractive woman with a strong personality. No wonder she appealed to so many men, and no surprise she usually went on to dominate them. If he didn't watch out he'd be under her spell too, and Cathy would die laughing if he told her. It was time to take charge.

'Mrs Constantinidi.'

'Ursula, please.'

'Better keep it formal, Mrs Constantinidi. Tell me about your own relationship with your sister over the last few months.'

'Well I hardly ever saw her; when she was down here it was too far out of town for me, and when she was up in London she was in Downing Street and I don't like going there … all those serious looking people pretending to care about us. I've no time for politicians, they're all liars.'

'But you did see her from time to time nevertheless?'

'Hardly ever, actually.'

'And when you did, you got on alright?'

'Of course ... oh I know what you're at ... you've been talking to Julia haven't you.'

'Mrs Henderson? Yes I have.'

'And she blabbed on about Rose and I having a bit of an argument. It was nothing. Julia's a menace; she can't keep her nose out of other people's business.'

'So you *did* argue?'

'We disagreed; Rose was acting the big sister, telling me what I could and could not do; it was ridiculous.'

'And you lost your temper and ...'

'And nothing. I lost my patience and shouted at her.'

'So you didn't hit her?'

'No ... well ... just a tap. She probably didn't feel it.'

'And what was the argument about.'

'Nothing. I can't remember.'

As the interview progressed Reynard became more and more convinced Ursula was only telling half the truth. She needed prodding harder.

'Ah you *must* remember.' he said, 'Surely if the reason for your dispute was as insignificant as you want me to believe, you'd not have hit her, and if it was important enough to merit a slap, which I think it probably was, you must be able to remember it. Now, Mrs Constantinidi, I have to warn you this is a murder investigation, so I'll ask you again "What was it that made you hit your sister?'

Unexpectedly Ursula began to cry. At first he thought she was putting it on, but then she disintegrated, and he realised she'd accepted her sister's death at last, that she'd never see her again. It was about Henry Finnerty.' she whispered.

'What about him?'

'Rose thought, no Rose *told* me, that Henry was to be avoided, that he'd a terrible reputation, and that somehow my seeing him would discredit James. I said it was a preposterous suggestion. For Goodness's sake we've known Henry all our lives ... way back to when we were children. We can't pretend we don't know him now. But she wouldn't listen just went on and on and on ... and, in the end, I slapped her to shut her up. I wish I hadn't and I deeply regret it now, especially after what's happened subsequently, but our little spat had nothing whatever to do with her death.'

'I see. And there's nothing else you can think of which might have led to your sister being poisoned ... nothing?'

'Not a thing, Inspect ... sorry Superintendent.'

'Do you see much of Mrs Henderson?'

'I can't stick her, any more than I can that wet blob of a husband she has, Lance.'

'Right. We'll leave it at that,' said Reynard, worried Ursula's outburst would get in the way of the enquiry, 'but,' he continued, 'if anything comes to mind please contact me.'

Ursula nodded and drained her glass. 'Sure you won't have one Superintendent; I'm having another?'

'Oh yes, quite sure. I must get back to the office.' he said, getting up from the chair and walking slowly back into the house.

Seaforth House,

Adelaide Crescent, Brighton.

Lance and Julia had spent most of the morning, once Reynard had left, compiling the lists of foodstuffs they'd eaten at the exhibition. They'd done it separately so their lists were not quite the same. This, they reckoned, was partially due to the fact that Lance had been more involved in talking to the exhibitors than sampling their products while Julia and Rose, as far as Julia could remember, had tried more or less everything they'd been offered. This, to a degree, was because they thought the sample looked appetising, but it was sometimes due to the fact they didn't like to refuse what they were being offered.

Each of their lists had two columns headed: "Nature of Sample" and "Company Involved". Julia's had thirty one entries, Lance's had twenty two … all of which, bar two, were also on Julia's list. There was no mention of samosas on either.'

'I see neither of you have put down a samosa.' said Reynard. 'You know, don't you, that we suspect the hemlock which poisoned Mrs Jellicoe was introduced into her digestive system in one of these things, or in something of a similar nature, that is to say, a filo or flaky pastry case with a savoury filling?'

They both nodded their heads.

'OK. These will be very helpful anyway.' said Reynard, as he quickly ran his finger down each of the columns on each of the lists. 'You are absolutely sure these are all you can remember, Sir? Only you told me there were a hundred and thirty exhibitors.'

'That's correct.' Said Lance, 'but less than half, fifty nine actually, were giving out samples.'

'And you Mrs Henderson, are you sure too?'

Julia hunched up her shoulders, raised her eyebrows, and held out her hands as much as to say ... 'I think so.' and then added... 'Yes, yes ... I'm sure.'

'Fair enough' said Reynard, 'So we have your thirty one, plus the two your husband had but you didn't, that makes thirty three ... right? How many of these were even remotely like samosas ... Sir?'

Lance scratched his head, 'None of them. I didn't eat, nor did I see, anything that looked even remotely like a samosa ... they're those little pastry things aren't they?'

'They are, Sir. Now you Madam ... did you come across any of them, or anything similar to one of them?'

'I didn't see any samosas, though there were a few other pastry based things I did taste. They're on my list and, as you'll see, most of them were open in as much as you could see the filling or contents. ... things like segments of pork pie, fruit tarts in various sizes, pizzas, flans, quiches, and of course ... sausage rolls. The only closed pastry sample I can remember eating that Rose didn't was a miniature Cornish pasty, and the only one I recollect her having that I didn't was a cheese straw.'

'OK. Your lists both look "thin" on the names of the manufacturers of the items you tasted, why do you think this is?'

Julia smiled, but Lance answered ... 'Good question. I

suppose we ought to have taken more notice of them.'

'Or,' said Reynard, mischievously, 'the companies involved need to review their advertising strategy.'

'Are you sure you won't have any coffee?' asked Julia.

'I won't, thank you. So you didn't eat, or see Mrs Jellicoe eat, anything like the samosa found in her stomach. How d'you think it got there?'

'The crowd was pressing closer and closer as we drew towards the end of our tour of the exhibits, Superintendent, and, in amongst that great mass of people, men with trays of tasting samples, some held high up at arm's length, were trying to force their way to the front. If they succeeded we had their wares shoved in our faces. It was becoming pretty frightening when Rose started to wobble and, the next thing, she was on the ground. There's no doubt in my mind she got the samosa during those last few frantic minutes as we neared the end of our tour of the stalls. We've talked about this very point over and over again, Lance and I, and we are both agreed Rose could only have taken a samosa without one of us seeing if she did so just minutes from the end of her visit.'

'Tell me a bit more about the crowd.'

'The oddest thing, Superintendent was the way in which it grew. When we first went into the garden it was like a procession; Lance and I were in the front with Rose, the members of the committee and council following us, and the public, if I can put it that way, straggling along behind us bringing up the rear. Every time we stopped the crowd gathered round and by the time we were nearing the end of the tour, there were as many people in front of us as there were behind. It was in the mass of people in front of us, walking along backwards so they could face us, that I saw men and women giving out samples, many of which we tried.'

'And the men and women with these …?' asked Reynard.

'… were mostly dressed up as butchers, fishmongers, waiters and waitresses, chefs and cooks. There were even a few in fancy dress and one or two in ethnic costumes.'

'You mean Italians, Indians … and so on?'

'Lance saw a man dressed as a cucumber.'

'Good gracious.'

'Could have been a gherkin, of course.'

'Any of them stand out as being particularly forceful in thrusting their stuff towards you, or trying to coerce you into taking stuff you'd rather not have eaten?'

'Several … though I did see one man, a chef, who appeared to be especially pushy with Rose.'

'What sort of things was he peddling'?'

'I couldn't see.' said Julia, 'All I can say was he was one of the men who was holding his tray high so the crowd couldn't get at it, and that he was dressed as a chef.'

'Ah yes … big tall hat and white chef's overalls, probably with blue and white chequered trousers … I know what you mean.'

'No, he had a red bandana round his head.'

Reynard's eyes lit up. 'Ahhh … now we're getting somewhere, a red bandana eh? I bet there weren't too many of those being worn. So he was in whites and…'

'Jacket only, a short one more like the sort a pharmacist or a dentist wears. I didn't notice his trousers, so maybe they weren't white. Mind you, I didn't expect I was going to have describe him or I'd have taken more notice.'

'And his facial appearance, his height, stature, hair?'

'Mmm ... can't remember much about his face except his eyes, they were darting about a lot. As to his general appearance, he was tall, over six feet I'd say, and skinny, and his hair was darkish, not black.'

Reynard looked at his watch. 'Crikey, I've got to get cracking, I've another meeting in half an hour. I'll come back tomorrow to see if you've remembered anything else?'

'Come early, I've appointments all day from ten onwards.' said Lance glancing at Julia, who nodded.

'Eight o'clock?'

'Make it eighty thirty and for an hour only, if you can.'

'Eight thirty it is; and thank you so much; you've added a lot to what we know. Can I ask you one more thing, Mrs Henderson ... it's about Mrs Constantinidi?'

'Certainly, what about her?'

'This is delicate ... she seems to think you were coming between her and her sister is there any truth in this?'

'Ursula doesn't like me and I don't like her much either, we've never seen eye to eye over a lot of things; it's no secret.'

'And?'

'And Rose tried to be the peacemaker.'

'And?'

'And she failed.'

'Did this upset you?'

'Not at all, but it upset her. She wanted Ursula and me to be friends but it was never going to happen, Ursula and I live on different planets. Look Superintendent I knew Rose from college days as I told you and, once or twice, I spent part of my holidays staying with her and her family. My connection to Ursula goes right back to then, to when she was schoolgirl. We never ever got on, I don't know why. The "Henry thing" was just the latest issue we differed on, I doubt it had much to do with poor Rose's death.'

'I see.' said Reynard, walking towards the front door to go. 'Well that's cleared that one up.'

☼☼☼

It was just on five thirty when Reynard got back to his office in Sussex House where he dropped his coat and went to tell D.S. Bradshaw of his progress. After that he returned to his desk, poured himself some coffee and took a Hobnob biscuit from his drawer. Before he got the chance to start on either though, or to gather his thoughts, his telephone rang; it was the Chief Technician from the Health and Safety laboratory. 'Superintendent Reynard?'

'Yes.'

'I've got something to show you, can you get over here?'

'I can; what is it?'

'Half a dozen Samosas loaded with hemlock and some chef's clothing.'

'I'll be with you in twenty minutes.' Reynard replied as he scribbled a note to Groves, asking her to hold back the squad meeting until he returned from inspecting "some vital evidence".

'Sounds like the boss is onto something, which is more than Next and I are.' Said Groves an hour later, as they waited in his office for Reynard to walk in. 'All we got was gassed.'

'What? How d'you mean gassed?' asked Edwards.

Best answered him 'The acrid stench of unwashed human beings, mate, that's what I mean. Annie Weaver's house is a refuse tip; it's packed to the ceilings with junk that must have taken years to collect. The Sarge and I'll be there for days sorting it all out.'

'So you didn't find much.' said Furness. 'I'm not surprised I saw the mess through the window when I was there yesterday.'

'Yes,' said Groves, 'we found nothing except a peculiar double existence we'll explain when the boss gets here.'

'The boss *is* here, Sergeant,' said Reynard, who'd walked through the doorway as she was speaking. 'so you can tell us what the double existence, you found, was.'

'Ah yes, Guv … Annie Weaver was a hoarder …. You cannot imagine the piles of stuff we found there; clothes, books, newspapers, kitchen equipment, blankets …'

'Yes, yes, we've got the picture,' said Reynard, holding up a hand as if he were stopping traffic, 'get to the point.'

Groves, upset at being stopped mid flow, hesitated a moment and then started again by telling the others what she and Best had discovered, and how they'd come to the conclusion there were two separate existences going on at the same time. 'Obviously there had to be an explanation for all the piles of stuff cramming the rooms,' she said, 'and when we decided to give our lungs a rest by going out of the house for a while so we could breathe some fresh air and maybe to talk to a few of Annie's neighbours, I thought of Alison Dandy. She's the lady next door who D.C Furness told us about yesterday. Fortunately she was in, and, though she's quite old, she confirmed what she'd told D.C. Furness and he passed on to us yesterday. You'll remember …'

Reynard rapped on his desk impatiently 'Go on … go on.' He said, 'get to the heart of the matter, Furness can interrupt if he hears something different to the conclusions he's come to, if any.'

'OK, Guv, here's the scene: Annie's sister, Geraldine, lived in the house since it was built in 1972, having purchased it when the road was being developed. She used to work in the Post Office as an accountant until she retired in 1994. Almost from the moment she stopped working she began to act oddly, in that she collected and kept all sorts of things which she said "might come in useful one day."

'I told you she was hoarder.' said Furness, trying to be helpful, but in the end only bringing frowns from his colleagues who'd already come to the same conclusion.

'As I was saying,' Groves went on, 'in tandem with her assembling the collection of rubbish we saw, she began to neglect herself personally, and to withdraw from everyone else in the road, gradually adopting the life of an unwashed recluse.'

Furness, even keener to remind the others he'd covered all this ground the previous day, broke in again. 'It's like I said, she was a hopeless head case ... I reckon ...'

Reynard turned on him. 'One voice at a time, *please*. When Sergeant Groves has finished you can all have your say, right ... carry on Sergeant.'

Groves nodded. 'The antisocial activity inside Number Nine eventually began expand into the garden, which was soon covered with junk too. The sight of the rubbish so openly exposed infuriated her neighbours who reckoned that, should they want to sell their house, the sight of her garden alone might put off a potential buyer. They protested to her through a series of stronger and stronger worded "round robin" letters, but they were all ignored. Within five years by thoughtlessness alone, she'd completely isolated herself from the rest of the community. And then she had stroke and her younger sister Annie, who'd just retired from her job as a housekeeper, came to live with her.

Soon people began to notice changes taking place: builders came in and converted the dining room into a twin bedroom for the two women; the en-suite shower room was created, and there was much more rubbish being put out for the bin men. While this was going on the garden was gradually cleaned up and re-planted and a further acceleration in the reduction of the heaps of stuff inside the house was evident. Geraldine didn't like it but she was too incapacitated to do much about it except complain to Annie, who took no notice of her. More and more refuse bags were put out every week for collection and eventually there was so much at the gate every Thursday morning a man from the Environment Protection Agency, accompanied by a representative from the waste disposal company came round to complain. This brought about a moderate reduction in the number of black bags waiting to be collected and, for a while, all went well. But then Geraldine died and, Miss Dandy told me, Annie, who'd been getting on better with her immediate neighbours, inexplicably began to slip into the same blinkin' groove of isolation from which she'd so painstakingly hauled her sister. She had no callers and seemed to have no friends. She spoke to no one she didn't have to and, at the time of her death, was as much an enigma as Geraldine had ever been.'

'Well it's an excellent report.' Reynard said, when she'd finished. 'Anything to add, D.C. Best; you were there as well?'

'Not a thing, Sir, this is the most puzzling case I've ever been on and I'm stumped for answers. Poor old Annie was as "bats" as her sister, but it's what she was doing down the garden "in the altogether" I can't work out?'

'And,' Reynard said, 'It doesn't look as though anyone else can either so … anyone got anything to say before we move on; you're looking thoughtful D.C. Edwards what's got into you?

And D.C. Furness, have you anything to add?'

Edwards suddenly seemed to have snapped out of his daydream and was about to speak but Furness beat him to it. 'On another subject, if I may, Sir, one of the cases we handed over to D.I. Lawrence's has taken a surprising turn. I was talking to the new chap who's on that squad, a big tall lad, Riggs is his name. He and I both play for 'The Brighton Blues' second team when we can get off.'

'Rugby?'

'Yeah, he's in the second row.'

'I see, so what about him?'

'Well I bumped into him twenty minutes ago, and he was telling me about a case he was on - his first.'

'And … come on, hurry up; we all want to get home some time this evening.' Reynard told him.

'No, Guv, it's just that he told me the victim in the case, a man who seems to have fallen from his balcony and died, was called Ramage. And I couldn't help wondering if it was the same guy D.C. Furness was investigating before our new cases came up and we had to hand over the uncompleted ones, including the one about a Mr Ramage and some falsified insurance claims.'

'Very interesting, but not our business any longer. Now, back to Annie Weaver; have you anything to say D.C. Furness?'

'Yes, I was thinking about the garden hose again; I've mentioned it before. I'm convinced it's got something to do with Miss Weaver's death but I can't put my finger on it. I mean she was hardly squirting water up into the air in the pitch dark and then stripping off her clothes and dancing in the spray as it fell to the ground. She was batty yes, but surely not that daft.

No there's something else, and I won't settle until I have an explanation for it.'

Reynard leaned across towards Groves and touched her arm. 'Give Edwards a dig, he's gone to sleep.'

As she was about to tap the Welshman's knee he opened his eyes. 'Maybe it was a punishment'

'For what ... going to sleep on the job?' Best began to laugh, 'the Governor caught you out there Taffy ... sleeping when on duty ... it's a hanging offence.'

D.C Edwards, unruffled by the Superintendent's implied rebuke and Best attempt at humour, just smiled. 'While you lot have been waffling on about rubbish and the state of Annie Weaver's house I've been thinking of what D.C. Furness keeps reminding us ... the garden hose ... because it's been troubling me too. And then I remembered something that happened a couple of years back which was reported in our local paper at home - The South Wales Gazette. When my mother saw the piece she realised the place involved was just down the road from us, a big gaunt grey four storey house, an orphanage run by nuns who, it seemed, sprayed boys who misbehaved with cold water from a garden hose. Now I know we're not talking about an orphanage or nuns here, but all the same ...'

'But all the same it's the only explanation we've had so far. Well done Edwards ... go back to sleep and see what else you can dream up! In the meantime I have something new to add; the Health and Safety boys have found something in the rubbish bags we put in the marquee: a white coat, a red bandana, a small tray, and six samosas with a strong presence of hemlock. We now know what our killer looked like on the day and, what's more important, we can say with certainty that the hemlock was put into the samosas deliberately by someone who wanted to see Mrs Jellicoe dead.'

'But we don't know why.'

'No we don't, but I think we can safely put the 'How' to

bed. I've told you this bit of news first because, in a way, it's the most important but I'd better also give you the gist of my conversations earlier today with The Lord Mayor, his wife, the Prime Minister ... and his sister-in-law, Mrs Constantinidi. The interchanges I had with these people, if followed up, could lead us to our killer, or show us Mrs Jellicoe was just unlucky to have been in the wrong place at the wrong time. When we come to hear of what Furness and Edwards dug out of the exhibitors we can sift out anything to do with the 'How' of the case and concentrate on finding the 'Who' and the 'Why'. Everything else we'll leave to one side. So, D.C. Furness and D.C Edwards, you have the floor. How did you get on today interviewing the exhibitors?'

'You tell them Dessie,' said Edwards, 'I'll prompt'

'OK,' Furness replied, before going on to describe their day with the exhibitors. 'If we leave out anything we asked, or got answers to, regarding what the Governor's calling the 'Hows' we had an almost entirely unproductive day, Guv. Of course this was because we spent most of the time cross-questioning people on the 'How' - which was the top priority yesterday morning. Outside this we discovered no one had seen anyone with samosas at any time, though a man from one of the Salmon Smoking firms told us he witnessed something odd, which is now likely to be of significance; a man taking of his jacket, removing a red scarf from his head, and stuffing both into a waste container on a side path leading to the shed the mowers are kept in. It's only a few steps from the back service gate, which might have been his exit route. In view of what the governor has told us it seems obvious this is the clothing Health and Safety found today.'

'Absolutely ... I agree.' said Edwards. And, from the facial expressions all around the office, so did everyone else.

Reynard had a satisfied smile on his face too. 'Not a bad day then,' he said, 'but a long one. So, to summarise position in the Jellicoe investigation: We're confident a poisoned Samosa was forced on Mrs Jellicoe by a tall thin man with dark hair and strange eyes wearing a short white jacket and a red bandana which he later stripped off and dumped, with the rest of the samosas, in a refuse container near the bin shed. After that, he probably slipped out of the gardens though the rear service gate which was quite close by.

The Weaver investigation is also in the early stages. We've uncovered the fact Annie Weaver was living in what had once been her eccentric sister's house; and that she was an odd character too, though not so bizarre as her sister. It's been suggested she might have been getting punished when she was stripped of her clothes, tied up, and showered with cold water, though for what reason we don't know unless it was to make a point regarding her personal cleanliness. I mean who wants a tramp living next door? We're guessing when we say this though, grabbing at straws because we don't actually know what the 'Why' is, and we haven't even started to speculate on the 'Who'. No, we're still flittering around on the edge on this one.

Anyway … it's getting on … so let's pack it in for today and, as most of the people we need to interview require a rest as much as we do, we'll let it go at that until Monday morning. Off you go, don't shut your phones down.'

Alan Grainger

DAY FOUR

Sunday 20th September 2009

Alan Grainger

Sussex Police Headquarters,
Sussex House, Brighton.

Sundays are almost sacrosanct in the Reynard household, only the most serious crimes are allowed to disrupt them. Reynard believes, and quite rightly so, that if one is prepared to consider oneself on duty 'round the clock' for six days a week, then Sundays ought to be reserved for rest and relaxation. In his case they always followed the same pattern: rise at nine instead of six thirty, do a few household chores until midday, wander to The Cricketers with Cathy for a pre-lunch drink and then amble another hundred yards to the carvery at The Dog and Duck for a bite to eat. Lunch would be followed by a walk along seafront, and they'd wind up at home lying on the bed napping. At five they'd get up, make tea, read the papers, do the crosswords, and watch the television programmes Cathy had recorded during the week. By ten, they'd be in bed with a night cap reading their books - a romance for her, a biography for him. And that would be it, another Sunday done and dusted; he wouldn't have swapped their rest day routine for a king's ransom.

This particular one had started off like all the others but, by the time he'd found a Phillips screw-driver of the right size so he could fix a loose door catch on a self-assembly cabinet he'd built the previous weekend, he was already drifting to thoughts of the cases he was trying to resolve.

Cathy could see how unsettled he was. 'Oh for God's sake, Foxy,' she said at last, 'go into the office if you must. I can see you're itching to get back to your case; there's no point our going to the pub while you're in this frame of mind.'

'I think I will, I left my notebook on my desk last night and there're a few things in it I can't quite remember. If I nip in for half an hour, I could still meet you at the Dog and Duck before they stop serving ... say at two. Alright?

'It'll be better than watching you mess about with that damned cabinet all morning and grumbling to yourself, you'll have an accident. Go on, I'll see you at two ... *in the bar!*'

Reynard smiled, gave her a quick kiss, and put his tools away. By ten thirty he was on his way to the office, and by ten fifty he was locking his car.

There were only a few vehicles in the car park and he recognised one of them immediately, it was Groves's dark red Megane coupé. Slightly puzzled, and never thinking for a minute anyone else in his team could be in the same unsettled state of mind he was, he entered the door, threw a salute to the desk Sergeant, and climbed the stairs to the C.I.D. Suite.

As he entered it he could see the tops of Grove's and Best's heads; they were just visible above the blue room dividers, as was that of another man he couldn't place. ''Ello, 'ello, 'ello,' he said, parodying a Music Hall policeman. 'What's going 'ere?'

Three head swung round. 'Blimey, Guv, It's Sunday!' Groves exclaimed, 'What're you doing in the office?'

'I'll ask the questions of you don't mind, Sergeant,' he

replied, 'What are *you* doing here ... and who's this?'

Best answered, 'The Sarge and I decided to come in for an hour to try to work out where were with our enquiry. We spent most of yesterday in the house but, in between, we each interviewed a couple of Annie's neighbours in Pendine Avenue.'

'And,' Groves continued, 'as we didn't finish until nearly seven last night, we thought we'd be better come in for an hour this morning to compare notes. We don't want to get caught out tomorrow when you and the other two question us.'

'And this gentleman is ...?'

Best answered again, 'He's Acting D.C. Riggs, Guv; he's on trial in D.I. Lawrence's squad. He was already here writing up his case notes when we arrived; he's been looking into a fatal fall from a balcony over a shop in Chichester.'

'Not a shop, a gallery.' said Riggs, 'it's a flat over a picture gallery.'

'I see. So you're all trying to get your act together and sort out your notes ... which is the reason I came in as well. *I* need to think my way through the information *I've* collected and get it in some form of coherent order; but I can't concentrate at home. How far have you got?'

Best laughed out loud, 'As far as filling the kettle, Guv.'

'Good idea; you lot sort the coffee out and I'll see if I can rustle up a few biscuits. Then, when we're settled, we can bounce the information we've got off each other and see what happens. After that we can go back to our own desks, write up our conclusions, and be out of here by one o'clock. How's that?'

'Does that include me?' asked Riggs, keen to be involved and not seemingly intimidated by the prospect of working alongside the team of the famous Foxy Reynard, even if it was only for the morning.

'It does, Constable, so tell us what you discovered.'

'About Mr Ramage?'

'No, about …'

'The man who fell was called Ramage.'

'Was he? Maybe he was the man we were investigating for fraud; I gave the case to D.I. Lawrence. We're not involved.'

'I know you're not Sir,' said Riggs a little disheartened by Reynard's apparent lack of interest. 'but I thought you'd like to hear what I found anyway.'

'Alright … but make it quick. We've a lot to get through and not a lot of time to do it.'

Riggs, cheered up at that and, restored his smile. 'The first thing I have to say, Sir,' he said, 'is that the Mr Ramage who fell to the ground from the balcony of his flat was not the Mr Ramage you were investigating. My Mr Ramage, if I can put it like that, the one who died was Mr Morgan Ramage. The one you were looking at regarding possible insurance fraud is Mr Brandon Ramage, Morgan Ramage's younger brother.'

'Ah, so the fraud case has not been compromised, and will continue to be pursued.'

'I presume so Sir, I'm not on it.'

'How come your Mr Ramage fell?'

'Well at first I thought it was because he was drunk, the evidence pointed that way; and a Sergeant Hawkins, who I met at the scene had already come to the same conclusion, as had another man who was there - a Doctor Vladic.'

'Ah yes we work with those two all the time, they're very experienced, and if they reckon he fell because he was drunk … that's what he did. What was the supporting evidence?'

'A wine glass stem in his hand, a half empty bottle of Shiraz on a table on the balcony, and a totally empty similar one lying on the floor just inside the room. Doctor Vladic says he has to establish the victim's alcohol level before positively concluding he was drunk enough to lurch against the balcony rail and break it.'

'He broke the rail; it must have been some lurch.'

'I dare say it was, but the rail was rotten anyway.'

'Hmm, so no apparent connection to the fraud your team is looking into.'

'On the face of it no, Sir.'

'But ...?'

'But, while I'm not happy contradicting the conclusion two such experienced officers, I did see one or two things which made me wonder if something else had been going on apart from drinking wine.'

'How long have you been with C.I.D.?' Reynard asked.

'A week Sir, this is the first time I've been out on my own; we're overstretched since taking over some of the cases you were working on, D.I. Lawrence says.'

'I'll bet he does.' said Reynard.

Groves, who'd hardly opened her mouth since Riggs had started to tell Reynard about Morgan Ramage, interrupted. 'What were the 'one or two things' that made you suspicious?'

'The state of the room for a start.' said Riggs, 'Furniture knocked all over the place, papers scatted everywhere ... some of them from the insurance firm concerned in the fraud in which Brandon Ramage is said to have been involved.'

'If he had had a few too many, he *could* have staggered into the furniture and knocked the papers onto the floor.'

'I know that, Sergeant, but there was just so much chaos.'

'That you think ... what?'

'That there was someone else there he was wrestling with ... maybe playfully, maybe more seriously.'

'His brother?'

'Could be; perhaps they were arguing about the insurance claim, came to blows, and Brandon shoved Morgan so hard he crashed against the balcony rail, broke it, and fell to the ground.'

Reynard looked at the young man admiringly, and slowly nodded. 'Not bad for your first taste of detective work, Constable, not bad at all. What're you going to do next?'

'Get my thoughts on paper ready to give to D.I. Lawrence in the morning, he'll want to take it from there I expect.'

'Yes, right, so the Mr Ramage who used to be ours, Mr Brandon Ramage, might have more to worry about than a few extra noughts on an insurance valuation ... interesting ...' said Reynard, 'but now we have move on to our own cases. Thank you for sharing that information, Constable and, in answer to the question I'm *sure* you came to ask me, *yes*, in my view Mr Brandon Ramage could be a violent man if provoked. I wouldn't put it past him to fight with his brother, physically fight I mean, though I doubt he'd have murdered him. If he did shove his brother off the balcony as you have suggested, it'll more than likely come down to being a manslaughter verdict.

OK, either of you two got a question for Constable Riggs before we let him go?'

Groves and Best shook their heads.

'That's it then, keep going as you are Constable, and you'll have a few people in this department looking over their shoulder. Well done again, and now you must excuse us.'

Riggs unfurled himself, straightened up to his full height, and strode off to his team's area, leaving Groves and Best in a state of mind bordering on disbelief; never before had they seen such a level of confidence in a trainee; the Super was right ... they'd have to keep an eye on him.

Reynard brought them back to earth. 'Right you two ... what have *you* got?'

Groves turned to Best and raised her eyebrows.

'No,' he said, 'you go first.'

'OK.' She replied, taking out her notebook. 'Well, briefly, for a start, we had a terrible time in the house as we told you last night. And we made no progress towards finding an explanation as to how or why Annie Weaver died. We *did* see the garden hose was out of place but, to be honest, we never associated it with Annie's death until D.C. Furness mentioned it. No, we concentrated on the house and the neighbours as you'd asked, Guv. And we didn't get far with either.

It'll take days to work our way through the house looking through all the stuff and hoping to find something which will shed light on the case. This is partially due to the fact there's so much of it, and partially because we don't really know what we're looking for other than her private papers. The neighbours weren't difficult, but they weren't a lot of help either because, apart from Alison Dandy, the Colberts, and the Winters, none of them knew much about the Weaver sisters. In the end *I* spoke to Miss Dandy, the lady next door; she knew Miss Weaver as well as anyone; and D.C. Best tackled the Colberts on the corner; they knew her and her sister even better. And we both spoke briefly to the Winters who had nothing to add to what they'd told D.C Furness the day before yesterday, which was that they'd neither heard nor seen anything the night Annie died. We can write them off as far as worthwhile information is concerned.'

'Is there any more coffee? asked Reynard.

Best leaned across, picked up the Cona jug and topped everyone up as Groves continued. 'I reported to you what Alison Dandy told me last night, so suppose I just summarise what I said and then let D.C. Best tell us how he got on with Colberts.'

'Alright, but keep it brief.'

'OK ... the house belonged to Annie's sister Geraldine, a retired accountant in the Central Post Office who became more and more introspective and eccentric as she grew older. Not long after her retirement she started holding onto things she was about to throw away and then, gradually, began to add stuff she 'rescued', from what her neighbours put out for their bins. When the house became too crowded to take any more clutter, she began hoarding it in her garden. Eventually, not only did neighbours complain but so did the council.

And then quite unexpectedly, having always enjoyed perfect health, she had a stroke; and her sister Annie, who'd just retired from being a housekeeper, came to live with her in a part of the house they had converted into a one bedroom flat.

When Geraldine died three or four years later, Annie quickly slipped into the rut her sister had once been in, letting the rubbish pile up again inside the unoccupied part of the house, though she kept the other bit, and the garden, tidy. This was the situation right up until she died last Wednesday night. She was a recluse, living alone in an environment, half of which was in pristine condition, and the other half ... well ... more like a corporation tip. It's obvious to me we must continue trying to find out how Annie died; it's our first priority. D.C. Furness suggested an extraordinary possible scenario last night, obviously there must be others.'

'You mean when he suggested water torture?'

'Well something to do with water anyway. But actual

torture? That's a bit far-fetched surely; why would anyone want to torture an old woman? She wasn't a spy, and she wasn't rich, no, we'll just have to keep looking for some other ...'

'Hang on,' said Reynard, grinning, how d'you know? She could have been a spy.'

'Governor!'

'All right she wasn't a spy but she could have been rich ... money under the mattress ... old people have been hiding money since it was invented.'

'It all comes down to discovering more about her prior to her moving into live with Geraldine I think; which is what I hope D.C. Best will be telling us he managed to squeeze out of the Colberts. In the meantime I've decided that tomorrow I'm going to spend the whole day looking for wills, birth and death certificates, passports, pension books, letters, photographs and anything which will reveal the history of these two women and, before you ask me, Alison Dandy neither heard nor saw anything untoward on the night of Annie's death.'

'OK.' said Reynard 'So a lot of work but not much progress so far. Now, D.C. Best, what have you to tell us?'

'Very little more than D.S. Groves as it happens, Sir, but there were just a few odds and ends which might come in useful.'

'Ahhh ... good.'

'Don't get too excited,' Best replied, 'they were mostly about Geraldine, not Annie, she was a close friend of the Colberts for a long time. In fact Mrs Colbert worked with her in the Post Office before she got married, back in the sixties.'

Reynard leaned forward, his arms folded; at last it seemed they were going to hear something of substance.

'For a while after they got married the Colberts and Geraldine lost touch,' Best continued, 'and then, by pure chance, they both bought one of the newly built houses in Pendine Avenue and the friendship, which was eventually extended to include Annie, as well, was restored. With tact, and certainly if the Sarge will go with me, I think we'll get a lot from Mrs Colbert. At the moment she's still in shock and she's frightened ... no, no ... apprehensive ... concerning opening up to me about her long time friend who, she admitted, had gone a bit doolally over the last few years. If we can establish a good rapport with Mrs Colbert I'm sure we'll find out a lot about Annie too.'

'That's fine,' said Reynard but have you anything *now*, anything which'll push us in the right direction?'

'The odds and ends!'

'Oh go on, Constable, don't string it out - what are they?'

Groves was hardly able to restrain herself from laughing; Reynard was well known for 'stringing it out'. Best was also amused, but chose a safer course by answering the question. 'They're from Ireland, Sir, the Weavers, though it wasn't apparent; Geraldine had no discernible Irish accent and Annie's was impossible to place. Geraldine was well off, it seems, but Annie hadn't a penny. And they were so far apart in age Geraldine had left home while Annie was still at Primary School.

They'd been all but out of touch for years, apart from an occasional holiday post card, or a letter at Christmas, until Geraldine had the stroke; which was a lifesaver for Annie who didn't own her own house or flat or anything like that and, as I said, she didn't have a bean. Strangely, they never got on I was told, sometimes hardly speaking to each other for days on end, yet sleeping in the same room.'

Reynard nodded and sat back in his chair scratching his head. 'Uneasy bedfellows as you might say.'

'They were, Sir.'

'Is that it?'

'So far.'

'Well we've something to think about now anyway. What're your plans for tomorrow?'

'We're sticking together in the house, Guv.' said Groves.

'Fair enough ... now do you want to hear how I got on and don't forget whatever I say is ultra-confidential, don't want "the powers that be" coming down on us.'

'You saw The Lord Mayor and the Prime Minister ... did you talk to anyone else?' asked Groves.

'The Lord Mayor's wife and the P.M,'s sister-in-law.'

'And can you tell us what they said, are you allowed to?'

'I am allowed, and I will; but things changed so rapidly yesterday. Half way through it, for example, the method the poisoner used was identified and then, later on, we got news of what he (and it was a "he") was wearing. As quickly as I asked questions, it seemed, they became redundant.'

'A wasted day then?' Groves asked.

'Not a bit of it, not as far as talking to the women was concerned anyway, and it was a privilege to be in a one to one with the Prime Minister, even if it was a business meeting and held under the most trying of circumstances. The Lord Mayor, Lance Henderson, is a decent enough man; I've met him once or twice before. Neither he nor his wife was able to throw light on any aspect of Mrs Jellicoe's death that would be any use to us. As to the P.M., well I didn't try to question him too much on his wife's recent state of mind; I felt it was too soon; I'll do it next time I see him. I left it to her sister, Ursula Constantinidi, to explain. My God, she's some woman, a real handful. Cathy, who keeps herself up to date on these things by reading the glossy magazines in her hairdressers, says Ursula Constantinidi is one of the leading lights in the current London social scene and a total contrast to her sister Rose, who was a much more reserved woman and preferred to keep out of the limelight. The most useful thing I learned in relation to our enquiries though, was that Mrs Jellicoe and Mrs Constantinidi had fallen out over the latter's involvement with a man called Henry Finner ...'

'Finnerty! I knew you were going to say that, Guv.'

'How could you possibly know?'

Best smiled, 'I go to the races with my girlfriend sometimes, and I've seen them in the enclosure. They're a flashy pair and their name comes up every time there's something dodgy going on. She's been married to other men, several times, but she's always with him.'

'Where d'you get all that from?'

'My girlfriend's like your wife, Sir, she keeps up to date with all that stuff by reading magazines in her hairdressers; she's always going on about this pair and the antics they get up to. I sometimes think she's jealous.'

'I wish I'd interviewed *you*, instead of Mrs Henderson, it would have saved time.'

'Sorry, Guv, I didn't mean to interrupt ...'

'Forget it, but for the benefit of Sergeant Groves ... you don't read glossy magazines, I suppose?'

'When would I get the time? No I don't.'

'Alright. This woman Ursula Constantinidi is a wild and impetuous high flyer according to Mrs Henderson. She had a major falling out with Mrs Jellicoe recently and they came to blows.'

'Why, Guv?'

'Why indeed. It was to do,' according to Mrs Henderson,

'with the fear that any scandal involving Ursula, because of her connection to Henry Finnerty and his doubtful betting schemes, might rub off onto Rose, and ultimately onto the Prime Minister. Rose obviously didn't want that to happen and they argued. Mind you, it was obvious to me Mrs Henderson had no time for Mrs Constantinidi anyway, so the account of the row between the two sisters may have been biased or exaggerated.'

'Was she close enough to Mrs Jellicoe to really know what the row with Mrs Constantinidi was about?'

'They were at college together, adjacent rooms in the residence, and they shared a flat in London for a while before either was married. And yes, they did know each other very well.'

'If there was physical violence between the two sisters, I'll bet we find it was at the bottom of this mystery.' said Groves.

'I agree it might be, but we can't be sure; we're not into speculation at this stage, we're still gathering facts The main thing now, as I see it, having identified the clothing the man who handed out the poison was wearing, and having been told he was tall and thin, had unusual eyes and dark or black hair, and probably left the Gardens by the back gate, is to find him. I'll be concentrating on that, and I'll have Furness and Edwards out on his trail as soon as possible tomorrow morning. And now,' he said, looking at his watch, 'it's time I was going. You'd better both go back to the house tomorrow, forget coming in here; I'll tell the others what's happening in your investigation. OK? Right then, I'm off.'

Alan Grainger

DAY FIVE

Monday 21st September 2009

Alan Grainger

Sussex Police Headquarters,
Sussex House, Brighton.

Groves and Best had gone straight to Annie Weaver's house, as suggested, and Furness and Edwards were already out checking for CCTV footage from every camera they could find in the vicinity of the back gate of The Pavilion Gardens, leaving Reynard sitting thoughtfully at his desk drinking coffee.

'Can I have a word?' It was D.I. Lawrence.

'Yes, come in Archie. Want one?'

'I won't say 'No'.'

Reynard pointed to a chair, took a mug from a desk drawer, lifted the Cona jug from the heating mantle, and began to pour. 'Milk, sugar?'

'Both. Are you alright for a few minutes?' Lawrence asked, and then, without waiting for an answer, went on to talk about the Ramage investigation. 'I believe young Riggs was in here chatting to you yesterday … what d'you think of him?'

'He's sharp and he's confident … not a bad lad, you're

lucky to have him. Why?'

'He thinks you invented sliced bread.'

'He's a bright boy!'

'No, seriously, I can't see him fitting in with my lot; they've been together too long for a newcomer to sit in easily, and I actually think they're already jealous of him and the initiative he's showing with regard to Morgan Ramage's death. I only put him on it on his own because I had no one else to spare and I was up to my neck in reports. Now he's got his teeth into it I don't want to discourage him by putting one of my more senior man alongside him, and I daren't leave him on his own; he needs guidance.'

'No.'

'God Almighty, Foxy, I haven't asked a question yet.'

'No, Archie, I know you haven't, but you're about to.'

'Can you spare someone to work with him?'

'You're so transparent! Look ... I would if had anyone to spare but the truth is I could do with a few more bodies myself; both my cases are proving hard to break open. Tell you what ... if I get one of them solved, or nearly solved even, I'll send you someone. Otherwise all I can offer is a Hobnob biscuit to go with your coffee and, as you know, I don't give those to just anyone.'

'How's the Jellicoe case going ... getting anywhere?'

'Slowly. We believe she was deliberately targeted and we know she was poisoned by hemlock in a samosa she was given by a man for whom we have a description.

We also have one or two bits and pieces of information indicating strife of various sorts between parties of which we know, and which might just be a factor. I've seen the P.M twice and I'll be seeing him again today, if he's free.'

'What's he like?'

'He's like you and me Archie, except he has kids and you and I don't. He's down to earth and likeable. I might even vote Conservative next time ... is that good enough?'

'So he's not the "lying deceitful bastard" you said he was last week, the day he handed out some home truths about the Police Federation in general, and a policeman's right to strike in particular. And don't try to pull the wool over my eyes, you're as true blue as it's possible to be, you always vote Conservative.'

'Yes, well ... more coffee?'

'No thanks. And keep what I said about Riggs in mind will you, he's worth encouraging.'

'A conclusion I'd come to myself, Archie.'

When Lawrence left Reynard followed him out; it was time to get some help, time to pull in the big guns.

✡✡✡

'Good morning, Foxy,' said Chief Superintendent Bradshaw, as Reynard walked into his office 'I was just about to go looking for you.'

'Something wrong?'

'No, I just want to know how you're progressing. I had Commander Simpson on a few minutes ago pressing me for answers and I didn't have much to tell him.'

'Ah well, my feet have hardly touched the ground since I last spoke to you on ... what ... Friday was it? If you've got fifteen minutes I'll lay it all out for you: our progress, our current position, and our planned next moves.'

'I'm listening.' said Bradshaw, pulling a note pad from

his desk drawer and picking up a pencil.

An hour later, with several torn off pages covered with writing before him, Bradshaw got up from his desk and began to pace about his office. 'You've done well, Foxy, everyone's done well, you've covered a lot of ground between you, interviewed a lot of people, and gathered a lot of information ... but it's not enough. The public are following this case and they want blood. The newspapers are hounding us for answers and giving us no space to find them. We have to step up a gear ... have you anything we can give them to keep them at bay?'

'We can involve them; ask them to help. In fact that's what prompted me to come to see you. If we release the suspect's description; the details of the clothing he was wearing and the route he took out of the gardens, and then ask the public to tell us anything they may have seen, we might get lucky. I was thinking of getting hold of that press officer Commander Simpson said we could have, Inspector Jane Elliot, and asking her to handle this so I could get back to asking questions instead of answering them. My two men are both out trying to track the man who gave Mrs Jellicoe the poison. They're checking all the CCTV coverage they can lay their hands on in the area around the back gate in the hope of spotting him. When we do, and we catch him, I expect we'll discover he was working for someone else; the person who has the grudge which prompted the murder.

Bradshaw, looking greatly relieved things were moving at the best pace which could be expected, nodded. 'If I can get her here for a meeting at two, say, can you make it?'

'Make it a bit later and I can.' said Reynard. 'I'm about to ring the P.M. to see if he'll let me look through his wife's personal stuff: her desk, her computer if she had one, that sort of thing. If he has no objection I'll do it this morning and then I must go to Eastbourne to see how Groves and Best are getting on. I was planning to be back mid-afternoon so if Inspector Elliot can make it for three thirty, I will too. Is that alright?'

'It's perfect, and relax … isn't it about time you began addressing me by my first name.'

Reynard sucked in a big breath 'Oooh, don't know about that, Chief Superintendent.'

☼☼☼

By the time he met Inspector Elliot at three thirty, Reynard had been to both Barton Court and Pendine Avenue; he was clocking up some mileage.

His first call had been on the Prime Minister and, as he drove up to the front door, he realised it was the fourth time he'd been there in three days.

'I had the coroner's office on earlier this morning, Superintendent.' the P.M. said, 'My wife's body's been released for burial so a deluge of advisors will probably arrive any minute. I don't need them; I've already decided it's going to be a private affair, family only … damned civil servants!'

'You have my sympathy, Sir.'

'I suppose you want to ask me some more questions - I've not got much time, but fire away.'

'No Sir, I came to ask your permission go over Mrs Jellicoe's papers.'

'Of course, her private room's at the top of the stairs.'

As he spoke a car drove up.

'Oh God, here they come.' the P.M. said.

'Then I'll go.' Reynard replied, and headed for the stairs

and a morning poking about in the turret room Rose used call "my little world."

James often asked her what she did all day up in her room. But she never answered, just smiled and did so, so provocatively, he was reduced to laughter. Had he pushed harder he might have found out she spent most of the time writing poetry; verses she never showed to anyone because she considered them too immature. She once sent one to a Woman's magazine and was astonished when it was accepted. But something else must have come up to take the space usually reserved for poems that week so she never actually saw it in print.

She also painted, water colours, views she saw in her head rather than real life scenes, and she read the papers and surfed the internet, in fact she often knew more of what was going on in the world than her husband did, which amused her immensely. One of her greatest pastimes was picking winners from the line up shown on the racing pages, but the horses she chose seldom won. James knew all this but let her think he didn't, it was more fun that way; *his* little secret was knowing she didn't know he knew *her* little secret.

When Reynard climbed up the narrow winding stair case leading to the turret room he felt the atmosphere changing; downstairs it was all hustle and bustle, with house staff and members of the secretariat constantly passing to and fro across the lofty atrium which served as the hall and gave access to the rooms. But up there in the turret it was all tranquillity, and Reynard could easily understand why Rose had picked the room at the top to be her own. It was hexagonal, and may have been added onto the original structure in Victorian times. One wall had been built into the south west corner of the house, and the folly so created rose to top the chimney height, giving the room an all-round view of the countryside; it was the most attractive bit of living space in the house, Reynard thought. There wasn't much furniture, but there was lot of light and it was very relaxing. When Reynard spied the old dark green velvet armchair he flopped straight down into it.

'Hang on,' he said, a few minutes later when he felt himself beginning to drift. 'this is no good.' And he got up again and opened all the windows.

Apart from the chair there was a mahogany escritoire, Chippendale he guessed, with cabriole legs at the front and straight ones at the back. There was also a second armchair and, on a modern folding table, all her painting stuff except her easel which stood, folded, beside the desk. On a second modern folding table, standing against the opposite wall, was her laptop, and beside it a small metal filing cabinet on top of which was her printer. Other than that there were a few reading lamps, a small bookcase, and what looked to be a brand new tilting office chair. Reynard thought he wouldn't mind spending his life up there in that room.

He had a quick glance in the boxes of brushes and paint on the 'painting' table and pulled out the drawers from the filing cabinet one by one so he could examine them. It first he thought he was onto something because the drawers were full of newspaper cuttings. But then, in the bottom drawer, he found a scrap book she was making, and realised she was just recording her husband's political career. None of the articles or cuttings appeared to be controversial; none could be construed as being a justification to kill. He put the drawers back and turned to the escritoire. Anybody else seeking information would have looked in it first but Reynard, renowned for stretching out the tension in any situation, forced himself to by-pass the desk and look at all the other things except the lap top, before he tackled the escritoire. And he only left the lap top until last because he was unashamedly computer illiterate.

The escritoire, with the flap down to make a writing

surface, revealed an array of small pigeon hole compartments and drawers and Reynard was practically licking his lips as he examined them. Two small drawers which were on one side of the desk's interior contained pens, pencils, rubbers, rulers and the like. Two similar ones on the opposite side were full of ancillary items: staples, paper clips, elastic bands and cellotape. Of the two wider ones in the middle, one was full of headed stationary and envelopes, and the other was crammed to the top with photographs. The pigeon holes which ran under the wider drawers had in them bundles of old letters and cards, unused Christmas cards of doubtful vintage, and several address books, notebooks and diaries. Reynard could hardly contain himself when he recognised the promise of these treasures. Anyone else would have dived in at that point, looking for a key clue which would unlock the mystery of Rose Jellicoe's death. But not Foxy Reynard. Oh no. If he could string things out to tease others he could do it to tease himself as well … and enjoy it.

He dismissed the Christmas cards, bagged everything else, and put it into his brief case to be examined when he got back to the office. It'd be two hours at least before he'd get to dig into the victim's private life, two more masochistic hours of exquisite torture for him to enjoy. Grinning with the pleasurable anticipation of what was in store for him, he picked up the laptop and brief case, descended the stairs, crossed the atrium to where the P.M. was talking to his secretary, stopped a moment to say what he'd taken, and then went back to his car and drove the forty seven miles to Eastbourne.

Groves's car was parked outside number 9, and he was just pulling in behind it when she appeared at the open front doorway. 'Packing up already? he asked, as was getting out.

She took a few steps towards him. 'No Guv, I'm just taking a breather to clear my lungs. Are you coming in or do you want me out there?'

'I'm coming in,' he replied, following her as she turned and went back into the house.

Inside the air was foul, but nowhere near as overpowering as it had been the day before. She led him straight though the hall and into the kitchen where Best was tipping photographs out of a cardboard box onto the table. 'I hope we're getting somewhere at last, Guv,' he said, 'this lot might help.'

Groves went to the dresser and picked up a cup. 'We've just had a cuppa, would you like one?'

'Er ... yeah ... why not? I'm a bit pushed for time so start telling me how you've been getting on as you make it.'

'Pour it Guv? It's made already. If you go out into the conservatory where the air's much better, I'll bring it out.'

'Nothing yet then?' he said to Best, as he walked past.

'Not a sausage ... but then I've just started.'

The air *was* fresher out there, much helped by the open double doors and the windows. He took one of the two chairs, sited with their backs to the wall of the house and facing out into the garden, and put Rose Jellicoe's lap top on the cloth covered coffee table which separated them. He'd brought it in hoping either Groves or Best could use their computer skills to coax it into giving up some badly needed clues. Hardly had he sat down than Groves came out with a mug of tea.

He tapped on the top of the coffee table. 'Down there please, and don't spill it. That computer's Mrs Jellicoe's and I don't want it swimming in tea. Can you have go at it sometime.'

'You'll have to learn one day.' she said shaking her head.

'Not as long as I have you to do it for me,' he whispered, "why keep a dog and bark yourself"?'

'Thank you, Guv!'

'Don't worry; I'm only joking. Any progress?'

'Some.'

'OK, what? But keep it short, I've to be back at three thirty; I'm meeting Inspector Elliot to agree a press statement.'

Groves nodded, 'OK, I'll do my best,' she said, 'we got here at about eight, the locals weren't awake by the look of their curtains, and we've been inside at great risk to our health ever since. First thing we did was sort out the rooms with the junk in, taking a guess that whatever Annie brought with her when she came here to live with Geraldine wasn't rubbish. We also assumed she'd had each room furnished normally before her 'junk phase' started ... you know ... beds in bedrooms and sofas in sitting rooms and so on. We went through the rooms one by one, splitting the contents into two parts: original furnishings and hoarded rubbish. By eleven, we had all the upstairs done and, as we'd examined everything as we'd handled it, we're pretty sure there was nothing up there to help the investigation.

Downstairs there was less to do because, apart from the sitting room, everything else was in the clean part of the house and much more accessible. We might as well have saved our breath as far as the sitting-room was concerned, it was packed with other people's rejects like the rooms upstairs and yielded nothing of interest. Even pieces of furniture buried under the hoarded material delivered nothing; drawers were empty, there were no framed photographs and no private or business papers, nothing of what you might call a personal nature except for the box of photographs D.C. Best is working his way through now.

'It had to be done.'

'Oh I know that, but I'm glad it's finished.' she told him, 'And now we're moving into the area we call 'the flat'; we have high hopes of coming across some worthwhile information there.'

Reynard put down his empty cup, sat back and folded his arms across his chest. 'Amazing isn't it Lucy, sitting out here looking out into the garden, that something so hideous happened behind that shed the other night?'

'I was thinking the same. 'It's no wonder the nurse who spotted her got such a shock. But we'll get to the bottom of it.'

'We'd better,' Reynard replied, rising from the chair 'because we're under the spotlight with this investigation every bit as much as we are with the death of Mrs Jellicoe. See if you can find something here we can call a clue to bring to our meeting in the office tonight, and try and squeeze something out of the laptop if you can. I'm off now; I'll see you at six thirty.'

Best was still looking through the photographs as Reynard walked through the kitchen to the front door. 'Anything?' he asked.

'Ach ... there *are* one or two we'll have to puzzle out. I'll bring them and any others I think might be of interest to the office later on.'

Reynard looked up at the kitchen clock; it was just coming up to half past two. 'I'm off then,' he said. 'I'll see you later ... make sure you have something for me.'

☼☼☼

He made the office with twenty minutes to spare and was seated in his chair going over the morning's events when Inspector Elliot appeared at his door. 'Ready for me?'

'Oh yes, come in.'

Sussex Police Headquarters,

Sussex House, Brighton.

'Are you ready to help me put a press release together yet, Superintendent?' asked Elliot.

'Sure,' Reynard replied, 'The information I have will to keep the newspaper hacks at bay for a while.'

'Brilliant.'

'But, much more important,' he continued I hope it'll also encourage the media to enlist the help of the public. The man who gave the poisonous food, possibly a samosa, to Mrs Jellicoe was wearing a waiter's short white jacket and had a red bandana round his head. We have this from two witnesses who saw him briefly but clearly. One described him as a tall thin man with dark, or black, hair. We also know he dumped the jacket and the bandana in a refuse bin by a wooden shed near a service gate at the back of the gardens, and we think he may have exited the gardens by that gate.

Someone, maybe many people, saw him, so, as to the help we need, can you knock something up for us using this information, and then add a request for anyone who saw a man matching the description at or anywhere near the Great British Food Fayre to contact us? Can you do this?'

'Of course I can, it's just what we need. I'll draft something and email to you. If you like it I'll call the press in and give it to them and I'll see an appropriate notice is sent round to be posted on all public notice boards and in all police stations.'

'Perfect.' said Reynard, who then headed for the CID suite where he found D.C. Edwards peering at a TV monitor. 'Aha, … so you got some?' he said.

'CCTV, Guv? Yes, we did better than we expected. D.C. Furness went straight up to the Traffic Department and got the location of all the cameras they had within half a mile of The Pavilion Gardens As it turned out they had them covering every major crossroads with the images not overwritten for seven days. They downloaded the ones we wanted onto discs and he's been up there most of the day examining them on the playback monitors.'

'Sounds promising; what are these *you're* looking at?'

'They're the ones I collected by walking along the possible route 'our man' took, looking for security cameras attached to privately owned commercial premises: shops, pubs, gated entrances to big houses. We worked out, early on, that when he left the gardens and went out onto New Road, whichever way he took he'd sooner or later have come within the range of the cameras at the crossroads at one end of road or the other.'

'And are these the ones Traffic have, and they'll have picked up vehicles and pedestrians?'

'They are and D.C. Edwards is currently looking at them.'

'So, if our suspect, and he is one now, had walked out onto New Road the cameras would have caught him, right? And if he'd parked his car in New Road, which is a one way one as I recollect then he'd have …'

'We'll have the car on the cameras at the junction of New

Road and Church Street.'

'Sounds good, but there must be dozens of cars passing along New Road at any time during the day and he could be in any one of them. For that matter he might have gone into one of the buildings on the opposite side of New Road to the gardens including the church, the pub ... even the hairdressers.'

'True, but we're hoping the camera has also aptured things a fair bit up the road towards the gate from which he exited and, if it has, we might see him getting into a car. There'll be a time showing on the camera shots as well, so we're going to look closely at the hour bracketing the time we've been told Mrs Jellicoe collapsed, and hope to see if he kept walking or got into a car when he left the gardens.'

'And then?'

'If he walked, we think we can track him on the discs I have here, the ones from the private security systems. If he got into a car we'll have him on the crossroads camera on the Church Street junction.'

'With a hell of a lot of others!'

'We know that, Guv, but we have to start somewhere.'

Satisfied each member of his team was on top of his job, Reynard retired to his office, rang Cathy to say he'd not be home until nine, and, with a cup of Costa Rican in one hand and a Hobnob biscuit in the other, he tilted back his chair and began the slow process of putting the jigsaw together.

The things he'd brought from Barton Court lay on his desk in front of him. They'd have to wait for another tantalising hour. In the event it was longer because, hardly had he begun to mull over what Edwards had told him, than Groves and Best appeared.

'Are we disturbing you Guv, because we think we have

something?' said Groves, who, without waiting for a reply, handed him two photographs: one of a middle aged woman in her mid-fifties or sixties standing beside a woman some years older. In the background was a long sandy beach. On the back it said "Geraldine and Annie. 1973".

'I think I saw that,' said Reynard, 'it was on the dressing table in the bedroom Geraldine and Annie shared. But it was in a frame then - right or wrong?'

'Wrong, Guv; this one was in the box I was sorting. The one you saw in the bedroom is this one.' said Best, handing Reynard a second photograph.

Reynard took it, and straightway saw how similar it was to the first except the women were much older. He turned it over and saw "Geraldine and Annie, 2001" written on the back. Before he had time to make any comment though, Best handed him a third print; it was of a headstone. 'Try this for size, Sir,' he said, grinning before turning to Groves and winking.

Reynard reached for the photo and walked to the window to see it more clearly and then, as he struggled to read blurred engraved lettering in the over developed print, he gradually began to smile. 'They must be the parents,' he said, 'listen to this.'

In loving memory of

Michael Orton Weaver (Mickey)

of Fairfield

1911-1973

And of his wife Eleanor Mary

1916-2001

'Just what we thought, Guv,' said Groves, 'and look at the dates; these photos must have been taken when Geraldine and Annie went back to their parent's home for their funerals. If they were, we now not only know who the Weaver sisters were, but we can have a stab at working out from where they came. All we need is to know where Fairfield is, and what they did between leaving it, and winding up in Pendine Avenue.'

'Very useful ... anything else to show me?'

'No, that's it Guv,' said Best, 'the rest of the photos were all to do with Geraldine only. I reckon her life could be traced through that box of photos, but it's Annie's we need to piece together ... and there wasn't a trace of anything personal of hers.'

'Bills, letters, bank account, passport?'

Groves shook her head. 'They must exist but ...'

'Did she have a computer or laptop?'

'The only thing we found other than her clothes was a purse with fourteen quid in it.'

'She must have had a telephone.'

'There was a telephone table in the hall, but no phone on it. Nor did we find a mobile; if she had one she had it well hidden.'

'Did you ask Alison Dandy how Annie managed her life?'

'Not in as many words, we tried to draw her out on that score but all she knew was that Annie only went out once a week to draw her pension and buy food but otherwise she stayed indoors or in her garden. She grew all her own vegetables.'

Edwards began to laugh. 'Y'know I like this old bird more and more, she's buried so deep we're going to need sniffer dogs to find out where she's hidden herself.'

'On which note,' said Reynard, 'I think we'd better leave it for today. Back here tomorrow, usual time. OK?

'OK Guv,' all but Groves replied.

'No home to go to?' Reynard asked her.

She checked to make sure the others had gone. 'It's a favour I want, Guv. Can you give me the whole team for a couple of hours to search the house? D.C. Best and I can't do another whole day in that stench. Two hours, Guv, please.'

Reynard, his face screwed up as though he was in pain, began to rub his chin. 'Hmmm ... I'll think about it.'

She smiled. 'Thanks.' she said, knowing that in appearing to have difficulty in making up his mind, Reynard was up to his usual tricks; drawing it out, putting off giving her an answer. He'd say "yes" in the end, of that she was absolutely sure.'

Alan Grainger

DAY SIX

Tuesday 22nd September 2009

Alan Grainger

Sussex Police Headquarters,
Sussex House, Brighton.

In the event, Reynard decided to go with Groves's suggestion, but he strung it out right up until they were seated in his office waiting for the daily catch up meeting to start.

'OK. Good morning all. Sergeant Groves has asked for an all-out effort in Annie Weaver's house today, and I'm inclined to agree with her. I want you all to go to there and, starting at the top, check through every one of those congested rooms until you're sure there's nothing there of use to us. Once your search has been completed I want you, D.C Furness, and you, D.C. Edwards, back here continuing your work on the CCTVs and following up anything you find. You and D.C. Best, Sergeant, can spend the rest of the day in the more civilised part of the house - Annie Weaver's flat. I'll be here all morning if you need to speak to me so … any questions before you go?'

'Riggs was looking for you, Guv.' said Furness.

'Fine, text him and tell him I'm here.'

☼☼☼

Best and Groves drove to Pendine Avenue in her car; Edwards and Furness went in his. Hardly had they gone than Riggs appeared at Reynard's door.

Reynard saw him through the glass panel and beckoned him in. 'Well, Constable, what can I do for you?'

'Nothing, Sir ... it's just to let you know I'll be at Mr Ramage's flat all morning.'

'Right.' said Reynard, inwardly smiling at the man's persistent attempt to ingratiate himself.

'If you like ...' Riggs began.

Reynard held his hand up. 'No, no ... hang on ... stop. Look I'm a bit pushed this morning, but in any event you should be reporting to your team leader, not me. I can't have D.I. Lawrence thinking I'm trying to poach you. We don't do that in this nick.'

'Fair enough.' said Riggs, completely oblivious to what others might have taken as a minor reprimand. 'I just thought I'd mention it to you.'

'Cheeky young sod!' Reynard said to himself, as the eager young policemen swung round and went back to his desk

On his own at last, Reynard tilted himself back in his chair and began to plan his morning. 'Bradshaw first,' he thought, 'tell him what's going on; Elliot next, to say I agree the public notice she sent me last night. After that I'm going to lock myself in here and go through everything I got from the P.M. and Ursula Constantinidi, or noted down at the Hendersons, or brought back from Rose Jellicoe's room at Barton Court.'

✡✡✡

His interview with the Chief Superintendent Bradshaw was short; the one with Inspector Elliot shorter still and, by nine, he was back in his office opening his note book.

'Let's see now ...' he mumbled, as he flipped over the pages. 'Ah yes ... here we are:

Rose Ann Jellicoe (maiden name Wyse); born 2.8.70. Ewehurst, Surrey; (sister Ursula born 14.5.74.)

Father, Ernest Wyse, and his brother, Frederick, partners in animal feed business near Epsom. Fell out over sales strategy in 1977 when Rose seven. Business sold to split partnership.

Father took family and his half of proceeds to Ireland where his wife, Jessica, Rose's mother, had inherited a farm outside Kildare. He found working it too demanding though and, after a couple of years, gave it up, built a warehouse in the yard, and went back into animal foodstuffs again.

The neighbouring stud farm was owned by man called Finnerty who had a son of Rose's age called Henry, the same man Rose and Ursula recently argued over.

Both the Wyse girls went to school locally and then to college in Dublin; Rose at Trinity (European History and Politics) where she became friends with Julia Fredericks, the English girl from Bath who later married a newly qualified solicitor from Brighton, Lance Henderson; and Ursula at Griffith College where she failed to take her education in Interior Design seriously and consequently never qualified. After Trinity, Rose continued her studies at London University (M. A. in Political Science) winding up as a Researcher, in the Conservative Party Central Office.

At around same time, and within two years, Rose and Ursula lost both their parents. The life insurance money they got, coupled with proceeds of sale of the farm and business, amounted to a sizeable inheritance. Rose invested her half wisely, but Ursula used hers to fund the extravagant London life style which ultimately rewarded her with three rich husbands, two of whom she'd quickly divorced.

While at Conservative Party Central Office Rose shared a flat on Clapham Common with Julia and, during this period, she started going out with James, a trainee Political Agent, she'd met in the course of her work. They married in 1995 when she was twenty-five. They have two teenage boys.

After marrying, Rose gave up her job to help James in his career and the higher he climbed, the more she withdrew. Her attendance at The Food Fayre being a rare exception, agreed to only because Julia was involved.

Rose had no political, governmental, or international contacts beyond those forged while in support of James and she had never been involved in political or international controversy. There was no obvious explanation for her death.

Reynard put down his pocket note book and closed his eyes. His interview with the P.M hadn't advanced his case one little bit. What could there be in Rose's life that he was missing? He tried to imagine her at the various stages of it, and then attempted to work out if, at any of them, there was a pointer to her death. But it was no good, and after ten minutes he gave up; there wasn't a single thing he could think of which might have conceivably connected Rose's life to her death.

Pushing to one side the, by then cold, mug of coffee he'd poured before he'd started his analysis, he tipped the contents of his brief case out onto his desk and spread everything out: a number of letters held together with an elastic band, a handful of photographs, a folder with pockets in it containing visiting and business cards, diaries for 2007, 2008 and 2009 ... and a well-used address book.

Did these few items hold secrets that would push him in the right direction to uncover Rose's killer?

He leaned forward, picked up the letters, and slipped off the thick rubber band. Most were in their envelopes and had reasonably distinct franking marks. 'Ah, good.' he thought, 'These things often give more information than the letter itself.' Half were from her mother; all were posted in 'Cill Dara' which, he assumed, was the Irish name for the town he knew as Kildare, the place in which Rose had once lived. They were all chatty notes written, as far as he could see, to give local and family news: a new puppy, a cousin married, the death of a neighbour - news of home and family.

He put them to one side and went to the rest, quickly seeing they were much the same except they'd been written by school and college friends. By the time he'd been through all the letters, there were only two left. Both, he felt, had interesting possibilities.

The first wasn't actually a letter at all, it was a postcard, and it was both vague and brief. 'Good luck. Hope all goes well. I'll be thinking of you.' It was signed 'Dimps' and had been sent, according to the post mark, from St Austell, on the eighth of August 1992.

The second wasn't a letter either, though it was tucked into an envelope from the Royal National Lifeboat Institute which had been posted in Poole a few weeks earlier. It consisted of a single sheet of paper on which, in large black marker pen letters was written ... 'You have ten days.'

He rocked back in his chair, his arms clasped behind his head. On his face was the first smile of the day; at last it looked as though he had something into which he could get his teeth.

'Won the lottery have you?' shouted D.I. Lawrence tapping on the Reynard's window as he'd walked past.

'I wish ...' Reynard replied, 'Oh, and while you're there, Archie, can I have a word?'

Lawrence pushed the door open, but he didn't go in. 'If you make it quick you can, only I've a ...'

'Riggs.'

'Yeah?'

'He keeps telling me things he should be telling you. Not that I mind, but I don't want you to think ...'

'I don't; he's just keen, wants to please everyone. How's the Jellicoe investigation going?'

'Slow, very slow.'

'Better put Riggs in charge then!' said Lawrence, laughing as he continued down the room towards his own office.

On his own again, Reynard reached for the wallet of visiting cards - every pocket was full, some even had two cards in them but, as he flipped through them, he saw they were mostly those of doctors and dentists, plumbers and painters, plus a load from hotels and restaurants. All looked innocuous, so he put them to one side and reached for the diaries, quickly discovering Rose had never used them to record what she'd done, but what she was about to do - they were appointments diaries in fact.

Every entry seemed normal; there was nothing unusual, unexpected, or in any way suspicious so he went to the photographs, which were mostly black and white prints. They and the address book were all he had left to go through except the lap top which Sergeant Groves had taken, promising to "have go at it" sometime during the morning.

He tipped out the photographs from a used envelope he'd taken from Rose's waste paper basket and slowly began to go through them. They were mostly family pictures featuring the children, but there were a few which must have been taken before she was married, some even as far back as her school and college days. He paid particular attention them; if her death was in any way connected to her past, there was just a chance someone in one of those photos might be able to help him.

9, Pendine Avenue,

Eastbourne, Sussex.

The second search through the crowded rooms had finished, Furness and Edwards were on their way back to the office to continue looking at CCTV footage, and Groves and Best were in the kitchen waiting for the kettle to boil; a cup of tea to wash down the dust was badly needed before they moved into the flat to continue their hunt for clues. 'What d'you really think, Sarge? Best asked. 'Was this an upset neighbour taking matters into his own hands, someone making a point about cleanliness?'

Groves shook her head. 'I've no idea. She wasn't being tortured to get secrets out of her, that's for sure. No, I think it's more likely a couple of teenagers, thinking themselves clever, who did it; a pair of thirteen or fourteen year olds who'll be half expecting us to come knocking on their door, and worried to death what'll happen when their parents find out what they did. Let's take our tea into the conservatory, we need a break.'

The sun was shining as they went out to the chairs either side of the coffee table and, momentarily dazzled by its brightness, Best tripped on the curled up edge of a Persian rug, stumbled against the foot of one of the chairs, and decanted his tea all over the tablecloth.

'Idiot, what d'you do that for?' said Groves, 'I'll get you another; while you clear up the mess.'

Best handed her his empty mug and, as she returned to the kitchen to pour him a replacement, he stripped off the cloth with the intention of taking it out into the garden to dry in the sun. But he never got that far because, as soon as it was removed he saw the box, a largish one, leather covered, old, battered, and red; it had been sitting on the table beneath the cloth. It didn't appear to be locked, so he lifted the lid. Inside there were stacks of papers and photographs, a desk diary, and an address book with no cover. Lying right on top, as though it had just been put there, was a bank statement. He picked it up. It was Annie Weaver's.

'Hey, Sarge.' he shouted, 'I've found her.'

'What?' asked Groves, as she came to the back door with his tea in her hand.

Best pointed to the open box 'Look for yourself, it's where she kept her private stuff. We've hit the jackpot.'

Groves put the cups down on the kitchen table and stepped out into the conservatory. 'OK.' she said, 'Let's have everything out, papers, diaries, the address book, the lot, and we'll soon see if we've got what we're looking for.'

'Yeah ... right.' Best answered, sticking his hands into the box and sliding them under as many sheets of paper as he could and lifting them clear.

Groves couldn't contain herself when she saw what was underneath. 'Yes!' she shrieked, giving him such a shock he dropped everything he was holding.

'What?' he yelled back.

She didn't answer, she just pointed to the bottom of the box; it was covered with bundles of bank notes.

Sussex Police Headquarters,
Sussex House, Brighton.

The photographs sat on Reynard's desktop awaiting his return from C. S. Bradshaw's office. He'd been talking about his team's progress in the two investigations in which they were involved, and reassuring his boss that any apparent delay in getting a result was due to their having to check and double check every single thing they did.

To his surprise Bradshaw seemed pleased, 'I'm glad to hear it,' he said, 'we can't afford to make a mistake in either of the cases you're investigating because, as I'm sure you know from our chat with D.I. Elliot earlier this morning, the damned press will pounce on us if they spot us making one.'

'They always do.'

'It's your blinkin' name y'know.'

'My name? What about it'

'They expect miracles.'

'Oh … right … I'll see what I can do then. No, seriously, we're edging towards getting a suspect in the Jellicoe case and if we do they might give us some breathing space '

'You're talking about the guy with the red scarf on his head I assume, how far have you got?'

Reynard launched into his report, giving as much detail as he could, and suggesting the different directions their enquiries might be taking them. He began with the Jellicoe case. 'The position is,' he said, 'I'm handling all discussion with the P.M myself and, for the moment, I'm doing the same with the Lord Mayor and his wife. D.C.s Furness and Edwards are going through CCTV of the area around the gardens. They're using the description of the man we have from witnesses to help them spot him leaving the gardens, and if they …'

Bradshaw held up a finger when, through the open door, he saw Inspector Jane Elliot approaching.

'Are you looking for me, or Superintendent Reynard?' he asked, beckoning her in.

'Both.' she replied, 'I'm taking the opportunity to inform you I've already had some replies. No less than fourteen members of the public have rung in, in response to our request for help. All of them say they saw the man with the red bandana; one, as he was putting it on, and two, as he took it off and dumped it.'

'Now we're getting somewhere,' said Bradshaw, 'have you called them in for interview?'

'I thought I'd better let D.S. Reynard do that, after all he's the one who'll be seeing them. Did I do right?'

Reynard nodded. 'You did, and if you give me the list I'll get straight onto it. Great response, thank you.'

'Was there anything else you were going to tell me?' Bradshaw asked, as Reynard stood up from his chair.

'I was also going to give you the latest in the Weaver case,' Reynard replied, 'but with the reaction we appear to have got in answer to our appeal for help from the public, I'd better start telephoning straight away.'

'You're dead right.' said Bradshaw.

As a result of changing his planned morning, Reynard didn't get round to the photographs again until nearly lunchtime at which point, though he didn't know it, Groves and Best were on their way back to the office. They'd initially been inclined to rush back with the box, but common sense had prevailed and they'd curbed their excitement and stuck to their original idea of giving the flat one last going over. As expected, they found nothing, so they locked up and set off for Brighton, stopping briefly at the house on the corner to talk to Mrs Colbert, who'd previously been more than reticent about the Weavers. This time she was less so.

She told them Annie had worked for 'a good few' years as housekeeper to an unmarried clergyman 'up in the north somewhere' and, as she was seventy four when he died, she'd retired. It was Geraldine having a stroke a few months later which had brought her to Eastbourne and inadvertently rescued her from a life of poverty in a bed sitter with only an old age pension to support her.

Armed with this new information on top of having discovered the box, and knowing how pleased and relieved Reynard would be, Groves and Best were practically quivering with excitement by the time they pulled up in the office car park.

Reynard though, unaware of the surprise which was on its way, and having made the phone calls and arranged to see all the members of the public who'd telephoned in response to the appeal, had just got back to sorting through the photographs when, through the window, he caught sight of Groves and Best climbing out of her Renault.

Clearly they were on their way to tell him how they'd got

on and ... maybe ... as they were back so much earlier than he'd been expecting, they'd found something of significance.

He slid the photographs into the top drawer of his desk and sat back, watching them as they entered the big open planned office, ambling along in his direction and talking animatedly to D.I. Lawrence who'd come in with them.

Groves must have sensed Reynard was looking at them and turned to see he was beckoning them. 'Sorry Archie, we must go,' she said, 'Foxy wants us.'

'And what Foxy wants, Foxy must get!' Lawrence replied, as they advanced on Reynard's office; Groves in front, followed by Best, holding the box in front of him like an offering.

'Aha! A present for me! Good ... what is it?'

'Governor ... we've struck it rich. It's Annie's papers.'

'Whoaaa! This is more like ... show me.'

Best put the box down on the desk, opened the lid and swung it round. For a second or two Reynard didn't move, and then he leaned forward over the box as if he was using his nose to sniff out the secrets. After a pause while he savoured the prospect of what might be coming, he began to take the papers out ... one by one. First came the bank statement; he looked at it carefully then put it down again and took up the next; there were letters, certificates, legal documents, even old school reports, and he read every one, mumbling, "Hmmm, hmmm" .. and ... "Ah yes" from time to time. Groves and Best shuffled in their seats; willing him to hurry up and get to the money. But he wasn't to be rushed as he slowly worked his way down through the written evidence defining Annie Weaver's life.

He was halfway through the papers before he spotted what he thought was part of a bank note at the bottom of the box. Immediately he lifted the corner of the paper above it to check if he was right. But even when the note was mostly exposed he still made no attempt to lift off the rest of papers.

Best was all but screaming in anticipation of Reynard's reaction when he got down to the bulk of the cash, but Groves, guessing Reynard would torture himself and everyone else by delaying the final denouement, had her eyes shut; she seen it all before. And then, almost with reluctance, Reynard picked up the last few papers and exposed the money.

'Hello.' he said, displaying neither surprise nor excitement. 'So she *was* being tortured.'

Groves and Best, who'd expected a much more dramatic reaction, looked disappointed; Edwards and Furness, had they been there, would of course have been delighted; after all, they'd said the hose was important from the start.

'Any idea how much?' Reynard asked, running his fingertips over the tightly packed bundles.

Groves opened her eyes. 'Eight and a half thousand pounds we made it. But whose is it? And is it really the 'Why' for which we've been searching as you seem to be suggesting?'

'Two good questions Sergeant. I suppose the money might have once been Geraldine's, most of it anyway, but it would have passed into Annie's hands when she died. Regarding your other point ... yes, you could be right ... remember what I told you about old people and mattresses the other day; thieves know a lot of old folks don't trust banks and hide their savings; they're easy targets. Better get it down to the evidence store and have the officer in charge lock it in the safe. And get a receipt; we don't want it going walkabout!

As to all this,' he said, pointing to the heap of papers beside the box, 'cart it back to your desks and go though it; listing everything and adding your comments. How come you missed it before?'

'How did we find it, you mean?'

'Yes, is it a secret?'

'Put it this way, Guv, we don't ...'

Reynard, sensing a long drawn out story, cut her short. 'Later please, and no tales out of school; just get on with the job and bring me your summary as soon as you've finished it.'

When Groves and Best had gone, Reynard began to refocus on the photographs he'd so hastily shoved into the top drawer of his desk.

Pulling the drawer open again and lifting the prints out, he was soon busy sorting them into different piles, the first was mostly of pictures of houses and gardens, long distance scenic views, and the QE2.

In the second pile were a number of Jellicoe family snaps including a few of older people he assumed to be grandparents, uncles, and aunts. Others were of the two Jellicoe boys from their toddler years onwards.

The third and last pile, the smallest, was the one in which he was most interested. It consisted of pictures of Rose at various stages of what he assumed to be her premarital adult life. In all of them, there were other people too.

He went through the first pile again and, deciding they were of no help, put them in a new A4 envelope and shoved them in a drawer. He treated the second lot in a similar fashion, using his hand to sweep the pictures into its envelope before sealing it and putting it away; which left the third group of eleven to be examined more closely.

He started by spreading them out so they weren't overlapping eachother, and then, taking them up one at a time, he checked to see if there was anything written on the back.

If there was he put them to the right side of his desktop, if there wasn't they went to the left.

Satisfied that his best chance of getting something from the photographs was lying in front of him; he pulled open a side drawer and took out his magnifying glass. Guided by the names and dates on the back of the pictures he'd taken from those on his right hand side, he soon saw none were pertinent... which left him with just five prints, all without names on the back, on which to pin his hopes.

The first showed a group of a dozen or more people partying in a high ceilinged, sash windowed, room. Whoever had taken the picture must have done so without warning because nobody was looking at the camera. Several of the people were standing chatting; others were grouped around a fireplace apparently discussing the Christmas cards displayed on the mantelpiece. And there were three or four sitting on the floor. Everyone seemed to be holding a part full glass.

The second print was of two women, easily recognised as Rose and Julia when they'd been about twenty three or twenty four years of age. They were standing either side of the front gate of a tall red brick Victorian house with its name - VILLA BELMONTE - chiselled into the granite of the gate post. It was a name Reynard somehow felt he heard before, though in what context he couldn't remember.

The third and fourth photos were similar to each other, both being of Rose and Julia with a young bearded man. They'd clearly been taken on the same day, and Reynard wondered if the man could be James or even Lance.

The last print, the fifth, was of a group of six people. It had been taken on what looked like a cross channel ferry. In it, Rose and two other young women were standing at the ship's rail alongside three men in their late twenties. He thought one of the men bore a slight resemblance to James, and might have looked even more like him if he hadn't had a drooping moustache, a long pony tail, and a guitar slung round his neck.

So it came down to five photos ... but what were they telling him? He picked up the second one again and checked the name on the gate; it was clear enough, VILLA BELMONTE. If this was the house in which the party in the first shot had been had taken, James might recognise the name, might even be able to place the house. None of the men in the first picture looked remotely like him; maybe he was taking the picture.

Reynard sighed, nothing obvious had come out of his first look at what he'd thought was going to be promising He put the picture down and wrote a note on his pad to remind himself to ask the P.M. and the Lord Mayor if any of the pictures included either of them. And he was just about to look at the second one again when Riggs knocked on his door and walked in.

'Excuse me, Sir,' he said, 'but, as I was passing your window, I couldn't help noticing you were using a magnifying glass. May I borrow it for a minute when you're finished; I'm going through photographs too ... dozens of them.'

'Doesn't anyone in your team have one?'

'I don't know Sir, they're all out. I only need it to check some details in two photos; I'll have it back in a flash.'

'You'd better; I'm just about to go for a bite in the canteen.' said Reynard, handing him the magnifier, 'Make sure it's on my desk again within the hour.'

'Of course, Sir, no problem, It'll be here quicker than that.' Riggs answered, taking it and swinging around to return to his desk, a huge grin on his face as usual.

Reynard watched the young man striding back to his desk, and smiled. 'Policemen *are* getting younger!' he said to himself, picking up his mobile and texting D.C. Furness, to ask him where he and D.C. Edwards were.

The answer came straight back. 'In a shop on the route "our man" took. We're checking CCTV. Do you want us back?'

'Not later than four.' he texted back, getting up from his desk and making for the canteen.

☼☼☼☼

It was seldom he found himself near HQ at mealtimes so he didn't normally eat there; settling for a sandwich at the nearest pub if he felt hungry. On this occasion though he was soon tucking into a mountainous serving of cottage pie alongside Archie Lawrence, a man whose judgement he respected. It gave him the opportunity to mention Riggs. 'I like him, Archie,' he said, 'but every time I turn around, he's there with his big smile and his offer to help. Have a word with him will you? He's going to do well in his job because he's bright as a button and dead keen, but if he doesn't calm down he'll put people off.'

'I know … he hangs around me like new puppy. But I don't want to destroy the good I see in him, the enthusiasm and the willingness. Mind you, I'll have to choose my words carefully if I'm going to cool him down without upsetting his confidence. Leave it with me, Foxy, I'll have chat with him when the moment's right. Is that OK with you?'

'Of course it is. How's he getting on with the case?'

'Ramage?'

'Yes. I heard he got right up Geordie Hawkins nose that first day when he turned up alone; I'd like to have seen it. Geordie can be a bit too big for his boots sometimes. Vladic told me it was very funny.'

'I'll bet it was. No, Riggs is mostly over there by himself unfortunately, I only get over to see what he's up to a couple of times a day but he's texting me all the time; Christ you should see his fingers flying over those phone keys.'

'Don't ... all my lot are quicker than me. So he's managing, that's good. Pity he started when we're so busy; a week or so back we'd have had more time on our hands.'

'How're your investigations going?'

'Slow but steady, though I sense we're on the verge of something ... I just don't know what. Back to Ramage though ... I understand this guy who dived off his balcony was the brother of the Ramage I handed over to you, the insurance fraudster. D'you think they were both at it; fiddling claims, I mean?'

'I don't know,' Lawrence said, as a grin began to spread across his face. 'You'd better ask Riggs!'

☼☼☼

Groves was waiting for him when he returned to his office 'Good lunch, Guv?' she asked, trying to hide the excitement which had been building up in her, in advance of what she was about to reveal. 'I've just put on a new jug, want some?'

'Sure, the grub in the canteen's good but the coffee's lousy. How're you and Best getting on with the stuff you found in the box?'

'He's doing it now, but it's slow work. He's listing every document, as you suggested, and adding his comments as he goes. When he's finished I'll jot down my own remarks and we'll bring it to you to see what you make of it.'

'Right so ...?

'So I've been having a go at Mrs Jellicoe's laptop.'

'Oh ... right ... and?'

'And I now know why she only had ten days!'

'Really, why?'

'She owed a heck of a lot of money ... six thousand pounds, and it was long overdue. I found letters in her email file.'

'From whom?'

'A company called 'Off The Course.''

'Bookies?'

'Sounds like it.'

'And you got all this from her laptop?'

'After a while I did. The problem was I didn't know her password. I tried all the usual combinations based on family stuff; names and birthdays of children, husband, parents and so on, which was hard enough because I only had Google to help me. And then I wondered if it was something much simpler, something with low protection. It was.

Apparently she was prepared to accept the risk of minimal security in order to have a password she could remember. It was pretty naïve of her; I got into her data quite easily once I started trying the names of places.'

'Places?'

'Towns where she'd once lived.'

Reynard's face lit up. 'Kildare!'

'Not quite ... the Irish version of it you saw on the postcard - Cill Dara - but in lower case and no spaces ... cilldara.'

'You're a genius, a bloody genius. So what did she bet on to lose so much money ... a horse?'

'A lot of horses, I reckon, but I don't know enough about betting, or racing, or horses for that matter, you'll need an expert to unravel and interpret the correspondence I found.'

Reynard was so pleased he couldn't keep his face straight. The breakthrough he'd been praying for had come quite suddenly ... but would it be enough, would it lead him to Rose's killer? 'This is terrific stuff, Lucy,' he said, 'I think Furness and Edwards are getting close to identifying the man we're after as well, and I can now see he might turn out to be a contract killer, acting on behalf of an unscrupulous bookmaker.'

'I was wondering about that too.'

'Anyway it's progress ... and now it's about time I found a few decent clues myself. If I don't, I'm going to be upstaged by my own team. Think of what that'll do to my reputation.'

'I don't think your reputation's in much danger Guv, you're a long way ahead of the pack. D'you happen to know if there's a "horsey" person in C.I.D.?'

'A "horsey" person? Yes, of course I do, so do you, there's one on our team. Didn't Furness say he often went to the races with his girlfriend when we were talking about Henry Finnerty? Oh my God, I wonder if Finnerty's involved? That's all we need, a high profile character like him as a suspect. Hell's bells. Anyway, enough of that; it's time we started getting some order into our investigation, time for us to pool our information and put together a story explaining why Rose Jellicoe died and then finding out who killed her. Summon the troops, Sergeant, have 'em all seated in here in an hour. OK.'

Groves didn't actually salute, though she did toy with the idea. 'They're all in the building, Guv, I can get 'em here in half an hour if you like ... twenty minutes.'

'Make it half an hour ... no ... tell 'em to be here at four o'clock like I told the others.'

As Groves rose from her seat, Riggs knocked at the door.

Reynard smiled for a change, and beckoned him in.

'Here you are Sir, fifty minutes.' said Riggs, holding out the magnifier.

'On the desk please.'

As Riggs stepped forward to place the glass down beside the photographs, he suddenly froze, his stiffened forefinger pointing at one of them.

Reynard's smile faded. 'What is it?'

'That photo, Sir. How did it get onto *your* desk?'

Reynard picked up the print depicting the party scene and scrutinised it more closely. 'This one? What's wrong with it?'

'Nothing; it's just that I've been looking at an identical one about two minutes ago … one I found in Mr Ramage's flat.'

'What!'

'I've got the same picture on my desk, Sir. Do you know who they all are?'

Reynard shook his head. 'The people? No, do you?'

'I only know their first names, and *they* were hard enough to decipher. Whoever wrote them on the back of the prints had terrible hand writing. That's why I needed the magnifying glass.'

Reynard suddenly saw the funny side of the conversation and his lips began to twitch. 'I'm glad I could help you, Constable!' he said, 'Go and get the photo.'

When Riggs returned a minute later with the picture in his hand, Groves and Reynard were still laughing.

Reynard took it, nodding slowly when he realised Riggs was right; it *was* identical to the one on his desk.

'We were just about to have a cup of coffee and a biscuit.' he said, 'How d'you like to join Sergeant Groves and I in a little celebratory snack?'

'Oh ... yes ... thank you, Sir.' Riggs couldn't believe it; he was about to drink coffee with the famous Foxy Reynard, and at his personal invitation; his mates'd think he was making it up.

'Good,' Reynard replied, I'm sure Sergeant Groves won't mind doing the honours while you scan and print off the back and front of the photograph for me.'

'I've already done it Sir, copied both sides when I was collecting it from my desk.' Riggs said, handing Reynard two sheets of paper.

'Let's see what we have then.' Reynard answered, checking the names on the back of the picture against the faces on the front of it. 'This is Lennie, and this is Joy next to him. And this is ... wait a minute I can't read your handwriting ... oh yes, it's Charlie; he's sitting on the floor with Ewart and Ambrose. And then there's Maggie and Julia, they're both on the sofa; she hasn't changed much! And then at the mantelpiece we have Alicia, Roddy, Peter, Rose, and ... I can't make this out ... 'er ... oh yes ... Morgan ... Crikey it's *Morgan Ramage* ... Rose Jellicoe and Morgan Ramage knew each other.'

'Hang on,' said Groves. 'Rose's picture was found at her house wasn't it? And Morgan's picture was found at his. And they both died within twenty four hours of each other so, assuming 'our' Rose is the one in Morgan's photo, and vice versa, and they clearly are, then the deaths must be connected too and we have another 'How' on our hands. This time it's 'How' are they connected?'

'Can I say something, Sir?' asked Riggs.

'Certainly ... what is it?'

'They might have known each other years ago but that doesn't mean they still knew each other. I'm in dozens, maybe hundreds, of photos taken at parties, or matches, or at school, alongside people I hardly knew then, and have never seen since.

This could be a similar situation, that's all.'

'He's got a point, hasn't he Sergeant?'

'Of course he has, and the fact they died with a day of each other could be just a coincidence too. All the same ...'

'Don't mention that word "coincidence" to me ... I don't believe in them but, if you like, we'll leave all options open for the moment ... another biscuit, Constable, you deserve one?'

'No thanks,' said Riggs, picking up his mug and drinking the last of his coffee, 'I'd better get back. If I see anything linking the people we're interested in I'll tell you.'

As soon as he'd gone Groves started to giggle. He thinks he's a big boy now,' she said, 'it's a wonder he didn't suggest you shared *your* information with *him*.'

'He *is* bright though, Lucy, you have to admit it.'

'Too bright perhaps?'

☼☼☼

Furness and Edwards were in the Traffic Division office, one floor above the C.I.D. level where they normally worked. They were using the better viewers Traffic had to go through the discs they'd brought back from premises on New Road, the thoroughfare onto which the back service gate and car park of the Pavilion Gardens opened; and they were getting excited. After hours watching the filmed traffic movement on the crossroads at either end of New Road the day before, they reckon they had one or two possible sightings of the suspect to explore more thoroughly now they had use of Traffic's higher resolution screens. They hadn't seen or spoken to anyone else in the team since the day before, and had no idea how *they* were faring.

'Bet we nail him first.' said Edwards, sitting back and

watching Furness taking his turn at the close work.

Furness said nothing; it was hard concentrating for hours on end, tiring for his eyes. They'd had their first stroke of luck the previous day, right at the start of their search, when they'd seen a short heavily built man come out of the gate into New Road and cross to the other side, right in the middle of the time bracket they'd been given. The picture had been taken by a camera at the cross roads where New Road and intersected with Church Street. The lens was aimed at the traffic at the junction, and only showed distant things indistinctly; nevertheless they felt fairly confident they'd seen the suspect exiting the scene of the crime.

He'd disappeared when he went between parked vehicles on New Road, opposite the gate, one of which was a furniture removal van. A few seconds later they'd seen a car, or some other small vehicle, pull away from the kerb not far from where they'd seen their man cross the road, and slot into the traffic between a bus and a high sided lorry. It wasn't possible at that stage to say whether the man was in the car any more than it was possible to say he'd gone into one of several commercial premises, a block of flats, or even the churchyard. The discs they'd subsequently secured from four shops, the entrance gates to the block of flats, and the car park beside the churchyard showed no sign of him, which encouraged them to conclude he had been in the vehicle which had pulled into the traffic behind the bus. These were the discs they were re-examining on the higher resolution screen, hoping to find more about the vehicle they suspected he was in.

'How many more have we got to do?' asked Edwards.

'None. These are the last; they're from all the crossroads he might have gone through once he left New Road.'

'And the vehicle, d'you still think it might be the Land Rover, the light coloured one we saw behind the bus as it went east on Church Street. Pity we don't have colour photographs?'

'Well there was only one vehicle between the bus and the lorry when all three turned into Church Street so, yes, I do.'

'What'll we tell Foxy?'

Furness removed the disc he'd been watching and switched off the monitor. 'We'll tell him we're fed up looking at these bloody screens. Come on I've had enough of this, we'll have a bite to eat and then go and find him; I think he's around.'

Creakwood Stud Farm,
Dial Post, Sussex.

Sam Midleton had left Creakwood at twelve and was knocking on Barney's front door in Peabody High Row, a grand name for a run-down street, an hour later. Mrs Truscott let him in; a small pale woman with unkempt hair, who, by the smell of steam drifting through from the kitchen, must have been doing the washing.

'Is he up?' Sam asked, well used to finding Barney was still in bed, even at that time in the afternoon.

Mrs Truscott, who had little to laugh about in her life, cackled. 'Barney ... up ... you're joking.'

It wasn't a surprise; Barney was a nocturnal man, a man whose day started after long after midday and ended long after midnight. He was a dealer in job lots he'd say, if people asked him; a trader in factory rejects and seconds. Indeed every bit of spare space in his house was packed with his stock, very little of which had clean provenance and for none of which was there an associated receipt. He was a smart man though; dapper and always well turned out in a well pressed suit. Though short and tubby, he walked like a Grenadier Guardsman; indeed he saw himself as one despite not reaching five foot five, a cocky little barrel-chested man with bags of presence. Henry had known him for years; he was one of many similar men living by their wits on the fringes of crime, and an automatic choice for those tricky little jobs from which Henry needed to keep his distance.

Barney often had to keep his distance from "the action" too, and to facilitate this he had his own ring of contacts, men to whom he'd sub-contract responsibilities given him by Henry.

The natural habitat of such men is the race track, the pool room, or the pub, and Barney was always to be found within striking distance of one of them; a popular man, frequently ridiculed behind his back by those who used him. In a way Henry was similar, but whereas he was a high class chancer who never got caught, Barney was small time crook who was often found out. Barney did a lot of jobs for Henry, the sort which, if not actually dirty, were at least questionable. They were a matching pair with Henry the puppeteer and Barney the puppet.

Sam, who wasn't a real confidant of either, tried as best he could to keep a foot in both camps. He'd side with Henry when he was with him, and with, Barney when in his company; he was no mug.

The particular purpose of the present visit, like all others, was unknown to him though, nor was it to the rest of the staff at Creakwood but, when they saw the way Henry rushed Barney into the house as soon as he got out of the Land Rover they at least knew something was "up", and they began to speculate.

'I don't see either of them getting richer whatever it is.' Sam said to Tommy, Slipstream's groom, as they stood chatting and watching Tracey lead Black Coffee back into her loose box.

'Nor more do I.' Tommy answered, 'but I bet it's some fantastic betting scheme again, one involving Barney taking all the risk and Henry taking all the money. That'll be the theory anyway, in reality it'll have no more chance of succeeding than I have of winning the lottery ... less probably.'

'Where's June?'

'Oh I meant to tell you, Henry gave her the afternoon off, and she's gone home to tart herself up.'

'Why ... is she entertaining him tonight?'

'She thinks she is! She said he'd told her she could have the afternoon off if she came in this evening to 'help with a new mare he's expecting.''

'What? That's rubbish; we've no mare coming in.'

'I know we don't ... but you know June.'

'Yeah ... and I know Henry!'

Sussex Police Headquarters,
Sussex House, Brighton.

Riggs had gone and the others, were seated in Reynard's office, with a mug of coffee in their hand. It was the first time in almost a week they'd all been present for the catch-up meeting and, to their surprise, just before they started, D.C.S. Bradshaw slipped in and took the last vacant seat.

Reynard nodded to him, obviously the "surprise" visit had been arranged, and then he tapped on his desk to get everyone's attention. 'The Chief's here to listen in at my request. OK? Right ... so we'll begin with a brief summary from everyone on what they've done and where they are ... Sergeant.'

Groves hastily popped the last bit of her biscuit into her mouth, put down her mug, and began. 'The Governor impressed on D.C. Best and me that we had to give the death of Annie Weaver the same diligence which was being applied to the death of the Prime Minister's wife. Well we've done that; and though we may be criticized at some time in the future for not solving the mystery of Mrs Jellicoe's death quickly enough, nobody will be able to accuse us of not putting in the effort.'

Reynard nodded, it was a point he was intending to make himself, and he could see from the expression on Bradshaw's face how pleased he was they'd taken his instruction seriously.

'Annie Weaver, an elderly, retired, housekeeper,' Groves continued, 'went to live with and care for, her older sister Geraldine, who'd had a stroke. And when Geraldine died, Annie stayed on in the house on her own.

Geraldine had become a hoarder as she'd aged, and Annie, having tried to change her, subsequently became one herself. When she was found dead in her garden, naked, we neither knew why she'd died or even precisely how she'd done so. We still don't, but we do have some indicators.'

'Did you find out what the hose had to do with her death?' asked Furness, who'd first seen something odd about it.

'I'm coming to that. After two fruitless days searching through the junk and finding nothing, we came across a box yesterday which we'd missed earlier. In it we discovered, not only a whole heap of Annie's private papers, but eight and half thousand pounds in used bank notes.'

Furness couldn't stop himself. 'There you go … that's what they were after, and they tortured her to get it.'

'Maybe.' Groves replied, 'At the moment we're just finishing going through the papers we found on top of the money, and hoping to learn more of Annie's background. We've already assumed robbery was the reason the thief was there, and that when he or she couldn't find it, some form of humiliation by stripping and squirting cold water on her was used to persuade her to say where it was. Obviously she didn't tell them; a brave and stubborn woman who died of heart failure due to shock, without giving up her secret.

We're now concentrating on the papers we found in the house, together with some new information we gathered from her neighbours. From these two potential sources of evidence we hope to identify a line of enquiry which will unmask the killer and lead us to him, or her.'

Edwards raised a finger. 'So what were the papers you found ... personal stuff or domestic bills?'

'Both: gas and electricity bills along with her bank statements, personal letters, photographs, death certificates, wills, old exam results and school reports.'

'Passport?'

'No passport.'

'Odd in this day and age.' said Furness.

'True, but Annie wasn't of "this day and age", she seemed to live in the past if her papers were anything to go by.'

Reynard swung round. 'D'you want to add anything, Constable Best?'

'No Sir,'

'Anyone else got a question?'

They all shook their heads.

'D'you have any, Sir?' he asked Chief Superintendent Bradshaw, who also shook his head.

'OK. So now it's the Jellicoe investigation, and I'll kick off by telling you we'd not got far either until yesterday when, all of a sudden, things started to break. Our slow start was mainly because we had to wait to find out if Rose Jellicoe's death was an accident or a murder; it was two days before we knew positively that someone had deliberately poisoned her.

Since then D.C.s Furness and Edwards and I have been trying to find out who did it.

We divided the work into two parts. I interviewed the high profile relatives and friends myself, knowing how sensitive our enquiries were bound to become. Principally I spoke several times to the Prime Minister, the Honourable James Jellicoe, the Lord Mayor of Brighton, Lance Henderson, his wife Julia, a lifelong friend of Rose Jellicoe, and Mrs Jellicoe's sister, Ursula Constantinidi. All provided valuable information, some of it sensitive, so I caution you to keep what I'm about to tell you to yourself. For example, Mrs Henderson told me Mrs Jellicoe recently had an argument with her sister Ursula that ended in blows; an unlikely reason for one of them to wind up dead you might think, but you never know.

I've also discovered Mrs Jellicoe owed a large sum of money, six thousand pounds, to be exact, to a bookmaking business called Off The Course, and she was being pressed to pay it. Finally, I came across a threatening note which may relate to this debt, but could just as easily refer to something else. Now,' he went on, 'before I go to the rest of my report I want to emphasise that I'm being serious when I say what I am about to tell you must never leave this room. Make sure it doesn't.'

There was quiet murmur of agreement and, when he heard it, he continued. 'OK, while I was in Barton Court, I also checked a lot of stuff in Mrs Jellicoe's private quarters ... correspondence, photographs and so on. We've plenty of material to work on, but there's more; the post mortem report we got from Professor Sir John Goodfellow, a very senior home office forensic pathologist, assisted by Dr Vladic, when added to witness statements we've collected, has led us to suspect that a man seen in a short white jacket and wearing a red bandana scarf round his head, gave Mrs Jellicoe a samosa containing hemlock poison. We know he left the gardens by the back gate, and Furness and Edwards have been following his trail. They can tell us what they've found.'

'You do it, Next,' said Edwards.

Best stuck up his thumb, then took up his notes. 'As the Governor has told you, Taffy and I have been tracing the movements of the suspect after he left The Royal Pavilion grounds. We have photos from the Traffic Division, files which hold the recordings of cameras covering all Brighton's crossroads. And we've collected CCTV recordings from premises on the route witnesses told us he took. So far, after hours of watching images on the high resolution screen in Traffic, we can say it's likely he left the gardens by the back gate, crossed the road, got into a light coloured Land Rover, and drove down New Road to the first junction where he turned East into Church Street, and headed for the A23.'

'Did you get its number?' asked C. S. Bradshaw.

'No sir, but as soon as this meeting's over we're going back up to Traffic to look at recordings taken at every subsequent major junction as far as the A23. With luck, we'll pick him up on one of them and get a clear enough picture to read his Reg. Number. We might know who the vehicle's owner is later today.'

'This is excellent,' said Bradshaw, as he stood up from his chair and walked to the door. 'I'm going now but keep me posted.'

'Anyone got anything else to say on either investigation?' Reynard asked, after the Super had gone.

No one opened their mouth and, within minutes, Furness and Edwards had gone back up to Traffic to recommence their study of CCTV recordings, Best had returned to what he and Groves had started calling Annie's "Box of Secrets", and Reynard, keen to interview the fourteen members of the public who claimed to have seen the man with the red bandana, made his way downstairs to the meeting room in which they'd been assembled.

Chief Superintendent Bradshaw, back in his office and feeling he had something to say which would be appreciated, rang the Head of C.I.D. Coordination, Commander Bill Simpson, and the Chief Constable of Sussex, Commissioner Colin Mustard, telling both of the progress Reynard's team had made

☼☼☼

By six o'clock, Reynard's team had made little further progress: Furness and Edwards, having viewed twenty two recordings covering the two hours either side of the time of Mrs Jellicoe's collapse still hadn't seen the Land Rover clearly enough to get its number. Best, working on the contents of Annie's box, hadn't found anything new. Groves, delving into a user name protected bookmaker's website was struggling to see how it worked. And Reynard, who'd had some very intense interviews with members of the public, had concluded that they had been good public relations exercises if nothing else.

But it had been a long day, and Reynard had had enough. 'We've had a good session,' he said to them in an email, 'but we're tired and not at our best. We'll continue tomorrow.'

Alan Grainger

DAY SEVEN

Wednesday 23rd September 2009

Sussex Police Headquarters,
Sussex House, Brighton.

Settle down, we've a lot to get through.' said Reynard. He'd been in since seven, preparing for the carry-over from the previous evening's meeting which was just about to start.

The whole team was present, and there was an air of expectancy that they were at last getting to grips with the essential facts in both cases.

It was a mood which didn't last long when Reynard got going. 'You may think we're making progress' he said, 'and, to a degree we are, but only at a snail's pace. We need to step up a gear and put flesh on the few facts we have. In the Jellicoe enquiry, for example, all we have is a description of a man, which would fit half the male population of this country ... tall, thin, and dark haired ... we need more than this.

Yesterday afternoon I spoke to the fourteen people who said they'd seen him in the grounds of The Royal Pavilion but, while they confirmed what we already know, they didn't produce anything new. The only lead we have, apart from the meagre description I've just given you, is his *possibly* being in a light coloured Land Rover, which *might* have left Brighton on the A23 going *God knows where*. If you call that progress, I don't.

We have to find out for sure if he was in that vehicle.

We have to get its registration number and see if the owner, or the passenger, if there was one, fits the description of the man we're after.

We also need the owner to account for his vehicle being in Brighton and close to the scene of the crime at the time of Mrs Jellicoe's murder. Getting answers to these questions,' he said, turning to Furness and Edwards, 'is your job today.

Yours, Sergeant, is to contact Off The Course and with them go through every item of business they did with Mrs Jellicoe: every bet, every result, every pay out. And when you have that, see if you can find anything which might have triggered the threatening note. Before though, get the lab to check the paper it's written on for fingerprints? Oh yes,' he said, grinning, 'and, whenever you get a chance, go back and squeeze those laptop files again, you never know what'll come out.

I'll remain on Mrs Jellicoe's murder as well. I telephoned the P.M. last night and he's agreed to see me again this morning. While I'm there, I'll have another chat with Mrs Constantinidi.

The funeral, he told me, is to take place on Friday; it's going to be very private: family and close friends only. Until then, he and his sons are staying at Barton Court but afterwards they're going back to Number 10. The purpose of my visit today will be to ask about the six thousand pound debt. When I get back I'll be working on the papers I found in Mrs Jellicoe's sitting room; there're still a few of them, and the address books, I've yet to look at. Oh, yes, and there's something I should have told you last night, but it slipped my mind. Thanks to the sharp eye of Acting D. C. Riggs, the young copper from D.I. Lawrence's squad who was with us yesterday, we now know the man who fell from his balcony in Christchurch was not only the brother of the Mr Ramage we were investigating, but an acquaintance of Mrs Jellicoe's. I'll be looking into this too when I get a chance.

As to the other investigation, we can't afford to let up there either, despite the fact I've had to steal Sergeant Groves to look at Mrs Jellicoe's laptop. You'll have to continue on your own for the moment Constable,' he said, looking at Best.

'I think we're all agreed the money, her sister's lifetime savings probably, was the reason Annie Weaver lost her life though we don't know for sure whether she was murdered or died of shock. From our perspective it doesn't matter, we have to find out who attacked her one way or other. The red box holds the answers, and I'm sure finding them will lead us in the right direction.

OK? We have to step up our effort. We still haven't a single suspect in sight. Now go and find me one. Any questions?'

Barton Court,

the P.M's private residence near Horsham, Sussex.

Reynard was met at the door by one of the P.M.'s sons, who seemed to be expecting him. 'Dad's in his office,' he said, 'would you like to come in.'

Reynard smiled he'd never quite imagined the office of Prime Minister being held by a man called 'Dad'. 'Thanks, I'm Detective Superintendent Reynard of the … '

'I know who you are Sir, you're Foxy Reynard aren't you, Dad told me to look out for you and take you straight in to him?'

'Right.' said Reynard, surprised by the boy's confidence. 'No school then?'

'Back on Monday.' the boy answered, opening the door and standing back to let Reynard pass.

'Ah, Superintendent Reynard, I'm glad you're here early,' said the P.M. 'I've a busy morning in front of me so I hope you're not bringing me a problem; I don't want to have to put off the funeral.'

'It's not a problem, Sir, I'm looking for information, that's all. But, as the questions I need to ask you and Mrs

Constantinidi are likely to be, well, sensitive, I thought I'd ask them personally.'

'Very considerate of you but I can't imagine what you're talking about. Rose wouldn't have been involved in anything controversial. How's it going anyway? Got anyone in the frame yet?'

'There's no controversy, Sir, it's more personal ... and delicate. And, 'er, yes ... well we're progressing ... but slowly. You know we're after a man who was wearing a white coat and had a ... '

'Red bandana, yes. Have you found him?'

'Not so far, but we're closing in on him. We know he left the garden by the back gate and that he crossed the road got into a Land Rover which we're now tracking by scrutinising every CCTV shot we can lay our hands on. We'll get him; it'll just take a bit more time.'

'Fine. So what are the sensitive questions you need to ask, really Superintendent, you make it seem as though the answers you're expecting will be 'erm ... unpalatable. What on earth have people been telling you?'

Reynard paused; how was he to ask a question he needed to ask without giving offence? In the end he came out with it straight: 'Can you tell me anything about the money Mrs Jellicoe owed?'

'To whom?'

'A company called Off The Course.'

The P.M. shook his head. 'Never heard of them, are you sure your information is correct ... Off The Course ... they sound like bookmakers and that wasn't Rose's scene. Her sister Ursula's yes, she's into horses, but not Rose, not since she was teenager anyway. Her folks had a small farm in Ireland, I believe

I told you, and they had a few horses she rode. Where did you get the information, and how much is she supposed to owe?'

Reynard told him it was six thousand pounds, and that Sergeant Groves had come across it when she'd broken into Mrs Jellicoe's email account. 'I'll be talking to the company later to get the full details, but I thought it'd be better if I spoke to you first.'

The P.M. looked shattered. Normally a very composed man, he was clearly shaken by what Reynard had told him. 'I appreciate you doing that, Superintendent, but this is something I'd rather sort out myself … if it's true. And if it's not …'

'There's more I'm afraid.'

'More? What more debts? This can't be right; there's a mistake somewhere. Rose'd never land herself in a mess like this. How much more?'

As the P.M. was speaking, Reynard withdrew the RNLI envelope from his pocket, took from it the sheet of paper on which the threat was written, and handed it to him.

'Where d'you get this from?'

'Mrs Jellicoe's desk. I nearly missed it … as you can see it was in a Lifeboat appeal envelope.'

The healthy complexion, which gave the P.M. his youthful look, paled as the implications of the evidence put before him sank in. Reynard could see he was genuinely mystified by what he was hearing. All the same, answers had to be got, explanations of the debt obtained, and some idea as to whether or not it was connected to the threatening note, and Mrs Jellicoe's death, worked out.

'Let's get this right,' the P.M. said, 'you have evidence showing Rose owed a bookie six thousand pounds; and you have what looks like a threatening note which may be associated with it. Are you sure this is correct?'

'I am, Sir.'

'And you don't want me to contact this Off The Course crowd to seek proof the debt was owed by her, or any details of it ... ah Superintendent I can't believe I'm saying this, this wasn't my wife, this wasn't Rose.'

'Prime Minister, I'd feel the same as you if *I'd* been confronted with something like this regarding *my* wife. I promise you I'll be careful, but I must ask my questions elsewhere if you don't have the answers I need. I have to have *all* the facts, however unlikely, if I'm to catch the man who murdered Mrs Jellicoe.'

The P.M. nodded. 'Any other bombshells?'

'I hope not ... Oh yes, do you know Morgan Ramage?'

'I don't, who's he?'

'It's a name that cropped up. Any chance your wife did?'

'I have no idea. Is he saying she owed him money too?'

'No, no, no, nothing like that.'

'Is there anything else then?' asked the P.M., in a tone which was noticeably cooler.

Reynard shook his head. 'Not for the moment, Sir, but I would like to talk to Mrs Constantinidi.'

'About the debt? She'll blab it all over the place.'

'Hmm. They had a little falling out which got unpleasant recently didn't they, your wife and Mrs Constantinidi, maybe the debts where what it was all about.'

'Superintendent, you know women, you're a married man. One minute they're in each other's arms, the next they're round each other's throats. It was nothing. Who told you ... oh yes, Julia Henderson; she and Ursula don't get on ... I mean *really* don't get on. Which reminds me, I have to get on too so I must let you go. If you come with me, Ursula'll be in the kitchen reading the paper. Take what she tells you with a pinch of salt; she's a woman with a vivid imagination and no sense. She's been married three times, for God's sake, and she's ... well that's another story.'

As he was speaking the P.M got up from his desk and led Reynard through the hall and into the kitchen.

Ursula was already there: sitting at the kitchen table, smoking a cigarette, drinking coffee, and reading a newspaper, while a woman behind her in a housekeeper's smock was at the sink peeling potatoes.

As the two men shook hands, the P.M. whispered, 'Remember what I told you, she's unreliable.'

Sussex Police Headquarters,

Sussex House, Brighton.

For almost an hour after Reynard left, Groves sat with her eyes glued to the screen of Rose Jellicoe's laptop, and her fingers flying over its keyboard. Occasionally she stopped to write notes on a pad she had by her side, or to print off email letters and sheets of paper with columns of numbers on them, entitled "OTC" (the initials of Off The Course).

When she'd extracted all the information of substance and left behind the requests calling for customers' opinions, and adverts for special offer ante-post odds, she went and found D.C. Furness, and asked him what he made of what she'd assembled.

It didn't take him long to give an opinion. 'Looks like Mrs Jellicoe started betting with Off The Course a while back. The records you've given me seem to go back to 2006 and she was betting regularly with them then. I happen to know the company; they're OK, and not the sort to threaten anyone. One of my mates uses them all the time as they quote better prices, something they can do because, with no shops they've lower expenses, and they use the extra profit to lengthen the odds and attract new punters.

Mrs Jellicoe's bets were usually a pound each way

during the first few years she was with them, and she generally lost. And then, about a year ago, she began to increase the size of her bets. By last Christmas she was betting in fivers and backing five or six horses a day. Sometimes she'd try a double, a treble, or a Yankee.'

'You've lost me.' said Groves, 'What's a Yankee?'

He told her, and gave her some examples, pointing out that big wins could come from combination bets, as could big losses. Gradually, with Furness's help, Groves began to see a pattern developing, and it was one of disaster; Mrs Jellicoe didn't lose every day but overall her losses were becoming greater and greater. By early summer she was losing as much as a hundred pounds some days, and showing no restraint. Her account with Off The Course was always cleared by direct debit payments and, Furness assumed, having never failed to pay what she owed, she'd been allowed to place bets without being questioned. He wondered if the company knew who she was.

Then, one day in July, having cumulatively lost over five thousand pounds since the beginning of the year, she made a massive 'on the nose' bet of a thousand pounds on a horse called Grey Prospect. Had it won she'd have cleared over twelve thousand pounds and been able to settle her out-standings, but it was beaten and her debt rose to over six thousand.'

'And they came looking for their money.'

'No, they emailed her when the direct debit payment didn't come through, asking her to contact her bank. Did you see any hard copy letters they wrote to her, or she wrote to them?'

'I didn't notice any … what bank was it?'

'That's the funny thing. Her payments seem to have been made by an outfit called 'Money Box Banking'. Is there a file for a company of that name?'

'The Governor has all her files; I'll go and have a look.'

A few minute later she was back. 'Is this what you want?' she said, 'I had a quick glance and it looks as though she had insufficient funds to cover the big direct debit payment.'

Furness took the file, it was quite thin, and he read it through from back to front in a couple of minutes. 'I can see what she did,' he said, 'she opened an account with Money Box Banking to keep her betting transactions separate from her household ones and, I presume, a secret from her husband. She started using it about three years ago with a lodgement of three thousand pounds which, depending on her success and failures, was gradually whittled down until, at the time she made the big bet on Grey Prospect, her credit balance had dropped to one thousand eight hundred and forty nine pounds, and clearly not enough to finance the direct debit charge raised by OTC.'

'And the threatening letter? Did Money Box send it?'

'I'm sure they didn't, but then we don't know anything about them, in fact I've never heard of them. It'll turn out to be one of those pseudo banks I expect; a small relatively local affair ... where is it?'

'Maidstone.'

'Maidstone, yeah. It'll be a cross between a bill paying service and credit union with minute resources and internet only.'

'In other words just the sort of company which might send a threating letter to defaulter in order to get quick action.'

'They'd more likely send in a debt collector; and those guys don't mess about.'

'It fits. You're dead right,' said Groves. 'You've nailed it. Brilliant. Wait 'til the Governor gets back.'

Furness gave a wry smile. 'I could be wrong mind you!'

Barton Court,

the P.M's private residence near Horsham, Sussex.

'Let's go through into the sitting room,' said Ursula, Mrs Johnson will make us some fresh coffee, I'm sure; this pot's cold.'

'Thank you.' said Reynard, following her into a sun drenched room and taking a seat on one of two sofas which faced each other across a long low table.

'What's this all about?' asked Ursula, 'are you here to ask me questions or to tell me you've found the man who did that dreadful thing to Rose?'

'Not the latter I'm afraid, not yet. But we *are* getting closer. No, I'm here to clear up a few inconsistencies and get your assistance, and the Prime Minister's, with one or two things I don't understand.'

'Good, we can't let this man escape. How can I help?'

'Before I start, Mrs Constantinidi, I want to tell you; no to re-assure you, that I fully realise some of the things I'm going to talk about may be difficult ... sensitive ... embarrassing even.'

'What *are* you talking about, Superintendent?'

'I'm talking about your sister's gambling habit for one.'

'Rose? She didn't have a gambling habit. She'd back the odd horse at Ascot it's true, so does everyone else; but I never heard her talk of casinos. In fact I can't even imagine her in one. No, you've got this one wrong Superintendent.'

'I see. And you ... do you ever back horses?'

'Fools back horses ... and I'm not one of them.'

'So you don't have anything to do with horses?'

'Of course I don't. I had enough of horses when I was a child. I know a few people who have a couple, and some of them are very successful.'

'Like Mr Henry Finnerty?'

'I wondered how long it would take to get round to him. It's Julia Henderson again, isn't it. She lied about a little tiff Rose and I had, and now this ... she'll bad mouth anyone just for fun.'

Reynard smiled. 'So you don't know about your sister backing a horse called Grey Prospect and, before you deny it again, Mrs Constantinidi, I should tell that you we have ample proof Mrs Jellicoe was a secretive and compulsive gambler who consistently lost money and died leaving a huge debt to a bookmaking company called Off The Course.'

Ursula looked at him open mouthed, but just for a moment, and then she calmly said 'You've been busy.'

'Of course ... what d'you know about a man called Morgan Ramage. He died in an accident last weekend?'

'I don't know anything. I've never heard of him.'

'Really, because your sister knew him?'

'Did she?' said Ursula, in a tone of voice that made it clear she'd had enough of his questioning. This suited Reynard very well; he crossed his arms, sat back, and looked her in the eye until she turned away.

It was an old trick he'd used before when trying to force reluctant witnesses to disclose what they were holding back. When he continued to say nothing, she first brushed an imaginary speck of dust from her trousers, and then began to fiddle with a button on the cuff of her silk shirt. Finally, seeming to concede to the pressure, she drew in a deep breath and let it out in a long sigh of submission. 'Alright,' she said, 'he lived in the flat above her years ago in London. I'd forgotten all about him until you mentioned his name.'

'And the six thousand pounds?'

'Had nothing to do with him.'

'You know Mr Finnerty pretty well, don't you? Go about a lot with him, despite being married to Mr Constantinidi?'

Ursula exploded. 'Bloody Julia!'

'So you *do* see Mr Finnerty regularly. What's he like?'

'I don't know what you mean by 'regularly', Superintendent,' she answered, 'or what you're implying. You're obviously aware I've known him since childhood, but what has this got to do with Rose's death? I hope you're not suspecting I had something to do with it. Or Henry. Oh you do ... don't you ... just because he has something to do with horses, and Rose used to have the odd flutter.'

'It was more than a flutter I believe, and tell me ... does Mr Finnerty have an interest in a horse called Grey Prospect? If he does it'll explain why ...'

'Why, what? You've gone too far. I'm answering no more questions. You twist every damned thing I say.'

Reynard raised his eyebrows and hunched his shoulders in an expression of innocence. 'I have to press the people I speak to sometimes, to get to the truth, Mrs Constantinidi; and I certainly don't think I have it yet in this case. There's something you're holding back, and it could be serious for you if I find you've withheld anything important.'

Ursula began to clench and unclench her fists as if she was preparing to attack him, but then, unexpectedly, he saw a tear trickle down her cheek, and he leaned forward, all attention, his arms across his knees and his hands clasped. 'She started betting,' Ursula said, staring at the carpet. 'because she got bored out of her mind at home on her own; the boys were away at school and James had joined the cabinet and was beginning to rise in seniority ... she was lonely. The gambling, which was financed by savings she'd made when she was working, started in a small way, just on the odd afternoon during the week but it went on for years. I told her she was mad; mad to do it, and especially mad to do it in secrecy. She wouldn't listen ... and she got deeper and deeper involved until she was gambling every day. I don't think James ever found out and I hope he never does. She was ashamed, but she couldn't stop. That's what the argument was about the day I slapped her; it wasn't about Henry at all. Now,' she said, wearily, 'I hope you're satisfied.'

Reynard got up from the sofa, laid his hand on her shoulder for a fleeting moment, then headed for the door. 'I'm only trying to find out who killed your sister, Mrs Constantinidi, I don't care whether she gambled or not.'

'You won't tell ...'

'Mr Jellicoe? ... only if I have to. I'll see myself out.'

As soon as he'd gone Ursula broke down, crying until there were no more tears to come. James found her an hour later. She was lying on the sofa staring at the ceiling and, before the day was out, despite promising herself he'd never know about Rose's secret weakness, she'd told him everything.

Sussex Police Headquarters,
Sussex House, Brighton.

Furness and Edwards were up in Traffic and they were whacked; their eyes were watering and their brains were befuddled. They'd checked dozens of crossroads recordings and not seen the Land Rover once. In the end they decided to break for a while and get a couple of cold drinks from the machine in the hall. On the way they bumped into Riggs, who was on a similar mission. 'Ah, the star of show!' said Furness, '*You're* making a name for yourself aren't you. Next stop Scotland Yard.'

'I got lucky.' Riggs replied.

'Yeah ... well ... just as long as you don't make the rest of us look idiots.'

Riggs smiled weakly and said nothing, not sure whether he was being baited or not.

'Take no notice of him.' said Edwards, 'he's jealous. What're you going to come up with today?'

Riggs gave him a rueful smile, 'I *have* got something as it happens ... but I don't know whether ...'

'Don't be stupid. What is it?

'More photos, but maybe ...'

'If you've found something, show D.S. Reynard. You can ignore my esteemed colleague here, he doesn't appear to know the difference between a Coca Cola and Sprite ... look at him.'

'I'm checking the sugar content, you should do it as well by the look of all that flab.' said Furness, as they walked back to check the last of the CCTV footage.

Riggs watched them go. Perhaps he'd better back down, leave the photos until he saw Reynard was on his own, no point in upsetting men he was hoping to work with by thoughtlessly upstaging them. Not that he needed to have worried, Furness and Edwards were about to shoot to the top of the charts themselves because, the minute they'd pressed the play button, they saw the Land Rover. It was caught by CCTV, stopped at traffic lights at the junction where the A272 crosses the A24 and its number plate could easily be read.

Within minutes they found it was registered in the name of Creakwood Stud Farm, Dial Post, Sussex.

'Bloody Hell.' said Furness, 'The Governor's going to love this ... if I'm not mistaken it's Finnerty's place.'

'Let's text him,' said Edwards, looking at his watch, 'he'll be on his way back by now.'

'Not yet. First we have to make a few copies of the frame showing the vehicle's number plate. Now we've found it, we daren't risk losing it.'

'Fair enough; so we'll say nothing to anybody until he's back. He's sure to call us together to tell us how he got on; that's when we'll do it ... we'll bung the C.D. on my laptop and surprise the lot of them. Brilliant.'

'Yeah.'

En route from Barton Court to Brighton.

D.C. Edwards was right, Reynard was on his way back but, what with one thing and another, he'd somehow missed his morning cup of coffee and his biscuit and had decided to stop at a seaside hotel and have an early snack lunch to compensate. He chose The Arden Hotel at Rottingdean, because of its long sea facing conservatory, found a comfortable chair, ordered a chicken sandwich and a pot of coffee, and settled to think about the progress, he'd made that morning, and he smiled; things had radically improved since he'd left the office, and there was little doubt the finger was beginning to point towards a person connected with horse racing.

The meeting with the P.M. had gone well, the disclosure of things about his wife particularly so. It must have been a shock if he really didn't know about her antics with Off The Course. But perhaps he did know and, in some misguided sense of loyalty, didn't like to admit it when he hadn't mentioned it when interviewed.

Then there was Ursula.

The problem with her was deciding which one was the real one, the arrogant and recalcitrant society woman, or the crushed repentant and tearful girl he'd caught telling lies?' He wasn't sure - the jury was still out.

The sandwich had been good: plenty of tender breast meat dabbed with mayonnaise tucked into slices of fresh baked bread. But the coffee was lousy and so tepid he didn't bother pouring a second cup.

When he'd first gone in he was the only one there, but it filled up quickly and, as luck would have it, a woman with a screaming baby took a seat at the next table.

He called for his bill and left.

Sussex Police Headquarters,
Sussex House, Brighton.

Down one floor in C.I.D., Sergeant Groves, having been through every file on laptop without finding anything of significance had joined D.C. Best working on the items from the red box.

'Where have you got?' she asked.

'Blimey,' Best answered, 'I hardly know.' and then went on to explain how, once the money had been put away in the safe as D.S. Reynard had asked, he'd gone on to divide the other items into two piles: Geraldine's and Annie's. He'd then subdivided each pile into official documents, personal correspondence, photographs, and general memorabilia. Geraldine's things were relatively few, and mostly papers, so they'd taken up little room and had been quick to check over. Annie's, because of the dozens of papers and photographs, not to mention the desk diary and address book had filled most of the space above the money and had taken a long time to sift through. By the time Sergeant Groves joined him, Best was about to start going over everything again, taking notes as he went.

'If we do it together, Lucy,' Best said, 'and we start with Geraldine's stuff; we should be through it before lunch.'

The morning passed quickly and, at the end of it, apart from a profile of Geraldine's life they'd built from what they'd found, they had only a few photographs, some pocket diaries and a handful of Christmas cards to show for their morning's work. The profile was interesting and it was written on a sheet of A4 in Groves's neat hand.

Geraldine Elizabeth Weaver

Born: Ardeskin, Co. Donegal, 1922. Died Eastbourne 2006.

Parents: Dennis Weaver, stone mason; Alice Weaver, cook.

School: Ardeskin National School, St Jude's Convent School.

Jobs: Shop Assistant Donegal Town, 1939; Shop Assistant Manchester Department Store, 1943; moved to accounts department 1946; Civil Service Entrance Exam (bookkeeping) passed with honours 1951; Post Office Eastbourne 1952; retired 1985; died 2006.

No evidence of social or community activities.

No evidence of marriage

Corresponded occasionally with younger sister, Annie. (Christmas and Birthday cards, Holiday Postcards).

Visited Donegal nearly every year to see Annie and other relatives, always stayed in same Guest House on coast road at Kinvara.

Left estate valued for probate at £285.000. All went to Annie.

'What d'you think? asked Groves.

'Yeah ... looks right to me. Now let's do the naked lady.'

'Ah, Next, that's not nice.' said Groves, glaring.

Seaforth House
Adelaide Terrace, Brighton.

Reynard found himself in the vicinity of the Henderson's house as he drove into Brighton and, on the spur of the moment, decided to see if Julia was at home.

Luckily she was, having just got in from a fund raising coffee morning with a basket full of home grown fruit, a pack of homemade muffins, and four loaves of freshly baked bread.

She invited him in and took him straight through to the kitchen. 'I hope you don't mind my bringing you in here, Superintendent, but I've bought far too much as usual, and I need to get most of these things into my freezer.'

'You sound like my wife, Mrs Henderson; she spends half her life at charity functions buying more than we could ever eat.'

'There you are then … but you didn't come here to talk about that I'm sure. Did you find out who killed poor Rose yet? '

'I regret to say we didn't, though I'm fairly sure we're getting nearer. It's in connection with my enquiries into Mrs Jellicoe's death that I'm here; I'd like your help in sorting out a few inconsistencies I seem to have got myself entangled in.'

Julia gave a little 'Huh.' and immediately regretted it when she saw the look of surprise on Reynard's face. 'Sorry, I didn't mean to give you the impression I'm taking Rose's tragic death lightly, I was thinking of you trying to work your way through all the contradictory things people must have told you. Not in malice d'you understand, but because they each saw events in a different way and envisage people in different contexts.'

'How true that is Mrs Henderson, and it happens all the time. Take this morning ... I was at Barton Court and ...'

'Oh dear, how's James, the poor lamb, and the boys?'

'Fine, as was Mrs Constantinidi.'

'Oh, yes, well...'

'As a matter of fact it was something she said that brought me here.' said Reynard, seizing the opportunity to get straight to the heart of the matter.

Julia shrunk wrapped the last of the muffins and began to wash the raspberries. 'What's *she* been saying?

'We were talking about Mrs Jellicoe's love of horses.'

'Rose? She hated horses; goes back to when she was a girl. Her father kept a few, they lived on a farm in Ireland, you know, and he used to put her up when he was breaking young ones because *he* was too heavy, and *Ursula* was too young.'

'She must have changed, because I found many connections to horses when we went through her things.'

'Really.' said Mrs Henderson, off-handedly, as though she wasn't interested. 'What sort of connections?'

'You tell me Mrs Henderson, if you knew her as well as you claim you did, then you must know about her considerable interest in horses. Mrs Constantinidi ...'

'It was only to amuse herself; she was lonely. James was so busy and the boys were at boarding school. She had to do something to pass the time. What's the harm in a little flutter now and again?'

'None, Mrs Henderson, until the little flutter becomes a habit that's out of control. You knew Mrs Jellicoe was getting deeper and deeper into trouble and you did nothing about it.'

'Are you interrogating me; I'm not going to answer any more of your questions? I thought you were working to find Rose's killer but you're trying to destroy her reputation instead. I'll have no more part of it. I knew Rose from when I was a fresher at university and will *not* have my loyalty questioned.'

'I'm not questioning your loyalty Mrs Henderson, you have misunderstood me. I want to harness it to get at the truth because I'm not getting it elsewhere.'

'From Ursula? Well what do you expect? You can believe every word James says, but not one of Ursula's.'

Reynard sensed Julia was calming down a bit. Perhaps because she was seeing she'd been wrong in keeping Rose's weakness secret, and he decided to exploit the changed atmosphere and ask more questions. 'It would be of great help to me,' he said, 'if you were to give me, in as few words as possible, a picture of your early friendship with Mrs Jellicoe: how it developed and matured as you went through your lives, the people you knew, the things you did, that sort of thing.'

'I'll put the kettle on,' said Julia, 'or would you rather a whisky, I've Scotch *and* Irish?'

'Tea will be fine.'

Julia nodded and, as she made and poured the tea, she told him all about her friendship with Rose.

'I wanted to study Philosophy and Ancient Civilizations

but I left it too late to get a place in Cambridge and took one on offer in Trinity College, Dublin, instead. Ireland was my second home you see; my mother came from Dublin and I had grandparents, uncles, aunts and cousins all living there. Despite pressures from within the family I didn't move in with any of them but took a room in the women's hall of residence, Trinity Hall. The day I moved in I met Rose. She was about to start a course on Politics and English. We soon discovered a mutual interest in playing hockey and quickly became friends. I spent three happy years at Trinity, much of it due to my friendship with her. And I spent so many weekends with the Rose's family, the Wyse's, I practically had my own room in their house, and was soon part of the weekend crowd she partied with … and I mean party, the Irish certainly know how to enjoy themselves, Superintendent!'

Ursula was about fifteen at the time and she resented me from the start; she was a schoolgirl while we were, or thought we were, twenty year old sophisticates. I think she saw me as an interloper who'd usurped her position as her sister's natural companion, but she was wrong, a twenty year old hasn't time for teenagers and Rose was no different. It had nothing to do with me.

When I was staying at the Wyse's, Rose and I would meet up with her friends and go dancing, or out to a pub to hear the music. Amongst the group who hung out together at that time was Henry Finnerty; his family had the next farm to the Wyse's. There was a sort of an on/off relationship between Henry and Rose which made Ursula even more upset for she had her eyes on him too and was making a fool of herself the way she threw herself at him. The odd thing, Mr Reynard, is that an outsider would have been unaware of the tensions between the sisters, even though it was evident to me.

During my last year at Trinity, Henry's father got into some sort of financial difficulty and he sold up, moved to

England, and set up again near Dial Post just south of Horsham, twenty five or thirty miles from here.'

'I know it. I've been to Mr Finnerty's place too.'

'Really? Yes, well ... I didn't see Henry for a long time after he moved to this country, but Rose kept touch with him.

I didn't see much of Rose either, because she went on to London University to study for her Master's while I went off to the other end of the world, back packing. I was away from England for three years and, when I got back, I found she'd got her extra qualification and was working in London. We teamed up and rented a flat over the basement bedsit in which she'd been living on her own. The house is in Clapham, and Henry used to appear from time to time, especially if there was a party in the offing.

Rose's parents had died while I was Australia, at which time Ursula was doing an Interior Design Course in Dublin. She abandoned it on their death, moved to London, where she joined Rose and I in Clapham, and started blasting her way through her inheritance in the hope of becoming a celebrity. And that's how it went on until we all got married.'

'All? Was Henry married as well?'

'No, I meant us three girls: I married Lance, Rose married James, and Ursula married a man called Evans, who turned out to be the first of her three husbands. She's had another couple since; she goes through them rather quickly.'

'Did your relationship with Ursula improve once you were only seeing her infrequently?'

'My tea's cold.' said Julia, 'I'll make another pot.'

'Not for me. What you've just told me has filled in a lot of gaps, but I still have a few questions.'

'Ask them Superintendent, before I regret what I've said.'

'Would you say Mrs Jellicoe's on/off relationship with Henry Finnerty amounted to an affair?'

'Sex, you mean? ... I don't know but I wouldn't be surprised. Not after she met James though, definitely not after that, she was too much in love with him.'

'And was Ursula having some sort of sexual relationship with Finnerty?'

'I've always assumed so, in between marriages ... and maybe during them; I wouldn't put anything past Ursula; she has no scruples.'

'And Mr Finnerty?'

'Henry ... huh ... he has less.'

'And what about Morgan Ramage?'

Julia's eyebrows shot up. 'Morgan Ramage, the art man in Christchurch who fell from his balcony last week? I saw it in the paper, what about him?'

'You didn't know him?'

'I don't think so, though the name's familiar.'

'Hmm ... d'you know what? I think I will have that tea, Mrs Henderson; I've a few more questions yet.'

As Julia poured, Reynard glanced at his watch; it was nearly two o'clock and, from the text message he received just before he rang the Henderson's bell, Furness and Edwards must have had a break through. Maybe they'd found the Land Rover on one of the other CCTV recordings and were bursting to tell him. Problem was, he wanted to continue his questioning of Julia ... what was he to do? In the end he decided to keep going, but as quickly as he could, and then go back to the office. He took a sip of tea and settled down to his prodding again. 'So, as far as you can remember, Mrs Henderson, you never met Morgan Ramage at any time in the past?'

'Since Lance went into local politics, Superintendent, I've met thousands of people, and I remember hardly any of them.'

'In that case it won't be a surprise to you when I tell you I have a photograph with both of you in it?'

'Not in the least, I'm often photographed in the midst of a crowd. There's one in this week's edition of the Argus of me and Rose at the food exhibition last week.'

'The photograph I'm talking about looks as though it was taken a good few years ago, possibly when you were sharing the flat with Mrs Jellicoe which you mentioned. Was the house called Villa Bellamonte?'

'My Goodness, Superintendent, you have been busy.'

'The picture I'm talking about was taken at a drinks party. There were about a dozen young men and women there, including you, Mrs Jellicoe, and Morgan Ramage. Now do you remember?'

'Not really, I can't remember any parties, though we must have had some. But then we were in and out of each other's flats all the time when we lived in Villa Bellamonte. There were three art students living in the flat above ours, for instance, and we'd often congregate in one or other of the two flats at weekends. And yes, we drank wine, a lot of it; it was the happiest time of my life.'

'And was there ever more to it than drinking wine?'

'Inspector! What *do* you mean?'

Reynard smiled. 'So you've no *particular* recollection of meeting the Morgan Ramage who owned the art gallery in Chichester though you and Mrs Jellicoe may have met him at a party in your flat years ago. Right?'

'Right. And now I'm afraid I must ask you to leave. I'm opening a new shopping mall this afternoon and the ceremony starts in an hour.' Reynard stood up from the table.

'Of course. I should be in my office anyway. Thanks for the information and if you remember anything else, ring me.'

Sussex Police Headquarters,
Sussex House, Brighton.

Furness and Edwards had gone off the boil by the time Reynard pulled into the car park, but their excitement was rekindled the minute he came through the door and walked over to them. 'Got caught up.' he said. 'So what's happened?'

'We found the Land Rover.' said Furness, gleefully, who then went on to tell how they'd spotted it on the CCTV, halted by traffic lights at the busy road junction, and how they been able to read the registration number and trace the ownership.'

'So come on, who is it? Who owns the vehicle?'

Furness looked at Edwards. Edwards winked. And the both said ... 'Henry Finnerty'

Reynard didn't react for a moment, and then he began to smile; 'I knew it!' he said, 'That bloody man has his marks all over this case. But I'll bet all the tea in China he'll wriggle out of it somehow. Got his address?'

'Yes, Creakwood Stud Farm, Guv, it's near Dial Post.'

'Grab your coats.'

Creakwood Stud Farm,

Dial Post, Sussex.

The Land Rover was right in front of them when they drove into the yard, and drew up behind it. Sam Midleton heard the doors of their car closing and came out of his office pulling on his jacket. 'Can I help you?'

'We're looking for Mr Finnerty, is he around?' said Furness, getting out of the car and flashing his warrant card.

Midleton nodded. 'Oh ... Police. What's he been up to?'

Reynard and Edwards had by then got out of the vehicle too, their identification in their hands ready to show him. 'Is he in?' asked Edwards.

'He was ... half an hour ago, but I don't see his car now.' Midleton replied, as two young women, clearly stable employees, appeared at the yard gate, each leading a horse. 'Seen Henry?' he yelled, but they shook their heads.

'He's gone to the village.'

They all turned round to see where the voice had come from. A man, with his head sticking over the half door of another loose box, was waving at them to draw their attention. 'He went to get stamps, he'll be back shortly.'

'Fine, we'll wait.' said Reynard, turning round and getting back into the car, having given a quick jerk of his head which Furness took as an instruction to ask about the Land Rover.

Before he got a chance to do so, though, Midleton said. 'Take a look around if you like, but don't go near the box where Tommy is; Slipstream's in there and he doesn't like visitors.'

Furness nodded, 'He's one of the stallions, I suppose.'

'More like *the* stallion.' Midleton answered, smiling.

'Oh yeah, Slipstream. I've seen his name on race cards.'

Edwards had wandered closer to the Land Rover while Furness and Midleton were talking and, having inspected its tax disc, was peering through the driver's window. 'Don't think much of your transport.' he said, 'it's ancient. I'd have thought a posh yard like this would have something a bit more up market.'

Midleton's smile broadened. 'Perhaps you'll have word with the boss when he comes back then; we've been trying to get him to scrap that old rattler for ages. Bloody thing, it's over fifteen years old.'

'And a rare mileage on the clock, I dare say. Is this the only transport you have?'

'The boss has a Porsche ... ahhh no, sorry, had a Porsche. Some lunatics in a van ran into it last week so he's currently in a banger the insurance supplied. And we've two horse transporters and a pick-up. The Land Rover's the runabout we all use.'

As he was a speaking, a Toyota Corolla came into the yard and a tall and smartly dressed fifty year old man got out.

'That's him.' said Midleton, beckoning Finnerty to join them. 'These guys're from the Police. They want to talk to you.'

Finnerty, who'd started towards them, stopped. 'You'd

better come into the house.' he said, swinging round to make for the back door only to come face to face with Reynard, who'd got out of the car again.

Reynard introduced himself and his companions, and they followed Finnerty into the kitchen.

'I don't think we've ever had a policeman here before.' Finnerty said. 'You have me guessing; what this all about'?'

'Mr Finnerty,' Reynard began, 'there's a Land Rover out there in your yard, which I believe belongs to you and ...'

'It's the company's technically, but go on.'

'It was caught on CCTV near a crime scene in Brighton last week, and we wondered if you wouldn't mind telling us why it was where it was when we filmed it.'

'That vehicle goes all over, where are you talking about?'

'New Road, behind the Royal Pavilion Gardens.'

'Is this to do with Mrs Jellicoe's death; she was friend of mine you know. It was a tragedy. My God ... the way she was murdered, very upsetting ... a lousy cowardly act. I'd like to get my hands on the bastard who did it. Have you got anyone for it yet, Superintendent ...'er?'

'Reynard.'

'Not *Foxy* Reynard?'

'The Land Rover, Mr Finnerty. Why was it in New Road just after Mrs Jellicoe was poisoned?'

'I don't know! I wasn't here that day; I was at Gatwick Airport at the time she died. It's easy to check; my car was run into by a van full of currency thieves, and I was helped out of the wreckage by a policeman and interviewed extensively afterwards. I missed my plane, actually, and had to catch a later one.'

'Who was driving the Land Rover on that day?'

'Hmmm ... I'll need to think about that. You're more likely to get the answer from Sam Midleton though; he's the man you were speaking to. He's my yard manager and knows where everybody is at any time of day.'

Reynard nodded to Edwards who went out to find Midleton and bring him in. When they returned, they asked him to think back and tell them who was driving the Land Rover on the day in question at the time the camera had filmed it. The answer they got surprised them. 'It was me,' Midleton said, 'I was in Brighton doing a few things for Mr Finnerty.'

'Near the grounds of The Royal Pavilion?'

'No, I was nowhere near there; I was down by the harbour buying rope in a ship's chandler's shop. I have the receipt ... I have the rope for that matter.'

'And you went nowhere else?'

'Dropped a letter off for Mr Finnerty, did a bit of shopping for myself; I live alone. I might be able to find the supermarket receipt I suppose. That's all.'

'Did you drive to any of these places via New Road?'

'I might have done, without knowing it. Where is it, I'm not familiar with the name.'

'Behind the gardens at The Royal Pavilion.'

Furness opened an envelope he'd been carrying, pulled out a photograph and slid it across the table so Midleton could see it properly. Finnerty stretched across, picked it up, mentally checking the registration number, and put it back down. 'Well,' said Furness, 'is this the vehicle standing outside in the yard?'

Midleton nodded. 'Yes ... but.'

'But what?'

'But that photograph wasn't taken in Brighton; those lights are just a mile down the road from here.'

Reynard grabbed the photo. Midleton was right. Furness, for whatever reason, had brought the picture taken at the traffic lights on the A24/A272 junction not ones taken near the scene of the crime. 'Where're the rest?'

Furness's face reddened. 'Sorry, Sir, I didn't bring them, because you can't read the Reg. number on them.'

'Idiot!' Reynard blurted out, and then regretted it; it wasn't like him to reprimand a less senior officer other than in private.

Midleton looked relieved ... but Finnerty was grinning; he was enjoying Furness's embarrassment.

Reynard, annoyed at Finnerty's gloating, shook his head. 'I'm sorry Mr Midleton, you can go. We'll be back with the other photos tomorrow and, in the meantime, be thinking of the route through Brighton you took last Thursday; we may be able to confirm it by looking at other junctions where CCTV is located. You two can go as well.' he said to Furness and Edwards. 'Wait in the car, I'll only be a few minutes, I want a word with Mr Finnerty on my own.'

Sussex Police Headquarters,
Sussex House, Brighton

Groves was finished with the laptop. She'd gone as far as she could and found nothing more of any consequence. Discovering the information about the gambling and, with D.C. Furness's help, tracing the way in which Rose Jellicoe had progressively sunk into debt had been the highlights. And anyway, if anything else arose, they could always go back and trawl through the files again.

After putting the laptop to one side Groves joined Best and, together, they set about compiling the profile of Annie's life, which had been modelled on Geraldine's but used up more paper.

'Let me check to see if we've missed anything.' Best said, holding out his hand for the completed sheet.

<u>Bethany Anne Weaver</u>

Born: Ardeskin, Co. Donegal, 1932. Died Eastbourne 2009.

Parents: Dennis Weaver, stone mason; Alice Weaver, cook.

School: Ardeskin National School.

Jobs: Kitchen maid, Sisters of St Audeline's Women's Sanctuary, Donegal, 1946: Assistant housekeeper St Jerome's Orphanage, Donegal, 1950; senior housekeeper St Jerome's Orphanage, Donegal 1958, Warden St Jerome's On The Shore. Kinvara Co Donegal 1968. Housekeeper to Monsignor Gerard Skelly, Formby, Lancs. 1979, Housekeeper to Very Reverend Christopher Mangan, Finchley, London; 1994; moved to nurse older sister Geraldine 2003; died 2009.

No evidence of social or community activities.

No evidence of marriage.

Corresponded only occasionally with Geraldine. (Christmas and Birthday cards).

Visited Donegal once or twice staying with Geraldine in Guest House in Kinvara.

Best handed the paper back to Groves. 'All sounds rather sad doesn't it,' he said, 'every time she got her nose in front something happened? Look at it: left school at fourteen, no secondary education - we don't know why. Got a job in a convent of some sort washing dishes, peeling spuds, whatever; works her way up to be the assistant housekeeper and then ... actually I thought the nuns did all the work in a convent.'

'So did I,' said Groves, pensively picking a long blonde hair from her trousers, 'but there were fewer and fewer of them so I suppose they took in local girls to help.'

'Hmm ... maybe. Anyway after getting up to senior housekeeper, she's transferred to this St Jerome's On The Shore place as its Warden, whatever a Warden is. And then ...?'

'And then she turns up in Formby where she's housekeeper to a priest, and then another in London, and finally, in 2003 when she's well over seventy, she leaves him to goes to nurse Geraldine … and we know the rest.'

'Do we? We have the dates she started all the jobs but we none when she left them. They were hardly seamless transfers, there must have been gaps; she could have been anywhere.'

'OK. You skim through all the papers again while I try to find out something about the convents and St Jerome's On The Shore. After that we'll tackle the desk diary and the address book. When I had a quick look at the diary before, it appeared to me as if it was a daily report book related to her work in St Jerome's.'

An hour later, thanks to some nifty work by Groves on the internet, and Best on the telephone, they knew much more about the institutions which had employed her: St Audeline's used to be a maternity hospital and children's home, St Jerome's was once an orphanage which looked after children born in St Audeline's who'd reached the age of five without being adopted. While St Jerome's On The Shore was an old dower house a rich landowner had gifted to the order back in the eighteen hundreds. For many years it had been used as a place of retreat and a holiday hostel for the nuns of St Audeline's and the orphans of St Jerome's, but it had been condemned as a dangerous structure following a severe winter storm in 1977, and was demolished the following year.

'She was heavy into religion, wasn't she?' said Best.

Groves nodded. 'Yeah, but as an employee, not as a nun.'

'St Jerome's On The Shore sounds interesting, I wonder what it's like.'

'*Was* like, you mean. From what I saw on the internet it's not much more than pile of rubble now. Shall we have quick glance at the address book and desk diary?'

'OK.' said Best, taking the address book. It was falling apart it was so old, and the first page, the one with the 'A' tab on, was missing. There weren't many entries; Annie obviously had few people with whom she corresponded and, within five minutes, Best was putting it to one side.

'I only saw two addresses which might be of interest to us,' he said, 'they were both for the first priest she kept house for after leaving St Jerome's On The Shore, Gerard Skelly. The first entry showed him living in Ballyshannon, County Galway, the second in Formby, just outside Liverpool. We saw that address on one of the other papers we were looking at earlier. Presumably Monsignor Skelly was working in Ballyshannon when she first went to work for him and, when he got moved to Formby, she went with him. Was there anything in the desk diary?'

'It's full of information but I can't make much of it; the entries are in a shorthand she must have invented herself, probably to make sure if it fell into the wrong hands her words wouldn't be understood. Seems fishy to me.'

'We'd better wait until the governor gets back before we try to decipher it let's grab a bite to eat, we missed lunch.'

'Always thinking of your stomach … alright.'

Creakwood Stud Farm
Dial Post, Sussex.

'Right, shall we carry on?' said Reynard sitting down again once Midleton had left the room.

'Will this take long, only I ...'

'The length of time, Mr Finnerty, depends on you.'

Finnerty smiled wryly, he knew what Reynard meant. 'I'm in your hands then, Superintendent,' he said, 'fire ahead.'

'Good. I want to talk to you about another matter concerning Mrs Jellicoe. I believe you knew her a long time so you might be able to help me. I've come up against a few inconsistencies which you may be able to assist me in ironing out.'

'I will if I can. Rose was a good friend of mine.'

'Like her sister?'

'Ursula? What's she been saying; that woman's nuts.'

'Yet you seem to see a lot of her.'

'Who the hell else have you been talking to ... oh yes, I know that pompous twit Julia Henderson. She doesn't like me, so

I'm not the least surprised she's been telling you all sorts of rubbish, how I've been a bad influence on Rose since forever. Listen, Inspector ...'

'Superintendent.'

'Superintendent, yes, Sorry. Look, I know I'm not everyone's cup of tea but I liked Rose and I'd never do anything to upset or embarrass her. Christ, I've known her longer than Julia, since way back in 1968 or 9 when she and her family moved onto the farm next to ours. But you'll know all this if she and Ursula have been talking to you; not that I saw much of Ursula back then, she was barely out of her pram.'

'Actually Mr Finnerty ...'

'Make it Henry, everybody else does.'

'Hmm. Perhaps not. No, I was going to say I've had a pretty good account of Mrs Jellicoe's life from her husband ...'

'James, poor bugger.'

'And from Mrs Constantinidi and, as you've guessed, from Mrs Henderson. Unfortunately while much of what they have told me is effectively the same story seen through different eyes, some of the essential facts, facts which may be of consequence, are radically different. It's those I want to ask you about.'

'Ask away, be my guest.'

'Fine. It's about your more recent relationship with Mrs Jellicoe that I'm interested; about her addiction to gambling.'

'She hated herself for it.'

'Did she? ... Tell me.'

'I know, I absolutely know, you have the wrong idea about me and Rose. Everybody does. I'm portrayed as a bad influence on Ursula, and hence a danger to Rose and her position as the Prime Minister's wife. It's Julia's hobby horse, and I know it infuriated Rose. It didn't trouble me though; I'm supposed to be a bad influence on everyone meet and a danger to the females of our species. I love it. I even encourage it. I tell you, it's got me more women than you could ever imagine ... and more enemies as well! Yeah ... there's a few guys out there I could name who'd gladly slit my throat. It wasn't like that with Rose though. I respected her as a friend and, to some extent, as the sister I never had.'

Reynard leaned forward, rested his elbows on the table, cupped his chin in his hands, ready to listen.

'I've surprised you, haven't I? A different Henry Finnerty is emerging ... well don't tell anyone, Superintendent, or I'm ruined.

When the Wyse's moved into the farm next to ours the families soon became friends; I assume you know Rose's maiden name was Wyse?'

'I do.'

'Yes, well, Rose and I saw a lot of each other, we were about the same age both loved horses. Ursula was just her baby sister and was never in our set. When my mother died unexpectedly in 1970, Mrs Wyse stepped in and kept an eye on both my Dad and myself. I should tell you, my Dad was a wild one, "Stirrups", he was known as, as was my grandfather; the direct opposite of Mr Wyse who was rather staid. All through my late teens this situation prevailed. I'd see a lot of Rose and little of Ursula, which I later discovered she resented. And then my Dad got into difficulty over taxes ... I'm telling it all as it was, Superintendent, this background stuff is important, as you will discover.'

'No carry on, it is helpful.'

'Well, the long and the short of it is my Dad had to sell all he had to pay what was being demanded of him.'

'The taxes?'

'Yes. And to do so he was going to have to get rid of the farm because all his wealth was tied up in it one way and another. When the news got out, he was harassed by people who, seeing the weakness of his position, tried to batter him down to get the place cheaply. Mr Wyse knew what was happening, and he lent Dad a lot of money to get the tax debt out of the way and give him the chance to sell in a more dignified way, and at a better price. I knew all about this and so did Rose. I firmly believe Ursula still doesn't ... and that's the way Mr Wyse would have wanted it. In other words Rose's father saved my Dad's skin and I'll never forget it. Now d'you see why I'd never do anything to harm any member of that family, not even Ursula, who knows nothing of this and who drives me up the wall sometimes.'

Reynard got up from the chair rubbing his buttocks. It had been a long story but had shown Finnerty in a better light. How was that to be squared with what subsequently happened? Was he being misled by what Julia Henderson had told him?

Finnerty also got up from his seat, 'Drink ...?' he asked, stepping across to the dresser, picking up two tumblers in one hand, and a bottle of whiskey in the other.

Reynard shook his head. 'Too early for me ... so your father sold up and he came over here and bought this place?'

'It was wreck when we came here but, slowly, slowly, over the years we got it up to what it is today. Shame is he died two years after we'd moved here so he never saw it as it is now.'

'You're not married?'

'Look around you Superintendent; this house is more like camp-site than a home. No woman would put a foot in place like this ... which suits me fine; I prefer my independence. No, I've managed to keep them at bay so far ... which reminds me ...' he said, looking at his watch.

'I'll not detain much longer, Mr Finnerty but I need to know about this little problem Mrs Jellicoe seemed to have been struggling with, and I thought you ...'

'You mean her gambling?'

'Yes.'

'I used to phone Rose fairly often, or she'd phone me. But I knew nothing about the mess she was getting into until she was making continuous losses. Even then I didn't know they were big, and I don't think James knew anything about it at all. It came out one day when she rang and told me what was happening and I, half-jokingly, suggested a tenner each way on a horse in which I had an interest ... it was entered in a race at York the next day. I told her it had fair chance and would be good price. But I'd no idea she'd plunge in with a thousand pound win bet until it was too late. The horse came second; lost by a short head.'

'Did she blame you for her misfortune?'

'No *I* did though, and then ... Oh God ... I hope I'm doing the right thing by telling you.'

'I'm not interested in your gambling tricks, Mr Finnerty, or indeed in hers, I guarantee it ... unless it has anything to do with her death of course. What were you going to tell me?'

'I'll take you at your word, Superintendent, because what I'm going to tell you doesn't reflect well on me. It's only that it just *might* be connected to Rose's death that I'm going to tell you.'

'Ah ... it was a little scheme was it? One of those for which you are noted. Go on, what was it?'

'The details aren't important. Suffice to say she was supposed to spread a series of bets over several bookmakers, placing them no earlier than ten minutes before the race. She said she would, but she didn't stick to her word. For some reason or other she put a single big bet on so early it was refused and the odds plummeted before any of my friends got their money on. Most of them backed off at that stage, which was lucky, because the horse didn't win anyway. But I was pretty pissed off with her for a day or two, it *could* have cost me a lot of friends I don't mind telling you. I rang her and told her so, actually shouted at her. But it was hardly a reason to harm her, let alone kill her.'

Reynard tapped the table-top with his forefinger as he slowly digested what he'd been told, and then he stood up. 'Thanks Mr Finnerty,' he said, 'you've cleared up a good few things I was beginning to get wrong, and you've given me much food for thought. I have to go but, before I do, let me emphasise how important it is for everyone, including you, to tell us anything they know about Mrs Jellicoe's life which might have had a bearing on her death.'

'Rest assured I will, Superintendent, and I hope you get him soon ... whoever he is.'

In the car, on the way back to the office, nobody spoke. Reynard was thinking of the revelations he'd just heard, and revaluing his views of Henry Finnerty. Furness was still smarting from the reproof he'd seen in Reynard's eye when he'd told him he'd only brought the one photograph; and Edwards, unsure as to whether or not he should speak up on Furness's behalf or remain silent, looked steadily out of the window and kept his mouth shut.

144, Peabody High Row,
East Jutland Street, Brighton

'Phone.' Yelled Mrs Truscott, her hand on the newel post as she looked up the stairs. Barney shook himself awake, trudged across the lino still half asleep, and leaned over the bannister. 'Who is it?'

'Your friend,' she said. 'He's on the land line down here.'

'Ah, fuck 'im.' he said. 'Tell him to ring back.'

'He said it was urgent.'

'Just tell him.' Barney replied, as he turned round and went back to bed muttering, 'who the fuck does he think he is?'

Ten minutes later there was a second call; Barney took it.

'Any sign of …?'

'Nah,' said Barney, 'they won't come here.'

'What about Gareth?'

'He's your pal. Anyway he knows which side his bread's buttered, he'll not say anything, so don't worry about him.'

'Right … but if …'

'They won't,' said Barney, putting down the phone.

The C.I.D. Suite, Police H.Q.
Sussex House, Brighton.

As they walked through the main office, Reynard in front and Furness and Edwards trailing along behind, Sergeant Groves saw them.

'Did you have any luck, Guv?' she asked, knowing from the look of self-satisfaction Reynard was showing that he had.

'Some.' he said, 'and we could have had more if D.C. Furness had been on his toes.'

Behind him, Edwards was smirking, but Furness was looking at her anxiously. For a moment she was inclined to tease him by not saying anything, but she could see he wasn't in the mood for it so she winked instead ... well, her version of a wink, one she executed by screwing up her face and closing both eyes.

Furness relaxed immediately and, by the time they were all seated in Reynard's office, the mood in the room was verging on convivial. Emboldened by the mood change and keen to get into Reynard's favour again, he launched into his apology.

'I made a mess of it Guv, and I'm sorry I embarrassed you. However, with Sergeant Groves's help, I think I might be able to make amends. While you were in the house talking to Mr

Finnerty, D.C. Edwards and I took a series of photographs of the Land Rover on our mobile phone cameras. We covered it from every angle and emailed the pictures to Sergeant Groves, asking her to see if the lab had any way of enlarging the photos we'd just taken, and the ones we got from the CCTV at the end of New Road. We were particularly interested to see images of the vehicle head on. What did you find, Sarge?'

Groves pulled several enlarged prints from an envelope she'd brought in, and laid them on the table. 'These are from the cameras at the junction at the end of New Road. It's the same vehicle Guv, no doubt at all. Look at the row of Race Course Members car parking stickers on the windscreens in both pictures; they're the exactly same. And look at the crumpled end of the front fender - also identical. It's just a pity we have no shots showing it actually pulling away from where we believe it was parked because, unless we find one, we have no way of telling if it wasn't just passing down the road at the crucial time … it could easily have been. Forensic tests allying it to the killer's clothes: the white jacket and the red bandana ought to help us.'

'It's good enough for me.' said Reynard, 'that man Finnerty's been lying and I've been completely taken in, bamboozled with a load of claptrap about being fond of Mrs Jellicoe when, all the time … OK let's think about this; we can't afford to keep making mistakes. So where are we?'

'Up the creek without a paddle' said Furness, emboldened by his re-instatement.

'Bright boy.' Reynard replied, grinning with the rest.

'It *couldn't* have been Finnerty anyway, Guv,' Furness added, 'he was at Gatwick Airport, and I doubt he made that up.'

'After today I wouldn't put it past him, but there's another way, somebody mentioned it last week; whoever it was wanted Mrs Jellicoe dead didn't have to kill her himself.'

'A paid assassin!'

Reynard nodded, 'It sounds dramatic and fanciful I know, but yes, any of the people we interviewed could have paid someone else to do the job. We're going to have to start again, go over every single bit of evidence we collected.'

There were groans all round, and the sense of achievement they'd just started to embrace, evaporated.

'Off you go then,' said Reynard, 'we'll compare notes before we leave this evening ... say at five. But if you come across anything you think significant, come in and tell me immediately.'

As soon as the others had gone, Reynard swung his chair round, tipped it back, put his feet up on the waste paper basket and, with his hands clasped behind his head, his favourite position for thinking, he closed his eyes. Unfortunately the peace which was so necessary to help him concentrate didn't last long though. Hardly five minutes had elapsed before, one after the other, three people came in. The first was Chief Superintendent Bradshaw. He asked for a progress report, saying he'd been expecting Reynard to call him all day, that he was being harassed by "the powers that be", and that he was far from pleased when Reynard told him their enquiries had led to nothing. He'd ordered everyone to go back to the evidence they had and to start again. 'Jesus, Foxy, you've let me down.' he said, 'Based on what you were saying the other day, I've been telling them an arrest was imminent. I'll be crucified if they discover we've made no progress whatsoever.'

'Oh I wouldn't say we've made no progress; we've come to a temporary halt that's all. You know what it's like; sometimes you're scooting along so fast you're almost out of control and the next thing, you hit a barrier and come to a complete stand still. that's what we've done in this case. Everything was going fine, we were heading in a particular direction at a rate of knots, confident were after the right man, and then our evidence began to crumble. We'll get going again soon, but we need to find the right direction.'

'That's no good to me Foxy; I want something solid I can give Scotland Yard. I want someone in handcuffs. Go and rattle a few cages, get this investigation moving again. Please.'

Bradshaw had hardly left when D.I. Elliot came in also looking for a progress report. 'I don't like chasing you Superintendent,' she said, but the press are beginning to turn on us. At the start they were all for helping ... look at the response to our plea for assistance they got us from the public when they headlined the case so prominently. But now they're beginning to question our slowness in getting a result. From experience, I know they'll soon be scoffing, and that'll make your job harder and harder. What can I do to help you move forward?'

Reynard shook his head, 'I doubt there's anything you can do at the moment except keep the newspaper and especially the TV reporters out of my way.'

'I'll do my best, Superintendent. Is there nothing you can give me; they need feeding?'

'We think it possible Mrs Jellicoe's death is in some way connected to another which took place recently.'

'A double murder! That'll keep them happy, who is it?'

'Sussex Criminal Investigation Department are not prepared to disclose any other details at this time.'

'Are you making this up?'

Reynard frowned and, when Elliot saw how serious he

was, she backed off. 'Thanks, Superintendent.' she added, 'I'll tell you how I get on later today.'

When she'd gone, Reynard tried to get back to his thoughts but he'd not even got as far as tilting his chair back when Riggs knocked on his door.

'Oh no, not now; I'm just about to go.' said Reynard 'Can it wait until the morning?'

'Sure.' said Riggs, not in the least put off.

Reynard nodded and, having abandoned all thoughts of having a few minutes peace on his own, set about texting his team to tell them he'd been called to a meeting, and that they should re-assemble in his office at eight the following morning.

With that done, he went home and, in the quietness of his sitting room, with his dog on his lap, he finally got the peace he'd been seeking. He didn't get much thinking done though, for within three minutes he was sound asleep.

Alan Grainger

DAY EIGHT

Thursday 24th September 2009

Alan Grainger

The C.I.D. Suite, Police H.Q.
Sussex House, Brighton.

Reynard was in at quarter to seven and found Riggs was already there, waiting for him. 'I know you're busy Sir, but I really need to …'

'Look, Constable,' Reynard said, displaying a degree of patience he didn't really feel. Standing chatting to Riggs was going to eat into the few minutes he'd planned to be on his own readying himself for the team meeting due to start at seven thirty. 'I'm pushed for time right now; can you give me shout after ten o'clock when I'm more likely to be free?'

'I can Sir but …'

'Later … please.'

Riggs's face fell; he'd been in the office since six thirty to make sure he'd catch Reynard before he got involved. Reynard sensed the disappointment when the young man's shoulders dropped so, despite himself, he said, 'Alright; just five minutes.'

Instantly Riggs's attitude changed; 'I can tell you in three, Sir, but thank you.'

'You should be talking to D.I. Lawrence you know, not me. If there's any overlapping the team leaders sort it out.'

'But I did speak to him, Sir; last thing last night, and he told me my best bet was to get in early and catch you before you got bogged down in the Jellicoe investigation.'

By then they were in Reynard's office and he was switching on the Cona coffee machine. 'Alright,' he said, 'sit down and tell me what it is you think I should know.'

'It's about Mr Ramage.'

'I thought it might be!'

'Doctor Vladic let me watch him doing a bit of the post mortem. Amazing. It was really fascinating …'

'Was it? Go on.'

'Well he showed me the contusions on Mr Ramage's head … close up.'

'Ha! He'd have a few of those, falling from his balcony.'

'But that was the point; he didn't fall because he was drunk; he fell because he was hit on the head with a bottle.'

'Did Vladic tell you this?'

'He worked it out from the shape of one of the contusions; he's very clever. The dent in Mr Ramage's head was in a place at the base of his skull Doctor Vladic reckons he could never have hit by falling, even if he tried. And then, when he looked at it more closely, he was able to see it was the size and shape a wine bottle might make. Showed me it all, he did, and when I told D.I. Lawrence last night he suggested the empty one I'd seen just inside the room on that first morning might have been the weapon. I went back to the flat and got it, and the finger print people at SOCO have since texted me saying they have a good set of prints for a right hand, but that they're not on any of our data base records.'

'So you've put two and two together … and … what?'

'No Sir, I just wanted to let you know. After all, the similarity I spotted in the photograph helped, didn't it?'

Reynard was about to reply, but then he hesitated. Riggs thought he was going to be dismissed, but it was only the sight of the team congregating at Groves's desk which had caught the Super's eye.

'Were there any more photographs, or letters, in the flat you think might suggest a connection between Ramage and Mrs Jellicoe?' asked Reynard.

'Photographs, yes, plenty of them; I told one of your lads I'd found some yesterday, would you like see them, they're on my desk, I can soon get them?'

'What made you believe they'd be of interest to me?'

'Mrs Jellicoe's in some of them.'

'*Is she indeed*? Hmm. You'd better get them then. Any papers of interest; letters and so on?'

'Not really; everything I saw was either a domestic bill or a business letter … not much good to us. There were a few from an insurance company about damage to some of the furnishings in the gallery, and there were one or two from his bank and so on; all pretty uninteresting and of no use to us apart from a file of letters from the insurance company saying the R&R gallery in Brighton, the one run by the victim's brother Brandon Ramage, had made a claim they were refusing settle.'

'The one which is being looked into already.' said Reynard, looking at his watch pointedly, and standing up, hoping Riggs would take the hint and go. 'I'll tell you what,' he said, 'Edwards is a rugby pal of yours isn't he? I'll ask him to go over there with you this afternoon and you can have another good look round. How's that?'

'Perfect, Sir. Thank you.'

As Riggs left, the others came in; it was still a few minutes short of seven. 'Sorry about the delay,' said Reynard, 'Let's get straight down to it. Last night we'd got to the point where we were stuck in both investigations; every promising lead had fizzled out. We'd collected a load of information, but we'd got no nearer finding out who'd killed our victims let alone catch 'em. Investigations often come to a halt like this ... and a fresh approach has to be tried.

I'm going to give you a résumé of what happened at the interviews *I* conducted yesterday, and each of *you* can then tell us what you found on *your* day. After that I propose we change round. I'll stand back to oversee and coordinate progress in both cases, but each of you'll switch from the case you're on, to the other one we're looking into. Understood?'

Groves saw from their expressions that the others were of the same opinion. 'You're right, Guv, we need the switch; it'll keep us sharp. We may not be too far from a break-through in the Weaver case, but we still need a few links to tie it all together.'

'Hear, hear,' said Best, 'I've had enough of the revolting stink in that house to last me a lifetime.'

Furness and Edwards were of a similar mind; they'd spent so long looking at CCTV recordings anything else'd be good.

'Fine.' said Reynard, 'I dare say you've already acquainted each other with what you'd done up until yesterday, so let's whip through the updates and get down to working out how we're going to move on. One last thing ... *I'll* still be dealing with the P.M. and his household. The funeral is tomorrow and I'll be there in the background, observing. No one else is to go anywhere near Barton Court or Downing Street without my express permission. OK, let's get on with it. Let's nail these villains.'

They didn't rise from their seats for an hour, by which

time the notes Sergeant Groves had taken covered three pages of her notebook.

Reynard got the ball rolling by giving them a run down on the previous day's meetings he'd had with the Prime Minster, Mrs Constantinidi, and Mrs Henderson. He told them that, one way or another, he'd heard so many views of the same events from them, and been witness to so much back-biting, he'd been hard put to tell which, if either, of the women was telling the truth about what had been going on prior to Mrs Jellicoe's death. 'However,' he said, 're: James Jellicoe: he's been so bound up in his job he didn't know much about his wife's life. He strikes me as being totally innocent of any involvement in her death or in any of her activities which may have led to it.'

'Like her gambling habit?'

'Exactly, and the debt she owed.'

'What about the women; Mrs Constantinidi and Mrs Henderson. D'you ...?'

'Liars, both of them ... to a degree anyway. There was some correlation of the relationship each had with Finnerty, way back in the past ... but there were plenty of contradictions too. The overall conclusion I came to, especially after talking to him, is that in pursuing Mrs Jellicoe's gambling habit, we may still have the best chance of working out the identity of her murderer.'

'D'you think Finnerty did it, or not?' Groves asked, as she put down her pencil so she could massage some life back into her fingers.

Reynard shook his head, 'I'm pretty sure *he* didn't kill her, and I can't see a strong enough motive to make me think he wanted to. No more do I think he commissioned anyone to do it for him. The same goes for the two women. OK, Finnerty was angry over a fancy plan of his which got upset when Mrs Jellicoe didn't do what she'd been told to do, but nobody lost money. No, for me, Finnerty's scam's just a red herring. Now ... about switching over ...'

Furness, who'd spent hours tracking the movements of the Land Rover, clearly wasn't happy when he thought his efforts had been so quickly dismissed. 'Blimey, Guv, my eyes are worn out looking at that bloody screen, and now you seem to be suggesting I was wasting my time.'

'Of course I'm not. That vehicle was too close to the place we expected it to be, at the time we anticipated, for it not to be somehow connected. It's just that a new approach might find out what we've so far missed.'

'Yeah, like the man who did it for a start,' said Edwards, ever the joker, 'the guy in the white coat and the red bandana ... in the gardens ... with the samosa ... he sounds like a character out of Cluedo. We'll be looking for Mrs Peacock and Colonel Mustard next!'

'Well if you do, you won't have far to look, Taffy; Colin Mustard's the Chief Constable and his office is upstairs.'

It was the light relief they needed, even Reynard joined in the laughter. 'Right,' he said when they'd settled down again. One more thing; Constable Riggs was in here just now and ...'

'Trying to worm his way in.' said Furness.

'No, to give me another bit of interesting information; Morgan Ramage wasn't killed by a drunken fall from his balcony, but from being hit over the head with a bottle and pushed off. Riggs found the bottle, and SOCO got a good set of right hand fingerprints from it. And, as there *is* that marginal connection between Mrs Jellicoe and Ramage that we saw in the photograph Riggs came across, I've decided one of us ought to go to Ramage's flat with him and see what else can be found .'

'I'll go.' said Edwards, I know Lofty well; we both play

for the Blues Seconds ...'

'Which is what I thought when I told him you'd be available after lunch.' said Reynard. 'In the meantime, you and D.C. Furness had better show D.S. Groves and D.C. Best how all that electrical gadgetry you used to view the CCTV footage works ... but only after *they've* handed *you* the red box. I'll be sticking with Rose Jellicoe's diary and address book this morning. Any questions?'

'Yes,' said Groves, 'are we taking over Ramage's death? If it's connected to one of our victims it makes more sense.'

'Let's walk before we try running, eh, Sergeant?' said Reynard.

Barton Court,

the Prime Minister's private residence, near Horsham, Sussex.

James Jellicoe was having his breakfast and thinking over the arrangements he'd made for Rose's funeral when Ursula unexpectedly appeared. 'Are going up to Number 10 this morning?' she said. 'Only I need a change of clothes. I've nothing suitable down here for tomorrow.'

'I'm not leaving here today.' James replied, 'I want a quiet one; might take the boys for walk and have lunch at The Marquis of Granby ... which is not your scene. Why don't you go up to town in the car that's taking the despatch boxes back to Downing Street? You can get a taxi from there to your place and come back down by train this afternoon; I'll get someone to meet you at the station.'

Ursula sat down opposite him, poured herself a cup of coffee, and started to butter a slice of toast. 'No I'll drive, and then I can go as I please without feeling pressed.'

'You can borrow my driver; I'll not need him today.'

'I'd rather take my own car.'

'Are you alright? Reynard was with you a long time.'

'As he was with you, James, and about as successful in

finding out who did it, I expect.'

'What do you think? I know we've not always hit it off, Ursula, but we have to stick together now for the boys' sake. Was there anything Rose was keeping from me apart from the horse racing business?'

'If there was she was keeping it from me too. I still think she was an unlucky victim of some crank who was trying to make a point of some sort ... but what it was, God only knows.'

'I can't help feeling it might have been something I did,' said James, 'but I don't know what.'

Ursula smiled. 'Life's a *bastard* isn't it?'.

'How did you get on with Reynard? Was he aggressive? Did he make you feel uncomfortable? What did he want to know?'

'Not aggressive but, in a way, frightening. All the time, I felt he thought I was holding something back; but I wasn't. And he went on and on about Henry.'

'Oh ... him.'

'You don't like him I know, but Henry's alright. He gets on my nerves quite often, as I do on his ... but it's soon forgotten.'

'Yes, well ... I'm going to find the boys, they need some fresh air. I'll see you when you get back.'

When James had gone Ursula topped up her cup and walked over to sit on the window seat to look out into the garden ... as Rose often did ... and before long she was weeping again.

The C.I.D. Suite, Police H.Q.
Sussex House, Brighton.

Edwards and Furness had gone off with Annie's Box of Secrets and the notes Groves had taken and joined Best at the CCTV monitor.

'I was thinking,' said Best, 'all the work the boys put in yesterday was in trying to track the man *after* he dumped the clothes and left the garden, wasn't it?'

'It was ... what are you getting at?'

'And they couldn't find a shot of him pulling away from the kerb, or one showing the registration number until it got to those traffic lights. How about looking for him *arriving?*'

Groves slapped her hand down on the table. 'You're right; they never mentioned that. And if he arrived and parked, he must have come *down* New Road because it's a one way street and he'd have been captured on the cameras at the *other* end. Don't let's get too excited, but you could be onto something.'

'Just what I thought; I'll go and see what Traffic have.'

When he returned a few minutes later he was grinning.

'You must have drawn a winning ticket.'

Best held up the two CDs he had in his hand and shook them in the air. 'I've won the Jackpot!'

The film from the first camera, showed the Land Rover approaching the junction from the town centre and then turning into New Road. The one from the second camera, showed it entering New Road and proceeding down it for a hundred yards and then pulling into a gap between parked vehicles. The rear number plate was clearly visible on the second shot, but it wasn't possible to see who was in the Land Rover vehicle until a man quit it and crossed the road. Even though the image wasn't clear it was possible to see he was carrying something. 'D'you think there's any chance he might have passed another camera elsewhere on New Road?'

'I don't know' said Groves. 'Dessie and Next told me they didn't look for anything above the gate, only below it.'

Feeling they might be about to make a major advance, Groves and Best drove to New Road and checked every building between the top junction and the place they reckoned the Land Rover had parked; and they were in luck. A block of flats, halfway along had two cameras, one with six clear pictures showing a shortish, well-built man, getting out of the vehicle with a box in his hand and something white over his arm. Disappointed they couldn't identify him, Best went up to Traffic and back-tracked the vehicle's progress through earlier monitored crossings. At one of them, the vehicle was stopped at traffic lights. There were only two cyclists in front of it so the driver and passenger could easily be seen through the windscreen. The passenger's features weren't clear but, when they showed the picture to Furness, he immediately recognised the driver as Henry Finnerty's yard manager, Sam Midleton, the man who'd embarrassed him the day before.

'Let's tell his nibs,' said Furness, but Groves shook her head. 'No,' she said, 'what we'll do is print off the evidence and show it to him at lunch time.'

Meanwhile, as Groves and Best were concocting their surprise revelation for Reynard, Edwards and Furness were puzzling over the entries in Annie Weaver's desk diary. They soon realised it was more than a diary when they saw 'Supplicium' had been printed in large letters on the front cover while inside was a list of numbers with dates and foreign words beside them, followed by a series of ticks. Edwards thought it was record of some sort, one Annie had inherited from a previous Warden of the hostel. 'I reckon,' he said, 'it's a confidential report written in a way to hide the information from anyone coming across it by chance.'

'Like nosy children, yes, it could be. I wonder if the entries in the first column are Irish social welfare numbers.'

'Shouldn't be too hard to find out; the Governor has contacts with the police in Ireland; they'll soon tell us.' said Furness, picking up the book and making for Reynard's office.

Five minutes later, he was back. 'No good. He rang his contact who told him the numbers definitely weren't Irish social welfare numbers.'

'That's a pity,' Edwards mumbled, rocking so far back in his chair he lost his balance and crashed to the floor.

D.I. Lawrence, who was standing a few feet away from him talking to Riggs, obviously thought it amusing. 'Oh dear!' he said. 'D'you want Constable Riggs to help you again?'

'I do *not*,' Edwards replied, getting to his feet, 'my problem needs brains, so there's no point in asking *him*!'

Everyone laughed except Riggs who, anxious not to upset anybody, picked up Edward's chair. 'D'you want a hand Taffy?'

'Oh alright … have a look at this.'

Riggs took the diary from him. 'It's a report book.' he

said after leafing through a few pages. But of what I don't know, my Latin doesn't go that far.'

'Latin?'

'Yes, someone's been having fun.'

Edwards turned to Furness. 'Surely Annie wouldn't have had any Latin, she left school at fourteen.'

'Don't ask me.'

They talked for a while without coming to any conclusion as what the diary had been used for and, in the end, put it back in the box and went for lunch.

✲✲✲

Reynard was comfortably rocked back in his chair in his 'thinking position', when he saw Groves and Best coming towards his office. They were suppressing huge grins, and he guessed they'd found something of importance. 'You'd better bring the other two in as well,' he said, stabbing his finger to indicate there was someone behind them. They turned, Furness and Edwards, who they'd seen in the canteen a few minutes earlier, were heading in their direction.

'Before you start, Guv,' Edwards said, as they took their seats, 'D.C Riggs was with D.C Furness and me before lunch, and he had some theories concerning the desk diary in Annie Weaver's box; have you time to hear them before we start, he's over there at my desk, having another go at it.'

Reynard smiled and gave a quick nod. 'The more the merrier,' he said, 'especially if, as I sense, we're about to make a leap forward,'

Edwards shouted to Riggs, who came over to join them.

'I believe you've solved the mystery of the diary.' said

Reynard, 'tell us what conclusion you've come to.'

Riggs, ever nervous, cleared his throat. 'While the others were at lunch and I was on my own, Superintendent,' he began, 'I tried to make some sense of ...'

'Yes, yes, the diary, go on.'

'No Sir, of the old lady who owned the box that contained the diary. Wasn't she in charge of an orphanage at one time?'

Groves answered. 'Part of one, you're right ... a retreat house and holiday home; a dual purpose building on the coast left to the nuns some years ago.'

'That's what I thought, and it made me wonder if the diary was a behaviour record of some of the people who stayed there. Look at the number of entries, there are hundreds of them; many more than would have covered her few years there.'

'And the Latin on the cover and the inside?'

'Ah, that's easy. I reckon some nun, years ago, devised the shorthand way of recording information in Latin so if it got into the hands of one of the children, it'd remain confidential. Miss Weaver, was it? She just carried on what had been done before.'

'But why in Latin not French, say?' asked Edwards.

'Who knows ... there was Latin everywhere in the Catholic Church in those days, I don't believe it has any particular significance for us. More likely it was a quirk of one of the nuns, a joke perhaps. The information covers those who stayed under, what I assume, is a booking number. It gives the room they were allocated and a tick when they paid.'

'Paid?'

'I assume the lay people who went on retreat must have made some sort of contribution, though the nuns and orphans obviously weren't charged. No, the only thing I don't understand is the title ... "Supplicium" ... which means 'execution'. Surely they weren't beheading people who didn't pay ... or pray hard enough!'

Reynard smiled, and then put up his hand; Riggs speculation had gone too far. 'Thank you Constable. All very interesting and, I fear, all very unlikely. Now Sergeant Groves what news have you ... something less fanciful I hope.'

Groves gave Best a sly wink, and delivered her bombshell. 'We have the Land Rover driving into New Road; six clear frames; absolutely dead certain. It drove into a vacant gap in the line of cars at the kerbside, remained there for half an hour while its passenger, a short sturdy guy carrying something white over his arm and a box in his hand, went into the Pavilion gardens. Half an hour later he came back out of with neither, got back into the Land Rover, which drove off.'

Reynard was on the edge of his seat with excitement, 'Passenger? Was *he* not driving the damned thing?'

'No, Guv.'

'Oh come on Sergeant, who the hell was at the wheel?'

Groves was in her element, turning the tables on Reynard, and dragging it out until *he* was about to burst.

'The driver was ...'

'Yes, yes, go on.'

'Henry Finnerty's yard man.'

'Ahhhh.' said Furness, 'the bastard who made me look stupid over that photograph.'

'Are you sure?' asked Reynard.

'Sure I'm sure; we could see them both quite clearly when the vehicle was stopped at the lights at junction at the top of New Road.'

'Did you recognise the passenger?'

'I think so.'

'Oh for God's sake, Sergeant, who was he?'

'You'll like this, Guv ... it was Barney Truscott.'

Reynard swung his head from side in semi disbelief. 'Oh God ... why aren't I surprised?'

'Why, indeed, aren't any of us surprised?' Groves added. 'And d'you know, Guv, I was just thinking about Henry Finnerty's "perfect" alibi. D'you think he could have manufactured it by deliberately driving into the path of that van so he'd be in the clear. He could still be behind the murder, as you said yourself.'

'What are you suggesting?' Reynard asked, his fingers keyboarding his desk top. 'Finnerty, trapped in his crashed car, is safely distanced from a crime he's set in motion when he dispatched Midleton, to instruct Truscott, to find someone to kill Mrs Jellicoe. Well, in the eye of the law, he's as guilty as the man who did it, the man who gave Mrs Jellicoe the poison. He was as complicit in bringing about her death as were Midleton and Truscott; they'll all have to pay the price. Great work all of you. Now let's go and capture them. I want Finnerty, Midleton, and Truscott behind bars by tonight and I want to be on the trail of the actual killer, whoever he is, not long after.'

'Shall I forget going to Ramage's flat with D.C. Riggs?' Edwards asked. 'Only he's all keen, and he *has* helped a lot.'

'Yes I know he has; you can carry on with him. Give the flat a final going over and, on your way back, pick up Barney Truscott for questioning. If he's not at home he'll...'

'I know where he'll be, Guv ... The Red Lion.'

'Right. And the rest of us'll go to Dial Post and collect Finnerty and Midleton.'

Groves stuck up a finger. 'You realise that'll leave no one working on Annie Weaver, don't you, Guv?'

'Once we have the man who killed Mrs Jellicoe in a cell, we can go back to the Weaver enquiry and follow up what we've heard today. OK, listen, it's a week since Mrs Jellicoe died, let's try to have her killer in a holding cell before the day's out.'

It was a forlorn hope for, when they got to Creakwood, neither Henry Finnerty, nor Sam Midleton, was there.

'Mr Finnerty,' Tommy, told them, 'has gone to London to a meeting, and said he'd not be back until late.'

'How late?' asked Reynard.

'God knows, he mightn't come back at all today. But I can tell you this, there's a valuable mare leaving here in the morning and he'll be back for that. I have his mobile number if it's urgent.'

'No, leave it; we just happened to be in the area and I wanted to clear up a few points. I expect to be passing through Dial Post again tomorrow; I'll call in then. And, 'er … Mr Midleton?'

'Sam? He's not here either; he got a call early this morning to say his Dad had been taken ill last night and was in intensive care in a Leeds hospital. He caught Mr Finnerty just as he was leaving and asked if he could have a couple of days off to nip up to see what the scene was. The boss OK'd it. Sam'll be back on Monday, first thing.'

'You don't happen to know where he lives, do you?'

'Southwater; about ten minutes' drive from here: Eleven,

Beacon House. It's a small block of flats near the station.

'Thanks,' said Reynard, turning to Groves as they left. 'You'd better check it in case he hasn't left yet. I'm going back to Brighton; I've just had a text from Edwards ... they've got Truscott.'

It took Groves and Best ten minutes to get to Southwater, where they quickly got confirmation of what Tommy had told them; Midleton had gone off in a rush the night before.

Apprehensive of breaking into his flat to search for clues without a warrant, they decided to head back to Brighton and watch Truscott being interviewed.

Interview Room Three,

John's Street Police Station, Brighton.

Barney Truscott was on one side of the table, Furness, Reynard and Groves were on the other. Reynard nodded. Furness leaned forward and switched on the tape recorder. For a long un-nerving moment there was deadly silence, with Reynard looking steadily at Truscott who was trying, but failing, to return the stare. It was a typical opening moment for a Reynard interview, one for which he was well known, one which Barney Truscott had experienced several times before.

Groves recited the names of those present "for the benefit of the tape" and then Reynard began. 'You have been formally cautioned, Mr Truscott but, just to make sure you have understood, I will repeat what you were told by D.C. Edwards when you were brought in: "You do not have to say anything. But it may harm your defence if you do not mention when questioned something which you later rely on in court. Anything you do say may be given in evidence." Do you understand this?'

'Of course I bloody do, but that woman's death had nothing to do with me.'

'That remains to be seen, Mr Truscott; this interview is to pursue that very point, to identify your connection, if any, with the death, by poisoning, of Mrs Rose Jellicoe in the Royal Pavilion Gardens, Brighton, a week ago on Thursday, the 17th September.'

Truscott, seemingly unmoved by the seriousness of his situation, turned to look out of the window. His display of disinterest failed to provoke a reaction from Reynard however, who went ahead and posed his first question.

'Where were you between two and three last Thursday afternoon? Think carefully before you answer.'

Truscott didn't hesitate. 'I don't fucking know, do I? Down the Red Lion I expect, or on my way home from it.'

'Are you sure, Mr Truscott? Would you like a moment to reconsider your answer?'

'No,' said Truscott. 'I remember now, I *was* on my way home because when I got there she had my dinner on the table.'

Reynard smiled. 'Think again Mr Truscott, I'll ask you one more time ... Where were ...'

'No wait a minute that might have been Friday ... yes it was it was Friday, fish and chips day.'

'So on Thursday you were where?'

'Dunno ... Red Lion, I'm usually there around that time.'

Reynard turned to Groves, and nodded. She took it as an invitation to ask the next question. 'So you weren't in the Pavilion Gardens at the time Superintendent Reynard mentioned?'

Truscott's eyes lit up and he grinned cheerfully at Reynard. '*Superintendent* eh, Mr Reynard? You *are* doing well. Gotta nice rise to go with it too, I'll bet.'

Groves tapped on the table. 'Answer the question please ... the Pavilion Gardens ... were you there? We have a witness who saw you handing money to another man in the middle of the crowd attending the Food Fayre.'

'He made a mistake, I wasn't in the gardens.'

'And I suppose you didn't get driven there in a sandy coloured Land Rover driven by Henry Finnerty's Yard Manger, Sam Midleton, and dropped off opposite the back gate?'

'No.'

'Or that half an hour later you returned by the same route and were driven off in the same vehicle by Mr Midleton.'

Clearly shaken, but trying not to show it, Truscott hesitated before answering: 'What day did you say?'

'Thursday the 17th ... last Thursday.'

Truscott rubbed his chin thoughtfully as though he were pondering over a huge decision. 'Yeah, come to think of it I did get a lift from Sam, I thought it was Tuesday, but I could be wrong.'

'Oh you're definitely wrong, Mr Truscott, we have you on CCTV in the Land Rover with Mr Midleton, and the film shots are automatically dated and timed. Who was the man you went to meet, the man to whom you gave the money?'

'What money? You're guessing. You don't know anything do you? I met Sam by chance, I thought it was Tuesday, but maybe it wasn't. And yes, I did slip into the gardens; Sam asked me to. He was supposed to meet this guy and give him an envelope from Mr Finnerty, but he was stopped on a double yellow line so he asked me to deliver it for him. And that's all. I gave it to the guy, went back to the Land Rover, and Sam dropped me home. If there was money in the envelope it's news to me.'

'Who was he?' asked Reynard, leaning across the table, intimidatingly which, unfortunately, only prompted a typical and entirely predictable response; 'How the fuck should I know?'

'Describe him, the man to whom you gave the envelope.'

'Taller than me anyway.' said Truscott, 'Six feet at least.'

'Six feet's not unusual, there must have been a lot of six feet men there that day ... how did you know him. Come on Mr Truscott you must realise we have a lot more than we've told you; we're well aware whether or not you're telling the truth.'

'I *am* telling the truth. I'd seen him before, out at Mr Finnerty's place, recognised him the minute I saw him. Same with him; he remembered me.'

'Does he work for Mr Finnerty?'

'He does things for him; not with the horses ... Sam and Tommy and the girls do that.'

'You have lot of stuff in your house.'

'What the hell's that got to do with it? I deal in factory seconds ... it's my stock.'

Reynard began to laugh. 'So it is. And it'll all be pukka won't it? All genuine. VAT paid and so on. I must go round and see what you have some time. Always looking for a bargain, me.'

Truscott, not quite sure how to take Reynard's remarks, didn't open his mouth.

'Yes, well ... Mr Truscott ... I think that'll do for the moment. You can go now, but don't leave Brighton without telling me; we may need your help again.'

'How the hell am I supposed to get home then?' Truscott asked Furness, as he was ushered out of the building. 'I'm not like you lot y'know, I don't have no car?'

'You'll manage,' said Furness, 'the walk'll do you good.'

Superintendent Reynard's Office.
Sussex House, Brighton.

I think you got as much as you're going to get out of our friend Truscott, Guv,' said Furness. 'It was easier than I thought, the idea of being in prison again was obviously more frightening than facing Henry Finnerty, even though he's all but shopped him. No, I can't see Barney Truscott being of much importance to us now. We have what we want out of him and the law will take care of the rest. What *is* important though, is his confirmation of what we'd guessed, i.e. that Finnerty is somehow behind Mrs Jellicoe's murder.'

Best shook his head. 'Hold on Dessie, he didn't actually say that, he just didn't deny it.'

'Same thing.'

'No, Constable,' said Reynard, who been listening to Furness's analysis with an amused grin. 'it is *not* the same thing. I don't think we're finished with Mr Barney "factory seconds dealer" Truscott, not by a long chalk. Did he come quietly?'

'Hah … he took one look at the size of "Lanky" Riggs, Sir,' said Edwards, 'and he came like a lamb.'

'Pity we didn't get Midleton as well; that'd have rounded

off the day. But we did get one thing; we got confirmation of the high possibility of a link between Finnerty and the famous tall thin man with dark hair.

Finnerty told me Rose Jellicoe had harmed no one but herself when she jumped the gun and placed her bets too soon, and that he wasn't flaming mad at her as Mrs Henderson had said. But his connection to the killer through *two* other people, which Truscott has now confirmed, was hardly the action of a man innocent of intrigue. Finnerty's still my top suspect for *plotting* the murder. The man who handed Mrs Jellicoe the samosa might have been the actual killer, and Midleton and Truscott were the intermediaries, possibly unwittingly, but Finnerty was the mastermind. Does that sit comfortably with you as a theory? Come on speak up.'

No one looked keen to be the first to comment; Reynard was famous for putting up provocative theories in order to flush out better ones, they weren't necessarily his true feelings. None of them knew whether this was one of his ploys or not.

Edwards, who'd only joined the team after being seconded onto it during Reynard's last big case, was the first to risk offering an answer. 'You could be right, Guv. Finnerty's a man with a temper. I saw him hit a jockey in the parade ring once, and my girlfriend, who knows about these things, told me when we were talking about him the other night, that he was in a punch-up in a London night club quite recently. It doesn't take much to upset him … no, my money's on him.'

'Thank you Constable … anyone else?'

Groves briefly lifted her hand. Reynard's theory had sounded plausible to her in every respect bar one … Finnerty's over-reaction to what, after all, was a small enough incident. No, Rose Jellicoe had seen a way out of the financial stranglehold she was in and, fuelled by desperation she'd plunged too quickly. Finnerty had lost the money he'd invested in greasing a few palms to set the gamble up, but it would hardly have been a fortune. 'Yes … gut feel … Finnerty's the one for me too,' she said, 'but I don't think we have the real reason yet … it certainly wasn't because Mrs Jellicoe, as you put it … jumped the gun.'

Reynard nodded *and* smiled, this was going well. 'Any more views anyone? No … alright, back here in the morning.'

Alan Grainger

DAY NINE

Friday 25th September 2009

Alan Grainger

St Oswald's Church,
Hooe, near Barton Court.

The service was over and the mourners had moved out to the graveyard for the committal. There weren't many people there, fifty at the most, including the P.M and his boys, Mrs Constantinidi, and the Hendersons; in fact there were more policemen hidden discreetly behind the hedge surrounding the church grounds than there were friends and family.

Reynard stood well back from the funeral party and probably wasn't noticed. He was there to pay his respects but he was also there to watch for anyone else observing from a distance. In his experience a killer was often drawn to his victim's funeral. In the event he saw nothing and was on his way to Creakwood by half past twelve where he hoped to find Henry Finnerty had returned.

His morning had started at eight when the continuation of the previous night's meeting got under way. 'Any further thoughts?' had been his opening words, but there were none. Irrespective of differences of opinion on motive, all thought Henry Finnerty was deeply involved. Reynard had conveyed as much to Chief Superintendent Bradshaw, who he'd bumped into as he was leaving for the funeral.

'So what's your next move?' Bradshaw had asked.

'I'm going to keep an eye on the mourners at Mrs Jellicoe's funeral for a start ' he'd answered, 'but I'll be back at Finnerty's place by lunch time where Furness and Edwards will be waiting for me. We're going to bring Finnerty in for questioning, see if we can shake the truth out of him. Ah yes … can you do me a favour, I'm a bit pushed for time. '

'Of course what is it?'

'Have word with Horsham nick and tell them I'll be there with a suspect around lunchtime, and I'll need an interview room and possibly a cell.'

That had been at eight thirty. He'd sent Groves and Best back to Southwater in case Midleton had come back from Leeds. If he had, they were instructed to bring him in too.

By ten fifteen he was at Barton Court, where he'd briefly spoken to the Prime Minister before preceding him and the rest of the mourners to the church. The first of them arrived not long after he'd positioned himself behind a huge rectangular stone tomb, fifty yards from the open grave. An hour later he left through the churchyard's only gate. He was the last to do so, and somewhat relieved he'd seen no one suspicious.

His arrival at Creakwood, an hour later, coincided with that of Furness and Edwards, thanks to some careful planning and a few text messages. Parked in the yard was the silver Toyota Corolla; Finnerty was back.

Tommy saw them drive in. 'Looking for the boss?' he said, 'he got back last night after all. D'you want me to get him.'

'No don't worry, I'll knock,' Reynard answered. 'I don't

suppose you heard from Sam Midleton?'

'Not a sausage. Look, if you're alright, I have to get on; we've this mare coming, as I told you, and I've few thing to do.'

Before Reynard had time to answer, Finnerty came out of the back door. 'Ah, Superintendent Reynard; looking for me?'

'Yes, Mr Finnerty, we've few more questions.'

'Can you come back, only I've got ...'

'No I can't. I want you to come with me ... I have more questions for which I need answers.'

'Wait a minute, I'm not going anywhere with you, or anyone else. I've an important client arriving here any minute and I have to attend to him first.'

'You're making it difficult, Mr Finnerty.'

'I'm making it difficult. *You're* the one who's making it difficult ... I want you to leave right now. You'll hear more about this ... a lot more. If you don't leave immediately, I'll be making an official complaint.'

'That's your prerogative, Mr Finnerty, and you'll get the opportunity to do it at Horsham Police Station, because that's where we're going ... Constable.'

Furness took a step forward.

'Henry Finnerty, I'm arresting you in connection with the murder of Rose Jellicoe in the Royal Pavilion Gardens Brighton on Thursday the 17th of September, 2009. You will be taken to Horsham Police Station for questioning and anything you say will be taken down and...' as his voice droned on, the look of astonishment on Finnerty's face changed to one of rage and, for a moment, Reynard thought he was about strike out. But he didn't, common sense prevailed, and he allowed himself to be led to Reynard's Volvo and put in the back, followed by Furness.

The shouting had brought Tommy and Tracey out from the loose boxes they'd been working in, and they stood, in shock, watching as the two unmarked police cars prepared to leave.

June, though, who'd been "helping" Mr Finnerty in the house for the previous hour, and was standing at a bedroom window buttoning her shirt, was in tears.

As the cars drove across the yard towards the lane and onto the drive leading to the road, Reynard's telephone began to ring in his pocket. He stopped the car and got out when he saw who the caller was.

'Yes, what is it Sergeant, we're just leaving with Henry Finnerty; we arrested him a few minutes ago. Can it wait, we're taking him to Horsham to be questioned, we'll be there in less than a quarter of an hour; you could meet us there.'

The reply he got was a long one and, during its ten minute duration, he spoke only occasionally, mostly saying 'Yes' or 'Right'. At the end of it he signalled to Furness that he was to get out of the Volvo.

'Problem, Guv?'

'No ... a change of plan. Here's my keys, I want you and Edwards to carry on to Horsham; I'll meet you there in an hour or so, to start the questioning. Before that I'll use your car to go to Southwater, where Sergeant Groves has found something at Midleton's flat she wants me to see.'

'Fair enough.' said Furness, handing over his keys, and getting into Reynard's car.

Reynard gave a perfunctory wave to the Creakwood staff, who were grouped at the door of Midleton's office, and set off on the ten minute drive to Southwater in Furness's Vauxhall Safira.

Outside Beacon House Apartments,
Southwater, Sussex.

Groves and Best were outside Midleton's ground floor flat with a woman who lived in a similar sized one on the top floor. She'd accosted them when she'd got out of the lift and seen them hammering on the door. 'You're wasting your time, he's gone,' she said, 'perhaps I can help you?'

Groves took out her warrant card and showed it. 'We want to talk to Mr Midleton, we knew he went up to Leeds yesterday but we were hoping he'd come back late last night.'

'You've got it wrong, I saw him early this morning, he was just tidying up before leaving for Leeds to take up a new job. Not that I knew him well, in fact we seldom saw each other, but this morning, as I came in, I'm a nurse in the local hospital and I was on the night shift last night, he was going out. He had a load of suitcases with him and was putting them in his car.'

'Hmm, I'd swear he said he was going to visit his father. But then, come to think about it, I heard it from people at his place of work; perhaps he didn't want to say he was leaving. Do you think he's gone for good?'

The neighbour wasn't sure but, as luck would have it, the landlord turned up, and he certainly knew Midleton had moved on. 'I just came round to see what condition he'd left the place,' he said, 'I've new tenants moving in a week next Wednesday.'

Alarm bells started to ring in Grove's head. 'When did he tell you he was quitting the flat?' she asked.

'Two weeks ago last Monday. He had to give me that, it was in his lease.'

The alarm bells were turning into panic. 'We need to examine the place before you re-let it. I'll get people here as soon as I can, but you'll have to put off letting a new tenant in.'

The landlord looked as though he was about to protest, but didn't. 'I can give you a week.' he said, handing Groves the keys. 'But I must have it a week tomorrow for sure.'

The neighbour, who'd stood in the background listening, moved to Groves's side. 'Is it something serious?' she whispered.

Groves smiled but, instead of answering the question, posed one of her own. 'Are you likely to be around today, only my boss'll want to talk to everyone who lives here?'

'I think so,' she said, 'I'm going to bed now, but I'll be up at four this afternoon if that suits.'

'It'll be fine. Now ... just before you go ... tell me exactly what Mr Midleton said this morning.'

'It wasn't much ... he just told me he'd been offered a new job which he'd decided to accept, and then he threw the last of his cases and a couple of plastic bin bags into his car and drove off, stopping for a moment at the rubbish skip over there to pitch the bags in.'

'Right, thanks.' said Groves, following Best into the flat and pulling her phone from her pocket.

The call she made was the one Reynard had received in the yard at Creakwood, the one which prompted his 'change of plan', and his swapping of cars with Furness. Her outlining the position to him, as described by the landlord, immediately brought the response she ought to have anticipated.

'I knew it!' he'd said.

☼☼☼☼

Things were moving by the time Reynard arrived in Southwater; Groves, having determined Midleton was driving a dark blue ten year old Peugeot 305 with the registration number YOT 575 CG, had put out a motorway 'stop and apprehend' request, alerted all sea and air ports, and asked SOCO to go over the flat for fingerprints and DNA. Reynard was highly complimentary when he got there.

'Thanks, Guv,' she'd replied, 'but I'm intrigued ... why did you say "I knew it" when I rang you?'

'Because I did ... did you not notice the expression on Midleton's face when he realised we didn't have a photograph showing the Land Rover's number plate other than one which was just round the corner from Creakwood? Anyone falsely accused of being near a crime scene would normally have shown signs of relief under such circumstances ... he didn't, he even looked pleased. I knew then we were onto something, but I couldn't see what.'

'Yet you arrested Finnerty, not him. Why?'

'I did it for a purpose ... I wanted to give Midleton a false sense of security he'd believe. I felt that as soon as he saw or heard of us bringing Finnerty in, he'd assume he was in the clear ... and that's when people make mistakes. It was a risk, but not a big one, though I confess I didn't expect him to disappear before we got a chance to squeeze him a bit.'

'Did *he* kill her though? That's what you're inferring. We

have no proof, and no evidence, to say he did.'

'Then we'll have to find it. We have the 'How', and now, I believe we have the 'Who'. What we need is the 'Why'.'

'But Finnerty, Guv?'

'Oh he'll bull and bluster, but he'll never make a complaint; he knows it would give us a genuine reason to poke about in his affairs and he wouldn't want that. Anyway I'm about to recruit him, he's changing sides though he doesn't know it.'

'You're joking!'

'I *am* not. When he sees we're after someone else, he'll fall over himself to be one of the good guys ... you'll see.'

Groves began to laugh. 'You're a cunning old fox, Foxy!'

Reynard tapped his nose with his forefinger, and grinned.

While they'd been talking Best had been down to the skip and recovered the bin bags. When he opened them, he saw they weren't the kitchen rubbish he'd half expected; they were almost exclusively pieces of paper.

'Tip 'em out.' said Reynard, bending to see what they'd got as Best cascaded everything out and onto the floor.

'Some juicy stuff here, Guv,' she said.

Reynard nodded, 'Yes,' he replied, 'you two can sort it out ... and make sure you have a good look round the flat again before SOCO get here. I'm off to Horsham to confer with Henry Finnerty.'

'Confer, eh? That'll surprise him,' said Groves.

Interview Room Two,
Horsham Police Station

Horsham had been chosen as the location at which Henry Finnerty was to be questioned because it was the nearest to Creakwood with a holding cell. Not that Finnerty was in it, a telephone call from Reynard had seen to that. He was in an interview room and wondering why he was there.

Furness and Edwards had arrived with him fifteen minutes after leaving Creakwood and, following a phone call they'd got from Reynard en route, they allowed their hard attitude to soften. By the time they'd got out of the car and into the building, Finnerty was beginning to sense a change in the atmosphere; the chilly silence with which they'd left the yard had been replaced with one tending towards affability. He wondered what the catch was.

The desk Sergeant checked him in without relieving him of the contents of his pocket, which further surprised him, as did the polite way he was conducted to the interview room. What was going on he wondered, as a cup of tea was placed before him? When he heard Reynard's voice outside in the corridor, he knew he wouldn't have long to wait before some sort of explanation was forthcoming. When Reynard came in he was all smiles.

'Thank God you played along, Mr Finnerty,' he said, 'it was important your staff at Creakwood thought you were in trouble. I *did* think of saying something to you, but everything happened so quickly I just had to hope you'd "twig" what I was up to, and not give the game away. I had to make it look as if I was bringing you in, d'you see, and the only way I could do it convincingly, was to actually do it, to arrest you there and then and cart you off. I do hope you understand.'

'Er ... yes ... of course ... perfectly.'

'We're after Sam Midleton.'

Finnerty breathed a sigh of relief. 'Ahhh.'

'And I knew he'd somehow get news of your arrest, and I hoped it would provoke a reaction from him. It did. He's done a runner, scarpered, which to my mind proves his guilt.'

'Yes, well I ...'

'His disappearing *is* a problem though, Mr Finnerty,' said Reynard, 'I won't deny it. I've tried to avoid giving him a reason to think we suspected him, because we still need one or two bits of proof validated. But this embarrassing misjudgement of mine has sent him running for cover. With your help we can catch him. We must get this man behind bars.'

Finnerty seemingly entering into the spirit of the thing, nodded wisely. Which was much to the entertainment of Furness and Edwards who, watching from the observation room, couldn't make out what the hell was going on. If Groves had been there she'd have told them ... Foxy was being Foxy!

Finnerty was every bit as puzzled as Furness and Edwards, but he was a wily man, and he played along with Reynard's extraordinary change of attitude to give himself the opportunity to work out why it was there.

'So let's get on with it, Mr Finnerty,' said Reynard, 'I

want you to tell me everything you know about Sam Midleton and, to ensure I don't have to call on you again, I'm going to get one of my officers to take notes as we talk. Is that alright?'

Finnerty said it was, and Furness was brought in.

During the next half hour, prompted by Reynard's questions, Finnerty told them as much as he knew about Sam Midleton which, when it came down to it, wasn't much.

Midleton, he told them, despite his lack of definable accent, was Irish. He'd run away from home at sixteen and got a job cleaning out stables at a racing establishment in Mullingar. It was there he got his first "hands on" experience with horses and quickly realised he had a natural empathy with them. The stables went into receivership and his job disappeared so he took a boat to England, arriving almost penniless in Liverpool at the age of seventeen. It looked like a bad start, but his luck changed when he got a job in a riding school on the outskirts of the city. That he was a natural horseman and could strike up an uncannily genuine relationship with even the most truculent of horses was quickly noticed by others in the business and, within six months, he'd been poached by a large livery stables in Chester where upwards of forty horses were kept. With so many animals, each with its own physical, mental, and psychological idiosyncrasies, he began to take an interest in the influence of hereditary factors, which naturally led him to look for a job in a breeding establishment. He found his first in a small yard near Goodwood and, after three years, applied for and got the job of Yard manager in Creakwood. He was still only twenty six, a young and talented man 'and,' said Finnerty, 'I depend on him greatly. If he has a shortcoming it's his inability to meld with the rest of the staff which makes things tricky sometimes.'

'He's loner then?' suggested Reynard.

'He's worse; he's a man with a chip on his shoulder that would cripple an ox. He brings silence to a room the minute he walks into it. I wouldn't tolerate his odd behaviour if he wasn't so damned good with the animals. But tell me, Superintendent, what makes you think he's capable of such a vile act as murder?'

Reynard shrugged his shoulders, 'It's a feeling.'

'Why d'you think he wanted to harm Rose Jellicoe, what have you on him, because I can't ...?'

'I'll get D.C. Furness to drive you back,' said Reynard, rising from his chair, 'but not a word about our conversation to anyone ... not a word ... I don't want it getting back to him until I have him locked up.'

As Furness and Edwards drove Finnerty back to Creakwood, they avoided conversation. This was partially because Reynard had told them to keep themselves to themselves, but it was also because they were as puzzled as Finnerty as to what the Superintendent was trying to achieve.

☼☼☼

Reynard went back to the flat in Southwater, as soon as Finnerty had left, to find Groves and Best in heaven; the rubbish had delivered a wealth of information once they'd pieced together the torn up paper.

'Well?' said Reynard. 'What have you got?'

'Look for yourself, Guv.' said Best, I've joined most of the papers together again with cellotape. You can ignore the big pile; they're all domestic bills and so on, relating to his recent occupancy of this flat. The small pile is more interesting because, as you'll soon see. there's evidence he was connected to Rose Jellicoe and to Morgan Ramage, and ... and wait for it ... I reckon he's also somehow connected to Annie Weaver as well, I found a bit of paper with her name and address on it.'

'Why am I not surprised?'

'Don't tell me you'd worked that out as well.'

'Of course I hadn't but, d'you know, Sergeant, I'm not ... "not surprised" ... that is. There have been so many twists and turns in all three investigations we should have at least suspected it. Have SOCO been yet, they should have been here ages ago?'

'At your service, mate,' came from the open front door.

Reynard turned round; it was Sergeant Geordie Hawkins and his SOCO boys.

'You know those finger prints you found on the bottle which came from the flat in Chichester.' said Reynard, 'we think they might belong to the guy who was living in this flat until yesterday. See if you can get a few here to match them. And then, as soon as you can, have another look around the house and garden in Eastbourne where that woman died; the same man could be involved there too. We're going back to Brighton to pull it all together.'

The C.I.D. Suite, Police H.Q.
Sussex House, Brighton.

They were assembled in Reynard's office, the coffee had been made, and the Hobnobs handed out. There was an air of 'a job well done' in the air, which they'd all have said was well deserved. Three amazing cases busted in a week … well nearly busted … and just over a week. Three murders which would go down in history because of their complexity and the fact that one of the victims was the wife of the Prime Minister. All they needed to complete their pleasure were three sets of matching fingerprints and Sam Midleton begging for mercy. But they were going to have to wait for; he hadn't been seen since saying goodbye to the nurse from the flat above him.

Edwards looked across the room to Riggs, who'd been included in the exclusive group because of his contribution, and he winked. Riggs stuck up his thumb and winked back.

'OK, let's get going,' said Reynard, 'we've had a good day today; in fact we've had two good days. A lot of progress has been made but we still have no one locked up. I don't propose to prolong this evening's meeting by indulging in speculation; rather I'd like to see the facts we've marshalled so far put into some sort of order. This'll help us frame our questions when we've got Midleton in front of us, and I hope that'll be soon. Now we've all worked on all three cases at some stage, so I propose to outline the situation as we currently know it. You may interrupt me as we go along if your view differs to mine. Right?'

He looked around from one face to another without seeing a response, so he continued. 'OK,' he said, 'we'll start with dates and times of death. Annie Weaver was the first to die at some time during the late evening of the 16th of this month. Rose Jellicoe died mid-afternoon the next day and Morgan Ramage very early the following morning. Three people whose lives appear to be connected by a thread we have yet to discover, let alone understand. Sam Midleton meant *something* to Annie Weaver, Rose Jellicoe, and Morgan Ramage, that much is certain ... but though we've found a possible link between the latter two in a photograph, we've come across nothing to associate either of them with Annie Weaver except the suspect himself and that slip of paper with her name and address on it that D.C. Best found in Midleton's rubbish. So what can the connection be?'

Reynard took up his cup, sat back in his seat, and slowly sipped as he waited for someone to speak. But nobody did. Not a single idea was forthcoming. Whether it was because none of them could think of one, or because anyone who had one in mind daren't voice it for fear of being ridiculed, he didn't know.

'Alright,' he said, at last, 'let's go home and get a good night's rest for when Midleton's apprehended, as he will be sooner or later, we may have some long hours to face.'

After the others left, Reynard went to see C.S. Bradshaw to give him an update. Bradshaw was both pleased and relieved; the pressure on him for a result, coming for all sides, been tremendous and fending off government officials and newspaper reporters had been getting more and more difficult every day. 'Your lot have done great work, Foxy, you're getting close.' Bradshaw told him, after listening carefully to every word of the report. 'Don't let there be any slip ups; if you need help, tell me; and I'll make sure you get it.'

'You know me,' Reynard replied 'I'd much rather handle everything myself but, on this occasion some heavyweight assistance might be appropriate. I was thinking of asking Commander Simpson to use his influence to get Midleton here quickly ... once we've found him, that is!'

'Which could be God knows when. Yes, it's a good idea. D'you want me to ring him? Here, I'll get him now, and you can talk to him yourself?'

Commander Simpson was still in his office at Scotland Yard when Bradshaw rang. Fortunately he'd been getting daily reports from Brighton so he was nearly up to date on the Jellicoe case and the possibility Ramage was in some way connected to it. But, when Reynard told him there was a slight possibility both were also linked to the death of Annie Weaver, he gasped. 'Thank God we kept her case to the fore in our press releases as well, gave it equal attention. No one'll be able to say we've been ignoring what might now turn out to be a pivotal factor in Rose Jellicoe's murder. Is there anything I can do to assist you?'

It was the opening Reynard was waiting for, and he seized it. 'We might need help in getting Midleton here when he's apprehended, and I was wondering if ...'

'Wonder no more, Foxy, when he's caught, wherever in the world it is, I'll get him to you as quickly as is humanly possible. Leave it to me ... all I need to know is where he's being held. Ring me at home if necessary'

Satisfied they'd done as much as they could; they walked down to their cars together.

'Here's hoping.' said Bradshaw, stopping at Reynard's car and proposing a toast by holding up an imaginary glass.

DAY TEN

Saturday 26th September 2009

Alan Grainger

The C.I.D. Suite, Police H.Q.
Sussex House, Brighton.

Midleton was stopped by police officers at the Brittany Ferry's Plymouth terminal while driving in a slow moving procession of vehicles inching its way through the customs and immigration towards the ship.

In his pocket he had a computer printout of a ticket for the 3.45 p.m. sailing to Santander, Spain.

He made no protest, but nor would he answer questions. A more senior officer was called and the arrest was made.

Reynard was finishing his supper when the call came through; steak and kidney pie kept warm in the oven, followed by plums and custard reheated in the microwave. Cathy had eaten an hour earlier. It was a regular performance, her having the supper ready at seven as asked, and then having to eat alone; his kept warm, or heated up again when he got there. They no longer argued about it. It was just the way things were.

As soon as he put the receiver down, he picked it up again and rang Commander Simpson who, as it happened, was *also* tucking into a re-heated meal in *his* kitchen.

As a result of the urgency the commander injected, Midleton was brought up to Brighton during the night, and was already locked up in a holding cell in John's Street nick when Reynard walked into the office at seven thirty the following morning. Groves and the others had all arrived ahead of him and were talking excitedly when he appeared.

'Guv,' said Groves, her whole face alight with the anticipation of what he'd say when she told him the good news. 'I've just taken a call from the custody Sergeant in John's Street ... they have him! He was stopped at the Brittany Ferries terminal in Plymouth last night.'

A lesser man might have said he already knew, but not Reynard; he preferred to let the little charade induce the team into thinking he was the last to know, and to enjoy the look of glee on their faces when he displayed exaggerated astonishment on his.

He didn't disappoint them, 'Whoahhhhh ... great.'

'And that's not all, Guv,' said Groves. 'I took the papers we discovered in Midleton's rubbish bags home last night and went through them again. Just as well I did, because it looks as if we'll be questioning him sometime today.'

'We will ... what did you find?'

'I spotted another connection between him and Annie Weaver we knew nothing about; a piece of paper, a sort of character reference, and it was stapled to two or three other references he'd got from previous employers. All had the name and address of the company he'd worked for except the last one ... it was headed 'St Jerome's Children's Home, Donegal', and signed by a Sister Celeste. Governor, it's obvious now that Midleton was brought up, or partially brought up, in an orphanage and, once I saw the importance of what I'd found, I texted Sergeant Hawkins at SOCO and asked him to hurry up the check of fingerprints found on the wine bottle at Ramage's flat.'

'The bottle that stunned Ramage, which at the time didn't match any on the national register?'

'Correct. I asked him also to re-check them against any they got at Midleton's flat yesterday, and any they found at Annie's house, if they went back. I haven't heard from them yet, but SOCO aren't renowned for early rising!'

Reynard stood for a minute, thoughtfully rubbing his chin as he took in what Groves had just told him. If all the prints matched, they had Midleton in the bag. With evidence of his presence at all three murder scenes, he must have killed all three victims; but why? That was the problem ... they had no idea why. 'OK, so let's have quiet chat ... my office ... all of you.'

'Can I come, Sir?' It was Riggs, he'd slipped in behind Best, un-noticed by Reynard despite his height, while Groves was talking about the fingerprints.

'If D.I. Lawrence says so ... yes.'

They all went into Reynard's office except Riggs who was looking for Lawrence. No one mentioned coffee or Hobnob biscuits; the excitement engendered by the overnight developments dispatched all such thoughts from their minds.

'First,' said Reynard, when they were all seated. 'I want everyone involved. Sergeant Groves and I will conduct the interview, and we'll do it at John's Street at eleven. The rest of you will be in the observation room, taking notes of things said which you feel ought to be explored. Two hours, with a break in the middle, ought to suffice. Right now we have to give the prisoner ... ah that sounds good, doesn't it ... the prisoner? Yes, we have to give him time to rest; he's been up all night and I don't want to hand him a chance of saying he was questioned when he wasn't fully awake. The hour or two we have before then will be spent on going over what we have against him and deciding how to use it.'

'You saw this coming didn't you Guv?' asked Best. 'I was watching when you were explaining to Sergeant Groves why you'd said you 'knew it', and it was obvious to me you'd made up your mind who'd done it ... and why.'

'That's very perceptive of you Constable, you flatter me. I certainly was getting close to believing Midleton was the culprit, but I didn't know, and still don't know, why.

Alright you can all go now. Check your notes again, revisit the evidence we've collected. Start from the beginning if you have to ... whatever way you tackle it, I want a list of questions you think we should ask in my hands by nine fifteen, now go ... no, no, not you Sergeant; we have to get our heads together and assemble the evidence we need to take with us.'

At ten o'clock, Reynard collected the suggested questions the team members had given him, and he and Groves went through them, occasionally adding one to the list they'd compiled. After that it was just a case of putting a few pieces of crucial evidence which they'd collected into envelopes, and telling Chief Superintendent Bradshaw they were on their way to John's Street.

Interview Room Three,
John's Street Police Station, Brighton.

Sam Midleton, looking washed out, sat slumped in a chair across the table from Superintendent Reynard and Sergeant Groves. Beside him was the duty solicitor he'd called for when brought in. In the observation room, D.C.s Best, Furness, Edwards and Riggs stood waiting for the drama to start.

Groves turned on the tape recorder and introduced those present. They were: Samuel Midleton and his solicitor, George Savage, Superintendent Reynard, and herself. Savage was well known to Reynard and Groves, a diminutive legal terrier who'd fight all the way. The accused man had drawn a lucky number when he got Savage.

'You were cautioned, Mr Midleton, when you were arrested in Plymouth last night,' said Groves, 'but to make sure you have understood what you were told I will repeat the words spoken to you at the time.'

She went on to repeat the familiar litany and then handed over to Reynard to commence the questioning.

'You are Samuel Midleton, recently of 11, Beacon House, Southwater, and an employee at Creakwood Stud Farm Dial Post, in the county of West Sussex, are you not?' he said.

Midleton didn't answer, so Reynard repeated the question.

Again Midleton didn't answer until his solicitor leaned over and whispered something, after which he mumbled, 'Yes'.

'Where were you on Thursday afternoon last, the 17th of this month, between the hours of two and four?'

'You know where I was.'

'Indeed I do, I have photographic evidence showing you at various locations while at the wheel of a sandy coloured Land Rover registration number ...'

'Yes, I've told you I was.'

'And with you, you had a man called Barney Truscott?'

'So what?'

'And he took a white coloured jacket and a white coloured box from your Land Rover and delivered them to someone in the Royal Pavilion Garden before returning for you to drive him away?'

'I don't know what he took into the gardens, whatever it was, it wasn't mine, I didn't give him anything.'

'I see. Tell me, what have you against Mrs Rose Jellicoe?'

'Me? Nothing.'

'Think again, Mr Midleton. We know the white coat was given to an accomplice, who put it on and then, disguised as a waiter working for one of the food companies pressed Mrs Jellicoe, who was tasting samples, to take a samosa containing hemlock. It caused her to collapse, and later, to die.'

'No.'

'No what?'

'No I didn't do it. I gave Barney a lift that's all. I bumped into him in a pub and he asked me if I was going back to Creakwood. I told him I was and he asked me for a lift home. Halfway there he asked if I'd stop for a minute or two, he had to nip into the gardens to give someone a message. I said I would that's all. I don't know who he met, or why.'

Reynard turned to Groves and nodded.

'Where were you between six pm and midnight on Tuesday the 16th of September?' she asked.

'No idea.'

'Alright, what is your connection to Miss Annie Weaver?'

Savage started hopping about on his chair. 'What's this got to do with your enquiries regarding the death of Mrs Jellicoe?'

'We're not sure, that's why we are asking the question. We know Mrs Jellicoe's death and that of Miss Weaver are associated in some way and we also know Mr Midleton has visited Miss Weaver's house recently.'

Savage practically shot out of his seat. 'You can't go dragging in all these wild allegations regarding a different case. My client has been brought in for questioning with regard to Mrs Jellicoe's murder. Please confine yourself to that.'

'It's true we are pursuing enquiries concerning Mrs Jellicoe today ... but there are other matters ... concerning other incidents, which impinge on the Jellicoe case. We need to see to what extent, if any, Mr Midleton was involved in them. If you wish us to caution Mr Midleton regarding them too we will oblige. It's up to you.'

'I need a moment with my client before I advise him to continue with this charade, Sergeant.'

Reynard intervened. 'Ten minutes do you, Mr Savage?'

'Er … yes … ten minutes. *And in private*,' said Savage pointing to the recording machine.'

Groves switched it off, and she and Reynard left the room to join the others in the observation room. The sound had been switched off in there too, so nothing of the animated conversation between Savage and Midleton could be heard.

'Out … everyone out of this room, please,' said Reynard, 'I don't want to give that little so and so an excuse to complain we were eavesdropping by lip-reading.'

They all left, but twelve minute later the team was back in the observation room and Groves and Reynard were taking their seats ready to start questioning again. Just before they went in, Groves got a text message from SOCO. She glanced at it and whispered in Reynard's ear, 'the prints at all locations match.'

The atmosphere was tense when they entered the room; Midleton and Savage had clearly disagreed over tactics.

Reynard raised his eyebrows, 'Shall we start?'

Savage nodded. 'But keep to the Jellicoe investigation.'

Reynard smiled, and turned to Groves. 'Carry on Sergeant.'

'What is your connection to Miss Annie Weaver?' she asked.

Savage glowered at her and was about to say something when Midleton answered. 'None, I don't know her.'

'You don't know her … I see. So you don't recollect coming across her when you were living in Donegal?'

'No I was only a kid then. I hardly remember anything of

my life at that stage. I was only ... well I was only a kid.'

'You must have been 'a kid', as you put it, for a very long time then,' said Reynard, wryly smiling. 'Alright, we'll put that to one side for a moment and move on to something else. Where were you on the night of the eighteenth of September this year?'

'The eighteenth?' Midleton looked up at the ceiling as if it was going to tell him. 'I don't know, at home I suppose. Yes ... I *was* at home I remember now.'

'So you definitely weren't in Chichester?'

Savage reacted immediately. 'Superintendent please stop dodging about all over the place, and concentrate on one issue only, namely that of Mrs Jellicoe's death?'

Reynard ignored him, and pulled a series of photographs from one of several envelopes he'd brought in with him, and slid them across the table in front of Midleton. 'These CCTV films were taken by cameras outside the Royal Pavilion Gardens. You can see from the times on them that you pulled in from the traffic and parked on New Road opposite the back gate to The Royal Pavilion Gardens at exactly two o'clock. Barney Truscott, your passenger, got out carrying a short white coat and a white box, and went into the gardens. Twenty minutes later he returned to you in the Land Rover without either the coat or the box and you drove off at two twenty two p.m. Mrs Jellicoe took and ate the samosa which killed her from a man in a short white coat and wearing a red bandana at about two o'clock to two fifteen p.m. We have witnesses who saw her take the samosa *and* saw her collapse.'

Midleton said nothing.

'Well?'

Midleton still said nothing. Savage did though ... 'What are you trying to get at, Superintendent? The photographs show my client stayed in the vehicle. He couldn't have given anything to anyone in the gardens, because he wasn't in them.'

'You have a point, Mr Savage, but not a very good one; numerous murders have been commissioned by people who didn't physically commit them, and may not actually have been present.'

'Is this what you are accusing my client of doing ... of paying some else to kill Mrs Jellicoe on his behalf. Why would he want to do that?'

'Mr Savage ... that's what we're trying to find out. Now can we carry on? Good ... Let's go back to Chichester for a moment. What was your fight with Morgan Ramage about, Mr Midleton?'

Savage was up in an instant. 'Who's Morgan Ramage for God's sake? Is this another diversion to confuse my client?'

'Only the late Mr Morgan Ramage of the R&R Fine Arts Gallery in Chichester knows the answer to that, and he's dead. Since you ask though, we have proof Mr Midleton was there the night Mr Ramage was knocked practically unconscious and pushed to his death off his balcony. D'you recognise the bottle in this photograph Mr Midleton?' he asked, pushing another print he'd taken from an envelope across the table.

'I've see dozens like that ... I bet you have too.'

'Not ones with your fingerprints on them I haven't.'

As the morning wore on, and more probing questions were fired at Midleton, Reynard could see him wilting. Even Savage looked tired. Reynard and Groves, scenting success, kept attacking and eventually Savage called a halt. 'I think I must speak to my client in private again. Can we have half an hour?'

'Of course,' Reynard replied, 'I'll send you in some

sandwiches and tea.'

Savage nodded, he wasn't enjoying trying to defend his client when he had no ammunition.

The police team retired to the canteen during the break to assess the morning's work. While they were there, they came to the conclusion that the case was drawing to an end. And it did ... as soon as they returned to the interview room. Midleton was slumped even lower down in his chair; he looked as though he'd been drained of substance.

Savage, on the other hand, was flushed with embarrassment; he'd never allowed anyone he was defending to give in before. 'I wish to ask for an adjournment,' he said, 'certain issues have been clarified for me during the break, and I'm at a loss to know what I should advise my client. I need to confer with others more familiar with the route my client now wishes to pursue.'

Reynard knew what had happened as certainly as if he'd heard the conversation Midleton and Savage had just had. It was obvious: Midleton wanted to confess, and Savage didn't know how best to handle it.

'You can have as long as you like Mr Savage, provided Mr Midleton agrees voluntarily to remain in custody.'

Savage nodded.

Reynard glanced at the clock on the wall; it hadn't been such a long morning after all.

Alan Grainger

THREE WEEKS LATER

Alan Grainger

14, Malvern Gardens,

Brighton, Sussex.

It was Sunday afternoon three weeks later; Foxy and Cathy Reynard had had their lunch in the pub and their walk on the seafront. They'd even had their little nap, and were lying on their bed looking at the ceiling and thinking of tea when Cathy asked how it had all ended.

'Come on, Foxy, surely you can tell *me*?'

Reynard yawned and stretched. 'Well it hasn't ended yet,' he said, 'not entirely. And it won't until the trial's over ... which'll be months away. But, as to telling you how it all started, and how things got to where did, OK, I'll try ... but it's a tragic story.'

'I knew it would be; I could see it was getting to you.'

'Human beings make choices, Cathy. Choices they somehow convince themselves are for the good of others, when in their heart of hearts they know they're only going to be good for themselves. It's what happened in this unhappy case. Three murders, and all stemming from an unfortunate choice made by a couple of students when they brought a child into the world and then abandoned it. Dress it up any way you like, it all boiled down to that.'

'So what happened; run me through it?'

'OK. Go back twenty seven years. Rose Wyse, as she was then, a post graduate student at London University, found herself pregnant after a party given by a boisterous crowd of art students living in the flat over her bed-sit. When she'd first arrived she'd been expecting to be sharing with her Trinity College friend Julia, but a last minute change in Julia's plans saw *her* hitch-hiking round Australia, and *Rose*, on her own, in a bed-sit in the basement of Villa Bellamonte, a house on Clapham Common.'

'And it was one of the art students who …?'

'Yes … Morgan Ramage.'

'And she wound up in his bed instead of her own!'

'She did.' said Reynard, 'and then, some weeks later, when she realised she was pregnant, she told him. He didn't deny his involvement and said he'd help her, whatever she decided to do. In the event she chose to have the child rather than have an abortion and, with the help and support of two Irish girls, old school friends, she went to Ireland and got herself admitted into a maternity unit attached to St Audeline's Convent in Donegal. She never told her sister, Ursula, who was at college in Dublin, and she never told Henry Finnerty, who was one of her best friends. No one knew she was there or even that she was pregnant, except the two friends who helped her, and Morgan Ramage.'

'So?'

'So she had the baby, a boy, who the nuns told her would be "found a good home".'

'Adopted, you mean?'

'Yes. He'd be given to an approved couple for adoption and that would be that; she'd never have to worry about him again. It was as though he was an aggravating spot, a blemish, which they were excising.'

'And she agreed?'

'She appears to have done; she never subsequently made any attempt to contact him as far as we could make out.'

'And then ...?'

'When she got back to London a few weeks later, the art students, including Morgan Ramage, had gone. She never saw or heard from any of them again; it was as if nothing had happened. I've since discovered that when he left college Ramage found dealing in other artist's work more profitable than creating and selling his own. This eventually led to his shared ownership of the R&R Galleries in Brighton and Chichester.

When Julia returned from Australia, she and Rose moved into a larger flat on Clapham Common where they were joined by Ursula. All three girls got jobs while living there and, one by one, they married; Rose to James Jellicoe, Julia to Lance Henderson, and Ursula to the first of her three husbands. After they married Julia and Rose still saw each other from time to time, but Ursula was so busy chasing rich men or painting the town red with Henry Finnerty, she might as well have been on another planet. And that was the situation until the baby boy Rose had had all those years before started formulating a plan to exact revenge on those who, in his view, had made his life such a misery.'

'You mean by punishing his parents.' said Cathy. 'Well, I suppose I can understand that ... however slewed his thinking. But to kill them ... no ... something else must have happened.'

'I hardly know where to start.' said Reynard. 'The baby had been given the name Samuel Midleton by the Mother Superior of St Audeline's. She'd chosen his Christian name from a list of boy's names, and attached the name of an Irish town for his surname. Midleton is in County Cork.'

'A novel way of doing it!'

'An odd one. Still, once he had a name he officially existed and was ready to be adopted. Only he wasn't. At that time there were more unwanted babies than families wanting to adopt. Children like him, waiting for a couple to pick them, were kept in a nursery attached to the women's sanctuary where they remained, if they weren't chosen, until they were five. After that they were transferred into the associated orphanage next door, St Jerome's Children's Home. Here, most of them stayed until, at the age of sixteen, they were placed in low level 'live-in' domestic service or hotel jobs.'

'I can't stand this, Foxy, it's too upsetting. I'm going down to get the tea ready. You can give me the rest of it later.'

Reynard was relieved; telling the harrowing story was draining him too and there was worse to come. He waited a while, then got up from the bed, ran a flannel dampened with cold water over his face, and went downstairs.

Cathy was in the sitting room unloading a tray she'd brought in from the kitchen: tea, fruit cake, and biscuits. 'So,' she said, as she poured, 'did he ever get chosen?'

'No ... that was the problem. If a couple had taken him none of the killings would have occurred.'

'Why didn't anyone want him? Have you any idea?'

'I think I do. It was bad luck really ... he was born with a speech impediment, a stutter, which attracted hurtful comments that affected his nervous system and brought an unsightly rash to his face and upper body. Prospective adoptive parents, took one look at him, and passed him by. Gareth Antrim, his only friend during his whole time in the orphanage, and throughout his life really; a skinny little dark haired boy who grew up to be tall thin man, had an even more difficult thing to deal with ...'

'Tall ... thin ... dark hair! ... So he was ...?'

'The man with the red bandana who gave Rose Jellicoe the samosa? Yes. His involvement with Midleton in a plot kill both sets of parents began one night when they'd been locked in the orphanage's garden shed for the night for "making a rumpus". They were eight years old at the time and, as they sat huddled together in that draughty old hut, they vowed to get their own back by killing those who'd abandoned them.'

'Their mothers and fathers, in other words. But surely this was childish talk?'

'Not to them it wasn't.'

'I assume Gareth Antrim is in custody?'

'Oh yes. Much of what I've told you came from him.'

'So they kept in touch after leaving the orphanage?'

'And continued to plot the murder of all four parents.'

'Was Antrim ever adopted?'

'No. At the same time Midleton was suffering from the hurt arising from his stutter, Antrim was trying to cope with an even more embarrassing congenital imperfection, Strabismus.'

'What on earth's that?'

'Strabismus. It's when your eyes don't move in unison. And because of it, *he* was never chosen for adoption either. Both kids had a miserable time in the home, the worst of them occurring when they were sent for their annual summer "vacation" to the orphanage's holiday house, St Jerome's On The Shore. Here a lay person was in charge, a thoroughly unpleasant woman called Annie Weaver ...'

'Not the same Annie Weaver ...?'

'The very same. It's hard to believe isn't it?'

'But, Foxy, you described her as 'a poor old lady'.'

'I was wrong; she was an evil old bitch who got some sort of gratification by hurting and shaming vulnerable kids left in her care. "Cleansing" or "Washing out the devil" as she called it, was her favourite torture, and she gave it for even the slightest misdemeanour. Both Sam and Gareth had plenty of it. She'd make them strip off all their clothes then spray them with cold water through the fire hose.'

'Oh, my Goodness. I'm beginning to see ...'

'Yes,' he said, 'But there was still more; she kept details of all the things she did in a book she'd entitled "Supplicium", one she used in private to pleasure herself by stimulating her sadistic memories. Midleton and Antrim told me everyone knew what she was up to, but daren't do anything about it. We found the book, but didn't realise what it was for a long time because of the title. It was only later, when we discovered one of the translations of "Supplicium" was "Punishment", that we could see she'd used the Latin version of the word instead of the English one in order to give the book an innocent look in a house where Latin was everywhere.'

'This is dreadful.'

'Yes, and it led directly to a plot to punish Annie Weaver as well as kill their parents.

'To punish her, not kill her?'

'From what they told me, they wanted to humiliate her in the same way she'd humiliated them. When they left her sitting in the garden chair they didn't realise she was dead.'

Cathy shook her head. 'She was evil; I can understand them wanting to put her through what she'd done to them, however bizarre it may seem to some. But tell me, what made those boy's childish dreams of revenge escalate into a plot to murder their mothers and fathers?'

'You mean when did their dream start to become a reality? I think it probably goes back to the day they broke into the Mother Superior's office and stole money from a locked cabinet to go to the cinema. They were about fourteen. After they'd smashed the lock and pulled the door open they found, not only money, but the personal records of all children born in the maternity home since the place opened. Naturally they copied down their own details, and it was this information which was so valuable to them when they came to seek their revenge.

'But that was years before, so how did they locate their parents and why choose poisoning by hemlock of all things?'

'Easy; they had their names from the time they'd broken into the Mother Superior's office, as I said, and it wasn't hard, with the aid of Google, to discover who and what they'd become, and where they lived. When Sam found Annie Weaver and Morgan Ramage lived within sixty miles of each other, he worked his way down England, job by job, until he got one at Creakwood which, he reckoned, was close enough to both for him to start thinking of bringing their plot into action. As to the choice of hemlock, I understand a horse in one of the stables Midleton worked in died from eating it. He must have picked up on the idea and then worked out a way of giving to her.'

'And Antrim's parents?'

'His father's in Canada but he hasn't yet found where his mother is. Anyway, back to Sam Midleton ... one day before he'd completed his plans for Annie Weaver and Morgan Ramage, he saw in the local paper that Rose Jellicoe was going to be in Brighton at the Great British Food Fayre and within easy range of where he was living. He could hardly believe it; this was going to be the best chance he'd ever have to even the score with the three people who'd condemned him to a life of rejection, loneliness and humiliation. He got onto Gareth Antrim and between them they set everything up.'

'I know it's awful, Foxy,' said Cathy, hunching up her shoulders and rocking her head from side to side, 'but I can't help feeling sorry for those boys. They had such a rotten life and ... do you know what? If I'd been discarded like that, and left in the care of people like Annie Weaver, well I might just ...'

'Ah, come on, Cathy, this is 2009 ... we've moved on. It's no longer "eye for eye, tooth for tooth", we've got the "the rule of law".'

'So we have,' she said, slowly shaking her head from side to side, 'and we all know what the law is!'

Reynard didn't answer; prompted by her unsettling previous comment, he was trying to work out how *he'd* have reacted if *he'd* been abandoned and left to the mercy of chance like Gareth Antrim and Sam Midleton.

Box Of Secrets

Alan Grainger

The towns, villages, streets and establishments mentioned in this book are a mix of the real and the imagined.

All the characters are fictitious.

Alan Grainger 2015.

Alan Grainger

With many thanks to
Edel O'Kennedy
for her critical help
and for sorting out my commas and colons.

About the author

Alan Grainger is an Englishman who emigrated to Ireland at the time when everyone else seemed to be going the other way. He got seduced by the lifestyle, married an Irish woman, and never went back. They have three children and seven grandchildren.

His business career ended unexpectedly early when his company was taken over and a whole new world of opportunity opened up. Ever since then, other than when he's watching rugby or cricket on television, he has been travelling, painting, and writing.

His journeys have taken him all over the world, provided him with much of the background material which features in his books, and allowed him to choose authentic sets against which he can tell his stories.

The following books also written by Alan Grainger are available from Amazon, Create Space, and other major online retailers in paperback and e-book formats. They may also be obtained by ordering through bookshops.

The Learning Curves

Divided from his father and frozen out of his home in Ireland by his new stepmother, sixteen-year-old Jimmy O'Callaghan runs away resolving never to return. With no one to guide and support him he finds himself with little option but to learn about life and love as best he can. He's aided in his quest for enlightenment success and happiness by an unlikely collection of worldly people, the sort he would never have encountered, let alone befriend, at home in Templederry. Starting off with the few pounds he'd stolen from the till in his father's pub the night before he left, and with little appreciation of how big a risk he was taking, his personality and determination ensure nothing is ever beyond his reach.

This book is the first of The Templederry Trilogy, and is partly set in the fictitious rural Irish town of Templederry, County Tipperary. It is followed by Father Unknown and The Legacy

Father Unknown

The fragile and sometimes volatile relationship between two brothers, Dick and Roger Davenport, is demolished forever when they find out something previously unknown to them about their beginnings. In the aftermath of the violence which follows their discovery Dick, strongly supported by his grandfather Archie, sets off in a new direction; one which brings him to Ireland on a journey of more surprising discoveries.

This book is the second of The Templederry Trilogy. It is preceded by The Learning Curves and followed by The Legacy.

The Legacy

When an heir hunter turns up looking for Charlie Cassidy and finds he's been dead for years he tells his son and daughter he has information which might connect them, through their late father, to an unclaimed legacy. He asks them if they'd like him to process their claim, but they think his fees are too high and decide to do the job themselves. It's a choice they regret when they discover their father wasn't the man they thought he was.

The Legacy is the third and last book of The Templederry Trilogy. It is preceded by The Learning Curves and Father Unknown

The same author's three murder/mystery novels other than Box of Secrets, featuring Detective Chief Inspector 'Foxy' Reynard, are available from Amazon, Create Space, other on-line booksellers, and bookshops.

Eddie's Penguin

When a young girl's quest to find the father she has never met becomes entangled in a police investigation into a series of seemingly unconnected murders she has no idea the information she digs up will ultimately lead to the uncovering of the last bit of the jigsaw the police are struggling to put together. Detective Chief Inspector 'Foxy' Reynard who makes his first appearance in this murder/mystery story leads the team from Sussex CID who ultimately solve the mystery and the crimes.

Deadly Darjeeling.

When Nelson Deep, a wealthy tea merchant, is found dead in his study in bizarre circumstances and Detective Chief Inspector 'Foxy' Reynard is called in, a solution seems inevitable. Such an assumption however makes little allowance for the dysfunctional and self-centred attitudes the D.C.I. uncovers as he attempts to unravel the strange relationships prevalent within the Deep family.

✵✵✵

Blood On The Stones

This spy thriller/saga by Alan Grainger is also available from Amazon, Create Space and other online booksellers and bookshops.

It's the story of two young men, once close as brothers, who fall out over a girl when they are in their twenties and go their separate ways. Their vow 'never to meet again' is forgotten though, when they find themselves face to face in the course of an attempted royal assassination.

Made in the USA
Charleston, SC
24 April 2015